You Can't Hurry Love

Nicole Mikell

First edition

ISBN: 9798999229717

Editor: Danielle Barthel

Cover Design: Gowtham T

For anyone that has ever felt like Ivy,
may you find a sturdy wall to grow, so you can finally reach your
light.

The graceful ivy, clasping the oak that supported it, would form a whole in which strength and beauty would be equally conspicuous.

— Mary Wollstonecraft

MUSIC PLAYLIST

This is the scannable code that goes along with the songs in each chapter!

It is in order so if you don't shuffle, you can just follow as the book goes.

Chapter 1

"Shape of You"

Ivy

I pause for a moment and hold eye contact with the beautiful woman standing across from me with watery eyes. Taking one small step towards her, I say, "So, Laurel, are you saying yes?"

She nods her head rapidly and bursts into tears. "I'm saying yes!"

Pandemonium breaks out around her from the declaration. Her mother and sister quickly stand to hug her as two of Laurel's friends applaud and cheer. I clap along with them.

"Congratulations." I smile at her—my heart warms every single time I witness this moment. "This calls for champagne," I add, and the group nods their heads in agreement. I excuse myself and back out of the room to head to the staff lounge.

My mahogany heels click against the old white tile floors, and I take my phone out of my flowy black dress pocket to turn up the music in the boutique. A classical piano cover of "Shape of You" by Ed Sheeran sounds out through the hallway speakers. One of the consultants, Zoe, pops her head out to give me a thumbs-up in thanks. She must be having a difficult appoint-

1

ment. It can get awkward and quiet during appointments when there are differing opinions, so the music is a needed background buffer.

I use my back to push open the heavy white wooden door to the staff lounge. Yesterday I acquired a splinter on the palm of my hand from the fraying door. It took me almost an hour to get it out after soaking my hand in warm water and using tweezers—I won't make that mistake again today. The girls have been complaining that I need to do some updating around the shop and after yesterday's injury, I can no longer deny that they're right.

I head over to the fridge and pull back the metal door handle before grabbing an ice-cold green bottle of champagne from the bottom shelf. Then, holding my breath, I remove the cork from the bottle. No matter how many times I do this, I still flinch when the pressure releases.

I shut the fridge with my heel and place the bottle on the circular table the girls eat their meals at, before heading to a wall of shelves. The shelves house various delicate items: glasses, plates, and a few accessories. Glasses clink against each other as I take them off the worn middle shelf and grab a serving tray. I place the first few glasses in a circle before adding two more and the champagne bottle in the center. *It needs something more*, I think. Glancing to my left I notice a vase full of flowers and steal a few sprigs of baby's breath from it, placing them on one corner.

Perfect, a touch of elegance for Laurel.

Satisfied with my work, I turn around and walk back out of the staff lounge, my left side weighed down slightly by the weight of the tray. I walk down the hallway with gowns on either side of me, lining the wall—truly a fairytale. Taking one final calming breath, I knock on the door and turn back on a bright smile before stepping into the room full of women once more.

"Champagne, ladies." I cheerily lift the tray in my arms before placing it on the glass table in front of them. Laurel steps down from the small wooden podium and lifts the front of her gown slightly as she begins to step towards me.

"I don't know how I will ever walk in one of these things." She chuckles as I pour a glass and hand it to her.

"Don't worry, I'll take your measurements when you're ready. Everything will be customized and altered so it will fit you like a glove. This gown is going to fit you better than anything else you will ever wear in your life. You are the *bride*, after all."

Hearing those words, her friends let out a cheer of excitement again and her mom a peep of a sob. I step back and grab a box of tissues from the side table by the window, and secretively hand them to her mother.

"Here." I smile at her gently. She pulls one out of the plastic container and quietly thanks me in response.

I could do this routine in my sleep and somehow it never gets old.

After they empty the bottle and snap a few photos, the appointment wraps up and I take Laurel's measurements. When I'm done, she gives me a huge hug before saying goodbye. I didn't know her two hours ago, but there is something about sharing a moment like this with another human being that makes you feel connected. This is something she will remember for the rest of her life—the day she found her wedding dress—and I'm the one who facilitated it.

After I wave goodbye to the group and shut the door behind her with a lock—she was the final appointment of the day—I crack my neck and slide off my heels, tossing them aside. Much better.

"Turn that shit off!" one of the consultants, Jade, yells from the back of the shop.

I laugh and pull my phone out of my dress pocket, knowing that she's referring to the horrible cover of a current pop song that's playing through the shop.

"What do you guys want?" I yell back, sitting down on one of the chairs for guests that is at the entrance of the boutique.

"Sleep Token!" Blair, the store manager decked out in Lilly Pulitzer, cheerily requests as she walks towards me.

"Heard."

I switch over the music as the three women finish putting the final gowns from their appointments back on the clothing racks in the main hallway. Then, one by one, they plop down on the couch across from me. After every Saturday shift, we have a quick meeting to go over the day's sales and any issues they might have encountered. Tuesday through Friday I usually only have one or two of the girls working in the shop with me, but on Saturdays, it's all hands on deck.

Jade pulls her long brown hair into a ponytail. "I had the mother from hell in an appointment today. She made her daughter cry because she told her she looked too heavy to wear a fitted gown."

I shake my head sadly as Zoe scoffs in disgust. "That lady needs to get a grip! Let the bride wear what she wants—it's her wedding. People like that make me want to tell them to...to... frick the frick off!"

Blair snorts and Jade cackles at Zoe's innocence and feeble attempt at cussing. It's one of the things that we love about her; she's too sweet to even insult someone in a way that would cut deep.

"Well, all we can do is try to give the bride the best experience possible. We can't control the people around her, but we can make *her* feel special," I tell them.

"Yup." Jade smiles. "The bride stuck to her guns and is coming back alone so I can take her measurements for the gown—the *fitted* gown that she loves."

"Good. I'm glad she's getting what she wants. That's badass of her to prioritize herself." I look at Zoe and then Blair. "Any questions or concerns from the day?"

They shake their heads in unison when a sudden crash sounds out, loud enough to be heard over the sound of the rock music playing, and not an "I just dropped my plate on the ground" crash but a "there's a tornado in the back of the store" crash.

I jump up from the suede chair and run to the back room, the three girls directly on my heels.

When we step into the staff room, I gasp when I see the cause of the sound. Every single shelf on the far wall has fallen like dominoes. Thousands of dollars' worth of inventory and glassware are now laying in a pile on the ground.

I stand in the doorway, shocked.

Blair begins to clear her throat from behind me. I know an "I told you so" is on the tip of her tongue.

I hold up a hand. "Not a word," I tell them.

I guess this is my curse for buying an old shop with obvious problems that the commercial realtor assured me were just part of its "quirks" and "charm."

Time to get this place fixed up.

Chapter 2

"Relax After Work With A Drink"
Ivy

"You're coming tonight, right?" my best friend, Olive, chirps from the other end of our phone call. Lying down on my bed, I stretch out and silently mouth *"fuck"* to myself. I completely forgot that I promised her and her husband, Hunter, that I would come to the show tonight. I'm exhausted after my long day at the store, but I haven't seen Olive in almost two months, which is crazy since we live less than ten minutes away from each other. Life has gotten increasingly busy, though, as we've grown older. It's even more chaotic because we are both business owners. I have my bridal shop, and Olive owns a bar, Whiskey Jane's—so finding time when we're both free is difficult.

"Yes, of course I will be there," I respond, overcompensating for my lack of enthusiasm with a faux cheery voice.

"Yay, but also cut the bullshit," Olive snorts. "What's wrong?"

"The store is falling apart," I tell her, knowing she can relate, because she had to make some major improvements at her bar once she became the owner.

"What happened?"

"Stockroom crash."

"The back shelves?"

"How'd you know?"

"I think someone attached them originally with super glue, Ivy. The wood was practically begging to crumble. Also, last time I was in there your ghost told me," Olive jokes.

"Oh my god. *Screw Barnaby*. He probably did it! He probably pulled out that final nail, just for some drama to entertain himself."

"That's what you get for falling in love with a building built in the 1920s—ghosts."

I know Olive is messing with me and that she doesn't believe me, but there are many unexplainable things that happen at the shop. I swear I have a somewhat creepy, but mostly just mischievous, ghost floating around Vera Bridal. I named him Barnaby with absolutely no logic in mind—it's just fun to say. Not to mention, if I named the ghost Mr. Crow, the original owner of this building, the thought of a potential spirit would be much scarier.

"But on a serious note, I need to figure out how to fix up the shop. I don't want something catastrophic happening while I have bridal appointments going on. I need all the positive reviews I can get since Vera Bridal hasn't even been in business for a whole year."

"I know, I get it. I would give you the contact to the contractor that fixed up Whiskey's, but they're booked months out usually and I know you don't have time to wait. I'll check with Hunter and see if he knows of anyone."

"Thank you." I breathe out a small sigh in relief. Olive has always been practical and a problem solver. Where I had been wild and spontaneous for years, she was always a solid rock, keeping the friendship intact and afloat.

"I don't like hearing you like this; it's not like you to be stressed. You're bubbly and a tad insane, remember that," she teases me, and I laugh, knowing she is right.

"Don't worry, I will come tonight *and* I will be accepting free drinks from you for the entirety of the evening."

"Deal," she responds. "Why else would you be friends with me? I've got to go though, I'll see you soon."

I tell her I love her before ending the call.

Almost a year and a half ago, I lived in Atlanta, so calls were all we had to maintain a friendship. I feel guilty that I haven't made more of an effort to spend time with her now that we live in the same town. Olive has never been a spiteful friend, though; she knows that life is busy.

I stand up, walk over to my closet, and look down at the piles of clothing begging to be worn. Picking up a slinky red dress that I haven't worn in years, I walk in front of my floor-length mirror to see what it would look like on me. I notice the cut-outs down both of the sides, basically making a V towards the crotch area—I throw it like it's on fire.

No, thanks.

Next, I grab a fitted black dress out of the same pile and try to brush out some of the wrinkles with my hand. I wouldn't say I'm the most organized person at home. If it's not work clothing, I'm not hanging it.

Professional me and off-the-clock me do not mix—they are two completely different women. I look over a few more items before deciding I will just wear some jeans and a crop top.

How am I supposed to know what to wear to go to my friend's bar to see a band play, whose lead singer I had one drunken hookup with while he was dressed as a Ninja Turtle?

Chapter 3

"Cherry Bomb"

Ivy

When I finally get myself ready and pull up to Olive's bar, it's almost eleven p.m. The parking lot is packed. It always is when Rinse and Repeat has a show—they draw quite an audience.

Wes, the lead singer, has a deep and raspy voice that gives the band a unique sound people can't seem to get enough of. It doesn't hurt that he's insanely hot. Like, chiseled abs mixed with a playful charm *hot*. He's perfect for the lead of a band; women swoon over him like he has the elixir to life—not to mention he's a pro skateboarder so tons of guys respect his talent as well.

I, on the other hand, can't take him seriously. He has a case of Peter Pan syndrome—he never wants to grow up. I spent many years dating idiots that acted similarly, and after our one night of sloppy passion, I told Wes *never again*. He respected my decision immediately, but still takes every opportunity that he sees me to harmlessly flirt.

Trust me, he is not doing poorly in the ladies' department,

9

so I'm sure his ego was not damaged for a millisecond when I friend-zoned him. I heard from Olive that he has been hooking up with a pair of best friends for the past month, so good for him—I guess.

I park my little black car on the outskirts of the lot and adjust my uncomfortably tight jeans once I stand up. My light pink shirt is cropped just above my belly button; it happens to be freezing since we are approaching the beginning of November, but I didn't let that sway my wardrobe tonight.

A blast of wind hits my face as I walk and I can't help but shiver; Mother Nature is rubbing salt in the wound of my bad outfit choice.

I'll be fine once I get inside with a bunch of drunk and sweaty bodies.

My long strawberry blonde hair swishes against my lower back and around my shoulders as I begin to walk towards the entrance, and I instantly feel a little better, a little warmer. My hair is my security blanket; it gives me a sense of confidence. I feel like I can hide behind my hair in situations where I don't feel comfortable, and flip it around to my advantage when I want to be flirty.

The booming bass and guitar seem to shake the whole bar from outside. I feel the electric charge from the live performance as I approach and pull open the heavy door. I'm instantly hit with the sound of Rinse and Repeat playing a cover of a popular Runaways song.

Stepping over the threshold into Whiskey Jane's, I'm immediately sardined in between a couple by the door and the wall.

"Oof," I grunt and try to move away from the sweaty, intoxicated pair. I clear my throat to let them know they are squishing someone, but they are deep in a make-out, completely unaware that they are holding me captive to their spit swapping.

Finally, the woman breaks the kiss for air, and I take that opportunity to quickly push past them. More people walk around me, and I duck underneath a man's hairy armpit to make my way through the sea of people towards the bar. This place is an absolute madhouse. Olive must be making a killing tonight; there has to be at least three hundred people in here.

I'm relieved when I make it to the counter in one piece and see a familiar face behind the bar: Hunter, Olive's husband.

"Hey, Ivy." He smiles broadly at me, his curly hair cascading around his face. "Olive is in the office. You can head on back." He motions his head towards the kitchen door while stacking some glasses.

I know my way around Whiskey Jane's; Olive worked here for ten years before she owned it.

"Thanks, Hot Dog."

He playfully scoffs at the nickname before turning his attention to greet some new customers taking a seat on the barstools next to me.

I found out from his buddies, Eddie and Wes, that "Hot Dog" was his childhood nickname after he threw up hot dogs at a birthday party. Being the ball buster that I am, I decided to partake in the name-calling. Hunter is basically a brother to me at this point—I've got to mess with him.

Pushing through the kitchen door like I live here, I wave to the two main cooks, Rob and Tate. Rob greets me warmly, but Tate is so deep in concentration at the grill that he doesn't even notice me. Rob chuckles and gives me a *this kid* look.

Tate started out working as a barback and has worked his way up to being a main cook alongside Rob in the past few months, so I know he doesn't want to mess anything up. He's a sweet but extremely goofy guy.

I walk over to the purple office door covered in stars and a blob that is supposed to be the moon. Olive and I painted it together last year when I moved back to Clairesville. I won't lie —it doesn't look great. The door appears like two fourth graders painted it. Her mother-in-law is much more talented when it comes to painting; she's an actual artist, so I'm not sure why Olive didn't ask for her assistance.

But we did have a blast decorating it together, so at least we have the memories to go along with the haphazard door.

I knock once before pushing the door open; that's the max wait time that she gets from me. We lived together for years which means I've seen every square inch of her body and nothing she could be doing in there could possibly surprise me at this point.

"Come—" she starts to call out and stops once she sees me. "Ivy!" she squeals, and jumps out of her swivel seat to hug me.

I step towards her to eagerly match her hug. "I've missed you." I squeeze her tightly.

"Enough affection," she teases, and steps back before giving me a onceover. She raises an eyebrow. "You look *hot*."

"Good."

"Trying to impress a certain lead singer?"

"Oh my god. No. You know I will never go there again. It was so...*sloppy and full of spit!*"

Olive shudders at the thought. "I can't hear any more, he's like family to me. I don't want to hear about *any* of his secretions."

I push my hair off my shoulder and laugh deeply.

I always make the story more dramatic than it was to poke at her. It really was basically a normal hookup—nothing insane. I just don't want to waste my time with a skateboarding, boy-band heartthrob with a line of women out the door.

"How's the night going?" I ask her, changing the subject.

She sits back down and slides a stool next to her for me to

sit on. I take the seat as she says, "Oh you know, the usual: Wes was hanging from some of the ceiling pipes during their second song, Hunter had to threaten him to make him get down, and I'm pretty sure we have maxed out the bar's capacity."

I make a "money" hand motion by rubbing my fingers together repeatedly, and Olive smirks.

"Oh yeah, we're making a lot of that tonight, too," she says, laughing.

"Are Eddie and Summer here?"

"Yup! They got here an hour ago."

"I'm obsessed with them."

Eddie is Hunter's other best friend, aside from Wes. He is tall, sexy, and broad—everything I would go for in a man. He's also insanely intelligent and financially stable. He developed his own app and has made a fortune from it. Slightly unfortunate for my sake, by the time I moved back here from Atlanta, he was already with his girlfriend, Summer.

They met when she was opposing counsel in court for a *total asshole* that used to work for Eddie who tried to steal the app coding to create his own software. The guy basically made an exact replica of what Eddie had already created, using Eddie's codes. He got nasty when Eddie confronted him about it and thought he could get away with it—so Eddie took him to court.

Eddie saw Summer the first day in court, walked over, and told her that he would buy her dinner after her client lost the case. She scoffed at his remark and told him it was completely inappropriate, but Summer confided in us a few months ago that she was absolutely turned on by his confidence in that moment.

In the end, Eddie did win the case, and also Summer's heart. They have been inseparable ever since their first date. So maybe I did miss out on a nice guy like Eddie while I was away, but I gained the friendship of both him and Summer.

Olive pulls me from my thoughts. "Let's go get a drink." She slaps her hands against her thighs and stands up.

I smile at her. "I thought you'd never offer."

Chapter 4

"Boyfriend"

Ivy

Following Olive out of her office, Tate takes notice of me this time when I walk past. He does a double take when he sees me and shyly tells me, "Hi, Ivy."

I give him a giant smile as I walk to the kitchen door and wiggle my fingers goodbye before pushing my weight against it and following Olive through the other side to go behind the bar counter.

"He's practically salivating at the mouth every time you're near," she shouts next to my ear, trying to speak above the band.

"Oh please, not true," I yell back. "He didn't notice me earlier. He was focused on the burgers."

"Yes, his first love." Olive laughs.

"Never come between a man and his meat," I joke, wiggling my eyebrows.

At that exact moment, the band ends their cover of Rob Zombie, so everyone hears me scream about man meat. Hunter looks at me like I have snakes coming out of my ears.

Olive pushes me away playfully. "I can't deal with you. Beer or tequila shot?"

"Always tequila. Make it a double," I say, not bothered by the confusion I just caused the nearby patrons. "Tomorrow's my day off."

"Heard."

Olive pours two giant shots and hands one to me before we lock eyes, clink the glasses together, and throw them back in unison. The liquor burns my nose and my eyes water as I slowly reopen them.

"Ooof," Hunter jokes from behind us. "It's going to be a dancing on the bar kind of night."

"I would do that sober," I tell him.

"We know," Olive adds. "You and Summer almost brought the entire place down when you two decided to have a *Coyote Ugly* moment last month."

"I heard my name!" Summer smiles broadly and pops up on the customer side of the bar top, leaning over to give me a hug. Her red ringlet curls brush against my arm as we embrace, and it tickles slightly.

She has Victorian era hair—basically porcelain doll hair. She's beautiful in a way that makes her appear straight out of a fairytale: fair skin and rosy cheeks with bright blue eyes.

I understand why Eddie was infatuated; if I was a man I would be, too. We are all waiting for the day that he pops the big question. I can't wait to put her in some wedding dresses.

Summer hops down from the counter and sits on a stool.

"Yes, we were talking about our bar-top dance parties." I grin at her. "Repeat tonight?"

"You know it. I didn't wear shorts under my dress for nothing."

"Can you guys at least wait till the older crowd leaves?" Olive snorts. "I don't want to be responsible for any heart attacks in my establishment."

Wes's band starts up their next cover, a punk version of the early 2000s song "Boyfriend" by Ashlee Simpson. The bar goes wild with uproar once more and I motion to Olive that I'm going to head into the crowd. She mouths *"good luck"* with a final smile before I walk around the counter and take Summer's awaiting hand.

We push through sweaty, aggressive bodies until I find a small opening in the commotion—we claim our spot. Jumping together in unison, we shout the lyrics at the top of our lungs. The moment is incredibly freeing. Everyone in the crowd is here for one thing: to let loose and enjoy themselves. Summer is dancing around to my left, and a tall, beautiful woman that I've never met before is on my right. Somehow within seconds the three of us end up bouncing together, laughing wildly the whole time as we sing the lyrics to each other.

Instant connection.

When the song ends, the woman takes a breath and waves goodbye to us before disappearing back into the crowd of people. I will probably never see her again, but that moment between the three of us was a blast.

It felt just like being a child on a playground and instantly making friends with a stranger from a simple game of tag. We don't get many moments like that as adults, and I resent it. I miss everything feeling so sincere and easy. Olive always jokes that I could befriend a wall, though. She tells me I'm the most social person she has ever met.

We scream out a few more songs before Summer turns to me and pushes her now sweaty, thick curls away from her face. "I'm going to grab some water and find Eddie. Do you want to come with me?"

"I think I'm going to stay here and dance for a little while longer. I'll hold our spot in case you want to come meet me back here," I tell her. She nods in understanding and then gives me a final joking shimmy before pushing through the crowd.

17

Standing on my tippee toes, I glance around and try to get a view of the small stage, but there are two giant men standing in front of me now. I try to squeeze around them to get a better view of the band but it's like a wall of solid rock.

These guys are big...also covered in tattoos. I'm now intrigued and I would like to see their faces.

For science, of course.

I lean up on my toes and tap the longer haired guy on the right with my index finger. The beast of a man turns slowly and looks down, his frame towering over me. Naturally, he is incredibly hot. His jaw is carved with sharp points, and his eyes are as dark as a starless night.

He's a tree I'd like to climb.

"What?" He scowls down at me.

I'm instantly taken aback by his rudeness.

Firmly planting my feet on the ground, I place my hands on my hips. If he's going to immediately be unkind, two can play at that game. "I can't see over your big head."

The other man next to him turns around hearing that and lets out a bark of a laugh.

"He *does* have a huge head."

This man is *also* incredibly chiseled and hot.

"Thank you. I'm glad someone agrees with me," I tell the muscular stranger with shorter hair.

He laughs again as the man with dark hair in front of me gives me a once over and grunts before turning back around. He seems completely unfazed and bored by the interaction.

I make eye contact with the short-haired guy and raise a brow like *"what's his deal?"* He chuckles before holding out a tattooed hand in my direction.

"I'm Ezra." He smiles, towering over my five-foot-two frame. I take his hand in mine, and we lightly shake.

"Ivy."

"Ivy, what a beautiful name."

He leans closer to me so I can hear him over the noise of the band starting up a new song. Ezra smells like peppermint and tobacco—the scent is unusually comforting.

He continues to speak, the words tickling near my ear. "You'll have to excuse my cousin. He doesn't get out much."

"Your cousin?" I look back at the grumpy man standing in front of me.

"Yeah. Donovan."

"I should have known you two were related," I snort. "You're basically built like two thick pine trees."

Ezra lets out a hearty laugh. "Pine trees?" His deep voice booms over the music. "Now that's one I've *never* heard before."

I hold his gaze.

"Come on, I'll let you climb up on my shoulders so you can see the stage." Ezra taps his back. I glance around to see if Summer is anywhere near, but she's nowhere to be found.

"Okay, kind, tall stranger."

Ezra laughs again before bending down and helping me get up on his back, then climb up to his shoulders. His cousin, Donovan, doesn't even glance our way as we are shuffling around next to him.

Good. Easier for me to ignore that grumpy jerk.

It's a shame that handsome looks are wasted on someone with a personality like his. A real crime to society because he is totally my type physically. I've dated one too many assholes in the past, though, so I instantly feel repugnance towards his bad attitude and extremely attractive appearance.

I spend the rest of the band's set on Ezra's shoulder's having the time of my life and screaming the lyrics. At one point, Wes even crowd surfs during a song and high-fives me as he passes.

The whole time, Ezra holds me like I'm light as a feather, not even flinching from my weight on his shoulders throughout the night.

What a *man*.

By the time Rinse and Repeat play their final encore song, I'm hoarse from singing and completely breathless. Ezra bends down to let me slide off the back of his shoulders and I step onto the ground.

"Thank you so much for that."

He smiles warmly. "It was seriously nothing. I've carried fish that weigh more than you."

"Fisherman?"

"You could say. My cousin and I own a fishing charter." Ezra nudges his head towards Donovan, who I realize is staring at both of us blankly.

"Wow! That's awesome. Maybe I can come see your charter sometime."

"Not likely," Donovan scoffs.

Ezra brushes off the comment while glancing down at me apologetically. "Ignore him. That would be fun. We just closed the charter for the winter season last week, but when we reopen in spring, hopefully you'll be our first passenger—on the house."

Donovan shuffles from one foot to the other before crossing his arms and holding the stiff stance he apparently loves so much. "We need to go. Cardinal," he tells Ezra with a stern expression.

This guy is a real ass.

Ezra pulls his phone out of his back pocket. "Oh shit, you're right. Sorry, Ivy, we've got to head out. It was nice meeting you."

The two goliath men start to step past me as Ezra continues, "When the winter season is over, give us a call." He pulls a dark leather wallet out of his pants pocket, takes out a small white business card, and hands it to me.

Anderson Fishing Charter

I glance up at Ezra. "Who's Anderson?" I ask playfully.

"We are," Donovan says, in a deep rumbling voice. I swear I almost see a hint of a small but vicious smirk on his lips. He starts to head towards the door, and the crowd seems to part for him as he passes.

"What a drama queen," Ezra says, laughing.

"He probably just spent an hour thinking up how to make a dramatic exit," I snort.

"Well, I do have to go. But seriously, don't be a stranger." He taps his finger against the business card I'm holding with their name and number. "Don't worry about Donovan. He's all bark, no bite."

I nod my head and smile. "Okay."

Ezra gives me one final look before putting his hands in his pockets casually and walking off through the crowd.

What an interesting night.

Chapter 5

"Light Up The Sky"

Ivy

I spent all Sunday in bed watching *Vampire Diaries* reruns and eating pizza, pretending like I didn't have a disaster to deal with at Vera Bridal.

The bubble has popped now that it's Monday and I'm standing outside the shop placing the key in the lock of my front door—I have to come to terms with the mess.

Once I'm inside, I set my purse on the aged cream front desk that was already here when I bought the building, then head back towards the staff room. When I make my way in, it's worse than I remembered Saturday night. There are at least sixty broken glasses strewn across the ground, and the jewelry that we kept stored on the shelves has been destroyed.

This is going to cost me a lot to replace.

Blowing out a deep breath, I pull a ponytail holder off my wrist and place my mop of hair into a messy bun. It's days like this that make owning a business difficult. Nobody else will fix this situation for me. It's my responsibility—I'm the boss.

"Screw you, Barnaby!" I yell out, as I grab a broom from the closet and slam the door shut with my foot. "I know it must

22

really piss you off to see a woman owning a business, but this isn't the 1900s. Get with the times."

I sound absolutely insane right now; I know this. I'm screaming at an imaginary ghost, in my shop alone, at nine a.m. on a Monday.

It *is* helping me feel a little better, though, I must admit.

Bending down, I start picking loose pearl earrings from a stack of shattered glasses and shake my head slowly with a groan. No one thinks about this stuff when you start a business.

Sure, people think about dealing with difficult guests or problems with an item in your inventory, but no one thinks about all the work that's unseen to customers. Permits and electric. Insurance and city rules. Landscaping and delayed deliveries. Your back shelf collapsing and ruining inventory. The little things that add up and pick at you behind the scenes.

Good thing I love helping brides find the perfect gown for their big day; if not, I might have burned this place to the ground by now.

"Music," I say to myself, feeling my drive lacking, and set the broom against a wall before going to grab my phone from my bag. The only thing that will give me motivation to clean up a mess that's going to end up costing me thousands of dollars in inventory and repairs—a good playlist.

I turn on my every-morning workout playlist, and the loud, industrial beat of "Light Up the Sky" by The Prodigy blasts through the ceiling speakers that line the hallway. I dance down the hallway, making a complete fool out of myself before finally getting down to business.

After two hours straight of work, I've swept up all the glass and jewelry and salvaged the items from the shelves below that were crushed in the disaster. Giving the mop one final pull across the floor, I feel satisfied with what I've accomplished and decide to call it a day.

My phone rings suddenly, and it echoes through the hallway speakers. I know exactly who's calling me thanks to the obnoxious train horn that Olive added for her contact info; we both gave each other the most annoying sound we could think of so that we rush to pick up the call instead of leaving it to ring.

I jog down the hallway to my phone on the counter and disconnect it from the speakers before picking up.

"Hey, beautiful bitch," I cheerily answer.

"Hello, my favorite little hoebag," she responds back, just as enthusiastically.

This is what real friendship looks like.

"What's up?"

"I found someone that can help you with the renovations around the shop. I can't believe I didn't think of him before—he's helped us at Whiskey's multiple times."

"Oh my god, that would be amazing. Yes, please give me his info, the sooner the better."

"I thought you would say that." Olive laughs. "I texted him earlier, and he said he can pop by your shop around noon to give you an estimate for the shelving and whatever else you're looking for."

"Ugh, you're seriously the best. You know that, right?"

"Yes, I do," Olive chirps back. "And intelligent and beautiful."

"Okay, too much," I tease her. "I'm already here, actually, so you can tell him to come on over whenever he's ready."

"Okay, perfect. Will do," Olive responds before changing the subject to a story about one of the bar regulars, Johnny, having his fourth and fifth grandchildren born today.

"Twins?! Man, his daughter is getting *busy*. What is that now, five kids in three years? I admire that woman's libido, especially in the trenches of motherhood."

"Seriously, I know!" Olive giggles.

We continue to talk about a variety of things and get so deep into our conversation that I don't even realize that forty-five minutes have passed until I hear a knock on the front door.

"Oh crap," I tell Olive. "I think the guy is here."

"Oooh okay! I'll talk to you later. You'll love him."

I thank her and hang up the call before heading to the front door.

As soon as I pull the door open, my eyes must deceive me, because I swear the douche from the other night at the bar is standing on the other side. I blink twice, but he's still standing there. His frame is taking up most of the doorway and towering over me, once again.

Dammit, it's Donovan.

Chapter 6

"Oh!"

Ivy

"**Y**ou're the bridal store owner?" Donovan scowls down at me.

I instantly feel defensive. "What's that supposed to mean?" I cross my arms and plant my feet firmly on the tile floor, marking my territory.

"You seemed a little unhinged the other night to be someone that *owns* a business." He glares at me through squinted eyes, judging me.

I know his type.

"How dare you," I tell him. "If you must know, I live by the motto 'work hard, play hard.' I'm allowed to be a boss and then let loose during my free time. It's honestly insulting that you think a person can only wear one hat. I can do *many* things well."

Donovan stares at me for a moment longer before relaxing his intense gaze slightly. "Are you going to invite me in so I can take a look around?"

I scoff, my arms still crossed. I have half a nerve to send this guy away. Why would I want to pay someone like him to do the work around my shop?

He raises an eyebrow slightly, challenging me.

"Whatever," I say as I scoot out of the doorway to let him walk inside. I really do need help around here, sooner than later.

As he steps past me, I give him a quick look over from head to toe, making sure to do it when he can't notice. Dark henley shirt with the sleeves rolled up, exposing his tattoos, and a pair of worn-in khaki pants. His hair is a rich dark brown that almost reaches his shoulders.

This man is so my type. The type that I refuse to waste time on anymore. I used to run towards assholes—red flags were my calling card.

I'm no longer that girl, though; I have priorities now. Priorities that don't allow me to melt into a puddle on the floor and fall apart slowly while my heart tries to heal from another horrible breakup. I haven't dated anyone since I moved back to Clairesville, and that's the way I like it.

At least that's what I tell myself most days.

Donovan looks around the old white wood-paneled shop interior. He walks over to a spot near the windows where I painted delicate green vines swirling around above the windowpanes. I saw the idea online and was trying to distract people's eyes away from the cracks in the wood.

"What did this place used to be?"

"A strip club," I tell him without even blinking.

He looks shocked for a second before quickly recovering and making his face blank once more. "You're fucking with me."

"I am." I smirk. If I have to deal with his sour attitude today, at least I can bust his balls in the process. "It was actually an antique store, and a hair salon before that, and originally a small general store."

Donovan nods his head and walks over to a splintered wooden wall. "Did you have an inspection when you bought it?"

"Of course," I scoff. "Do you think I'm an idiot? The inspection was clear other than minor issues, the guy said. A little water damage from a previous plumbing flood, some loose floorboards, and mostly cosmetic problems. Nothing insane apparently."

"You should have had the previous owner fix it."

"I bought it from the bank; it was foreclosed. I guess antique clowns don't sell well."

"You're messing with me again." Donovan squints his eyes at me.

"No. It was literally a clown antique store; it was called *Last American Honk*."

"I think I know why it failed."

Was that a hint of a joke from Mr. Grumpy Pants?

"Yeah, you've got that right." I smile. "So now it's my place, Vera Bridal."

He nods his head, and then we stand there for an awkward minute studying each other. The scowl never leaves his chiseled face.

"Follow me," I tell him, breaking the silence. "The staff room is the first order of business."

I step past him and lead the way down the hallway. I hear his heavy footsteps behind me; his presence is almost a little intimidating. I'm also wearing my usual comfy outfit for a Monday alone at the shop: yoga pants and a sports bra. I wasn't expecting to meet up with anyone here and I look like a perspiring mess.

Good thing I don't care what he thinks of me.

"I thought you owned a boat charter with your cousin?" I turn and ask him.

"I do. But when we close down for the winter season, I do this."

I cock my head to the side. "Really?"

"I like to stay busy," he murmurs.

I take the final steps down the hall and push open the heavy staff room door, moving out of the way for him to walk into the room. I follow and point to the large empty spot on the far wall where the shelves collapsed like an avalanche.

"There."

Donovan walks over and inspects the wall and knocks a few times before turning back towards me.

"The shelves weren't attached to the studs behind the wall," he says, frowning.

I throw my hands up in response. "I mean, do you expect a porcelain clown reseller to be a master handyman?"

He frowns even deeper which causes his eyebrows to knit together. "Show me the other issues."

I spend the next fifteen minutes walking him around the building, and with every new issue I show him, he seems to grow more exasperated.

When we finish going through everything, we head back towards the front door.

"I'll pay extra for the service if you lose the attitude." I raise an eyebrow.

"What attitude?" He scowls.

"You've got to be kidding me," I say, laughing in response.

Donovan heads towards the door, ignoring my slight teasing. "Write down your number. I will contact you by the end of the day with the estimate total."

Grabbing a pad of paper out of my desk, I quickly scribble down my phone number and hand it over to him.

"How long do you think the work would take you if I hired you?"

"Probably around three months."

"Geez. That long?" I groan. "We have appointments all week long. *Every* week."

"I thought you would only want me to come in when the shop is empty. So that takes into account the days you are closed and then after hours on regular business days."

"You would seriously work around the shop schedule like that?" I reply, unable to hide the relief in my voice. "That would be amazing."

"Sure." He shrugs, still no smile in sight. "It just might take a little longer than a normal job would take me with the weird hours."

"Okay, no problem," I respond quickly. "Whatever you think timewise is fine."

"I'll be in touch later." Donovan steps past me and walks to the front door. As he reaches for the handle, he turns back towards me one final time and tilts his head at me once before stepping outside.

I guess that's his version of a goodbye.

If I hire him—and I probably will—my goal is to make that grump smile at least once in my presence.

Chapter 7

"Summer Breeze"
Ivy

The next night I'm parked outside Olive and Hunter's house, waiting for her to come out. We are going out to dinner with Summer tonight, and I told her I would pick her up so she could let loose. Since she's always in work mode at the bar, she never gets to let her hair down and have more than one drink.

Olive steps out of her house and saunters down the walkway, which is surrounded by the garden that Hunter plants petunias in every year for her. Since it's starting to get chilly, this is probably one of the last weeks they will be in bloom before they freeze over.

She's wearing a large knit sweater and a skirt that clings to her long legs. Her dark hair is pulled into a tight bun—she always looks effortlessly cool and I tell her all the time that I admire that about her.

Olive pulls open the passenger door. "Hi!" She smiles at me warmly as she slides into the seat next to me.

"You're in deep doodoo," I tell her.

"What?" She instantly looks taken aback. "What did I do?"

"Donovan."

"What about him? He's great. I thought you two would hit it off."

"He's a total ass. I met him at Whiskey's on Saturday, and he was a turd to me there."

"A *turd*?" Olive snorts out a laugh.

I cross my arms. "Yes, I didn't stutter. A turd."

"Okay, well, I'm sorry. He is friends with Hunter and has always been great to us. Maybe a little serious and quiet at times, but he's harmless."

"Well, he sucks."

"So don't hire him."

"Oh, I already hired him this morning. I'm not going to let his asshole-ness keep me from fixing up the store—for a good price, I might add."

Olive laughs and shakes her head. "Of course you did."

I back out of her driveway as she continues to talk. "Maybe you guys just met on the wrong foot. What happened?"

I then explain to her the whole situation at the bar, and Olive stares at me, her mouth gaping like a fish by the time I finish talking.

"What?" I turn to look at her.

"Ivy! You told the man he needs to move his *big head*. You totally insulted him."

"Since when is telling someone they have a big head an insult? It could be so big because it's full of *brains*," I reply with a hint of smartass.

I knew exactly what I was doing—Olive knows this as well.

"Oh please." She rolls her eyes and gives me a snarky glance. "I bet you guys will end up getting along great."

"Never," I tell her swiftly, feeling stubborn.

Now that I've made that statement, I definitely won't be

telling her that I already made it a goal of mine to get him to crack a smile.

"He's your type," Olive says in a singsong voice. "Broad *and* tattooed.

"Does he have tattoos? I didn't even notice." I turn my car left out of her neighborhood and onto the main road. "I guess I couldn't see anything past his Scrooge expression."

"Now I *know* you're bullshitting me," she says, laughing. Olive and I have been friends for so long, she understands that I have a flair for the dramatic.

"Anyway," I say, changing the subject. "I can't wait to stuff my face with tacos and margaritas."

"Same. I wore the stretchiest skirt I own for that exact reason."

I glance down at my own outfit: skintight plaid pants and a tight black sweater.

"I fear I have planned poorly."

"You can take your pants off in the car after dinner."

"Great idea. There's nothing more freeing than driving in your underwear," I exclaim. "Truly exhilarating."

Olive looks sideways at me. "And how many times have you driven in your underwear before?"

"Dennis may have been a douche, but we had *fun*."

She groans when I mention my toxic ex-boyfriend I wasted years on. He cheated on me nonstop and always led me on. He actually ended up being cousins with Olive's husband, Hunter, which was an insane realization when we found out.

I continue speaking. "Trust me, I would tattoo 'idiot' on my forehead before I ever got back together with the likes of him."

"Good."

"What has he been up to anyway?" I ask.

Last thing I heard, he was in a rehab center for his drug and gambling addiction. He used to be a professional poker player, so I'm not sure what he does now that he has realized his addiction issue.

"Apparently he moved to Hawaii and has been teaching surf lessons at a resort."

"I didn't even know he could surf," I snort.

"Yeah, me neither. Hunter seems to think he's a changed man. Dennis wears tank tops and puka shells now and calls everyone 'brother.' He apparently is on some fruit-only diet, also."

I can't hold back my laughter. "That must have been *some* rehab facility."

This sounds nothing like the guy I knew.

A few minutes later we pull up in front of our new favorite taco spot in town, Taco-bout It, and I park in one of the few empty spots.

I see that Summer's silver Lexus is already in the parking lot. Our hotshot lawyer. She is always on time for every event, if not thirty minutes early.

We head inside, and the hostess escorts us back to a booth where we see Summer peek out from behind a large laminated menu and give both of us a big smile.

I slide onto the upholstered bench across from her as she scoots over, and Olive sits next to her. Summer is still dressed in her work clothes; she must have come straight from the office.

"Long day at work?" I ask her.

She grins brightly at both of us. "Actually, ladies, I just got my nails done." She dramatically lifts her hand and places it in the center of the table.

What I see first is a set of beautifully manicured mauve nails. What I see second is a huge diamond rock placed on her ring finger.

Olive notices at the exact same time I do; we both look up at her and scream.

Chapter 8

"You Know I'm No Good"
Ivy

One week later

One week ago, I found out one of my best friends is engaged; today I'm standing in a slushy puddle of mud with her looking at a chapel venue.

This is what happens when you own a bridal store—you immediately become the go-to person for all things bridal for anyone that has ever met you. I can't say I don't enjoy the time I'm getting to hang out with Summer, though. I've just got a lot of my own stuff filling my plate. I introduced her to a few incredible wedding planners, and I'm hoping she will hire one so that they can step in.

I glance at my phone. "I've got thirty more minutes till I need to leave and let the handyman in at the shop."

Summer ducks under a low tree branch as we continue to walk around the chapel grounds. She is at least eight inches taller than me, so I don't have to worry about getting smacked by the branch.

35

"Ah, yes." She smiles. "Donovan."

"Why are you saying it like that?" I scrunch up my face.

"Nothing, he's just your type. That's all." She winks at me.

"Why does everyone keep saying that?" I ask, exasperated. "*Was*. Was my type."

"Old habits die hard." She nudges me with her arm. "And *he* is a hard one to ignore."

"What do you guys all want me to do? Fuck him?" I shout and instantly regret it when I see two old women walking out of the chapel with shocked expressions.

"Sorry!" I bellow to them in apology, but the ladies just shake their heads in disgust as they head towards the parking lot.

Summer doesn't even seem bothered by the fact that I likely just embarrassed her. She straightens her navy blazer. "I hate this place anyway, it's a mud pit. Let's go."

We head to her car together, and once we get inside, she takes a planner out of her center console and marks off this location.

"Only twelve more places to try," she says, smiling.

"Aw man, too bad I have to go to work," I tease.

We get on the road, and she starts heading towards Vera Bridal, where I left my car earlier.

"I wasn't trying to make you feel bad back there. Olive and I just worry about you sometimes. We want you to find someone."

Trust me, if there's anyone that doesn't want to be left behind in the crowd of married people, it's me. I want companionship too—just like my friends. I used to be the one that was always in a relationship growing up and Olive never dated anyone. But how the tables have turned. She's married, Summer's engaged, and I don't even have a late-night booty call.

"I understand, but that guy is a total dick. I'm only using him for his fix-it skills."

"Apparently he's not that bad, Ivy."

I look at her with a firm expression, and she holds up her hands in surrender.

"Just saying. Eddie, Hunter, and Wes all love him—and you know two of those three guys have great judgment."

I can't help but laugh in agreement with her statement.

Poor immature, beautiful Wes. *Wes the Mess* is what all us girls secretly call him behind his back.

Ten minutes later we pull up to my store, and there is a large black truck in the parking lot. Of course, Donovan has a truck—it's in the douchebag dress code.

Summer pulls her car up in the lot right by the front door, and smiles at me. "Good luck," she teases.

I snort. "Thanks. He's the one that you should be wishing luck. We both know I can hold my own."

This makes her chuckle.

She has heard the story about me smashing my ex-boyfriend's front windshield when I found out he was cheating, the *final time* before I dumped him, many times.

I used to be a *wee bit* toxic in relationships as well—at least I can recognize my mistakes, though.

I tell Summer goodbye and grab my bag before pushing open the passenger door of her car. I instantly notice Donovan leaning against the Vera Bridal exterior window, waiting for me. I didn't even see him get out of his truck. I guess when you're that tall, you get to take half the steps of a normal person to reach your destination.

He looks good today.

He has on a grey sweatshirt, jeans, and work boots. There's something about men in winter clothes that is so hot to me; I love a man in a sweatshirt and a beanie.

His dark hair is casually pushed away from his face, putting his dark eyes and full lips on display. His features are unamused, like every previous time I've seen him, brows pulled together as he stares me down.

I decide today I will be professional and start everything out on a good foot, so I plaster a grin on my face and cheerily greet him.

"Good morning." I smile brightly at him. "Happy Monday!"

He grunts a response. "Another start to a long week."

"Let me guess. Do you hate Mondays, Garfield?"

"Ha-ha," he replies, his features barely moving as he lets out a monotone fake laugh.

That was close to a new emotion, right? Sarcasm.

I unlock the door and walk in, holding the door open so he can follow me. He picks up a large toolbox and wood panels that he had placed on the sidewalk outside. He texted me last night letting me know he had all the supplies and would be coming today to start building the new staff room shelves. I told him last week that I wanted to get that part of the job out of the way first so I could get the room back in order.

"You know the way from here," I tell him, and he nods before stepping past me and heading to the staff room.

I spend the next two hours catching up on some emails at the front desk, trying to not get too distracted by the sawing and hammering. Other than the sound of tools busy at work, I haven't seen or heard a peep out of him.

Deciding that I should go check on what he has accomplished today so far, I stand up from the front desk and walk down the gown-lined hallway. I shouldn't feel nervous about going in there and disturbing him—but for some reason I *am*.

I peek my head in and see him standing against a far wall,

wiping the sweat off his forehead with the bottom of his T-shirt. This has caused his full stomach to be on display. I wouldn't even call it a stomach—brick wall of abs is more like it.

It's not hot in here.

I clear my throat from the doorway. "Hey, just checking how it's going."

He lowers his shirt when he sees me, and it might just be my imagination, but it feels like it's in slow motion. I swear I can almost see a smirk forming on his face when he notices where my eyes are focused.

"It's going."

"Great. I was going to run and grab some lunch. Want me to get you anything?"

"No, thanks. I brought my own." He picks up a nearby water bottle he must have brought with him and starts to gulp it down.

"Okay, well...cool, keep up the good work." I pat the door frame and start to head out but stop when I decide I should talk to him a little more—break the ice. Like Summer said, if he's friends with all the guys, he can't be *that* bad. I might as well try to get to know him.

I turn back towards him. "So do you prefer the nickname Donnie or Van?"

He almost spits out his drink. "Neither," he says, scowling. "*Donovan.*"

"I bet you're *real* fun at parties." I cross my arms and raise a brow, egging him on.

Why do I love pissing him off so much?

Donovan takes a step closer to me before saying in a low tone, "I'm a blast."

He turns towards the wall with the shelving again and picks up a hammer and nail; he places headphones in his ears.

Alright, conversation over, noted.

I wonder what kind of music a joyful and smiley man like him listens to. Probably something really crazy like paint drying and snoring.

Chapter 9

"Toxic"

Ivy

Touching gently, I run my hand across the sturdy wooden shelves lining the whole wall that Donovan just finished moments ago. He went way above and beyond what I asked for. Every shelf row has a few built-in compartments on the end for storing smaller items with pull-out drawers. I had briefly mentioned how annoying it was trying to store the jewelry and lace swatches on the shelves in plastic bins—Donovan found a solution without even being asked.

Impressive craftsmanship.

Before I could start to say my thanks to him, he was packing up his tools swiftly and exiting the front door—not one for conversation at all.

I found myself wanting excuses all day to go into the room and see his grumpy but sexy face. I know he is just doing his job well by taking so much care and time with building the staff room shelves—it is his job, after all. But the deranged side of me wants to pretend like it was for me.

I wanted to at least speak a full sentence to each other today.

Should I care? Not at all. I *shouldn't* want attention from someone like him. His energy is so closed off, and he constantly seems angry. After the type of guys I've dated, I ought to be repulsed by his personality—and I was! Yet here I am, still thinking about him after he left.

I'm giving him too much power over my mind.

I'm a confident woman, and I know I can usually get male attention easily, so I think that's why it's driving me insane that he is still so uninterested after meeting multiple times already. The fact that he won't soften up and have a conversation with me, and that he seems so mysterious and cold, is reeling me in. I feel a little bit of my old ways bubbling up from under the surface.

Unfortunately, my interest has been piqued. I want to get to know him.

Toxic Ivy.

Toxic. Toxic. Toxic.

Chapter 10

"Touch Me"

Ivy

Two weeks later

The past few weeks have passed by in a blur of work and renovations. Donovan has kept his word and has shown up to do projects for a few hours around the shop four nights a week after appointments end. He also has been pulling full days of work on the two days we are closed.

I honestly couldn't ask for a better person to do the task—his work has been thorough and efficient, not to mention afford-able. So far, he has fixed up the staff room, sanded and repainted all the doors that were worn down from years of use, and completely rehung the bridal gown racks. Jade, Zoe, and Blair couldn't be happier with what he's done around Vera; they've been singing his praises to me every shift.

I made a few decorative changes when I first bought the store, like simple interior painting and covering cracks in the paneled walls with floral art—but I really wasn't responsible when it came to getting the shop ready. I was just dying to get the place open.

Vera Bridal is the *only* bridal store in Clairesville. Since it's a small mountain town, there aren't many options for brides at all. I previously worked at a bridal shop when I lived here, before my brief stint in Atlanta, but that location was out of town—over forty-five minutes away.

I knew this was an untapped market that I needed to fill for our little town and the surrounding areas, and boy, was I right. The business has been thriving.

I'm not even going to lie to myself and say I would change how I rushed to open the store. Seeing those first few brides get their dream gowns made the hurry feel worth it.

Now, almost a year later, I'm paying the price, though. Every expense I didn't spend back then to fix something is biting me in the ass at the current moment.

At least the ass taking my money is a fine one.

Stop it, Ivy! I tell myself, groaning out loud. I have spent these two weeks absolutely obsessing over a man that I've learned two facts about: he hates chives, and he is allergic to tomatoes.

These both seem like green flags to me.

Okay, so he despises chives? Great, he will never have onion breath. Big deal, a man can't consume a fruit that most people think is a vegetable. No problem, he's a simple man that can't handle lectins.

He didn't outright tell me these facts; that would have been too much conversation for his liking. I only learned these things after offering him some bruschetta from the Italian place across the street, before he scowled and told me "no," briefly explaining why.

Continuing to wipe down a shop mirror with a towel and glass cleaner, I grow more frustrated with myself by the second. It's 6:45 on a Tuesday night, and Donovan will be arriving any second. Tonight he is going to repair the racks in the fitting rooms and asked me to stick around for a little while so he can make sure the height is okay.

So here I am, furiously scrubbing the mirror in a light pink dress, waiting for his arrival. I may have worn a dress that usually gets me compliments for a particular reason. The reason might be that I want his eyes to linger on me.

I feel eager for his gaze and it's driving me insane.

Not even five minutes later, I hear the familiar two short knocks on the front door—the subconscious signal he's created to alert me that it's him outside and not an after-hours intruder.

Feeling slightly nervous, I take a quick peek at myself in the mirror and flip my head over to give my hair some much-needed volume. The strawberry blonde strands fall around my face, and I instantly feel calmer and poised—security blanket to the rescue.

"Coming!" I sing out and walk to the front door quickly before unlocking the top and bottom bolts. When I pull it open, I pretend like his appearance doesn't take my breath away momentarily. The more I'm around him, the more attractive I think he is—I know it's messed up to feel this much desire for someone who's only here because I hired him, but I can't help it. He doesn't seem to notice or care about what I do, anyway.

Donovan stands in the doorway, statuesque as always. His dark hair is down around his face, and he's wearing a beanie with a hand logo on it. I recognize that it's a skateboard brand from hanging out with Hunter and Olive.

Okay, am I learning a third fact about him?

I point up at the beanie. "Do you skate?"

He seems confused at first but then appears to remember what he's wearing. "Yes, that's how I know the guys."

"Oh cool." I smile and let him step past me to enter the shop. "Are you any good?"

"Yeah. I am." He's still stone-faced.

"I have a question for you." I shut the door and bite the inside of my cheek as I walk towards him. "Do you have the ability to smile?"

"Yes." Still expressionless.

"What makes you smile then?"

"Lots of things."

I snort. "Okay, let's hear them."

"No."

"No?"

"I said no," he repeats, and I swear he almost leans forward a little closer towards me as he says this—I think he's taunting me.

"Well then, *great* conversation," I say, and give a highly sarcastic fake "hurrah."

He seems unbothered by our exchange, like always, and walks off down the hallway to the first fitting station. I don't even think Donovan noticed my *look at me* pink dress.

I'm deeply offended that this man hasn't objectified me.

Chapter 11

"Hot Stuff"

Ivy

December

"Okay, so we are going to Seagull Bay, right?" Olive asks me from the other side of our phone call.

"Correct," I respond. "Summer said she wanted to do a beach town in Florida for her bachelorette weekend. Seagull Bay seems to have the best hotel and restaurant options."

"Fantastic. Have you contacted the other bridesmaids to make sure they're available?"

"Yes, Leena said she's on board and excited. Summer's sister won't be able to come, but Summer already knew that would likely be the case since she lives out of the country, and it's such short notice."

We are going on the bachelorette trip next month because that's the only time Summer will be able to take off after a big case ends. She asked me and Olive to be her maid and matron of honor, so we have now been automatically put in charge of planning the bachelorette weekend events.

Everything feels like it's moving so swiftly. I even joked with Summer the other day and asked her if this is a shotgun wedding, because most brides plan their wedding for at least a year in advance of their wedding date. She just laughed it off, though, and told me that she has been waiting her whole life for someone like Eddie and wants to be his wife as soon as possible.

They set their wedding date for this June—which is practically tomorrow in bridal years.

It's all very sweet to hear, but it's also incredibly stressful for her three other bridesmaids and a certain bridal store owner. She picked out the base of her dress a few days ago at the store and is paying an exorbitant amount of money to have the gown custom-made and expedited from one of the designers we carry.

Summer chose a silk satin fabric—very expensive—and wants a custom strapless bodice with a corset back and pearls starting from the back of the gown all the way down to the six foot train.

The designer said it couldn't be done, but with a little extra money and my adamant pleading with them to do it for me as a personal favor, voila, it's happening. It usually takes at least nine months to order and make a gown, so Summer is fast-tracking the process quite a bit. Especially for a dress that's so heavily customized.

She's lucky I love her ass.

"And you hired the male dancer already?" Olive asks.

"Affirmative. One of the *Sea-men* will be surprising us all at the hotel suite on Friday night."

"With a name like that, they've got to be good," she snorts. "I have ordered all the party favors: boas, wigs, and lots of penis necklaces."

"Perfect. I think we are really going to pull this off, even with the short notice."

"Same, but let's not pat ourselves on the back yet."

"Oh, Olive the pessimist. How I love ye."

"Shut it," she murmurs. "Realist is the *correct* word."

Moments later we end the call when I pull up to Vera. It's a Sunday morning, so the parking lot is empty, but I'm here so I can let Donovan in. I guess I might as well give him a key at this point, instead of coming up here on my day off—I trust that grumpy man. But on the other hand, it has helped me to accomplish tasks I've been putting off around the store.

Additionally, I think I've been using unlocking the door each day for him as an excuse to see him.

Am I delusional? I only spent two hours googling him last night—sounds healthy to me.

All I learned from my internet stalking was that he is thirty-two, his employee photo on the Anderson Fishing Charter website is super-hot, and he may or may not be currently living in Australia as a father of five?

That result might have been for another Donovan Anderson, but what do I know?

Like always, his black truck is waiting for me in the parking lot. I'm someone who's usually on time to places now...after years of practice. I used to be a mess and would show up everywhere an hour late—it drove my friends insane. Donovan is always at least fifteen minutes early getting here. I pretend it's because he wants to see me, too.

When I park my car, he hops out of his truck, grabs a bucket of white paint out of the back, and meets me at my driver's side door.

He greets me with a brisk head nod, and I smile at him as I lift two coffee cups out of my front seat cup holders.

"Good morning. This for you," I tell him, and hand one of the cups over to him.

He looks reluctant as he takes it, and holds the cup under his nose to lightly sniff it.

"Jeez Louise," I say to him with a laugh. "It's just coffee. I'm not trying to poison you." I raise an eyebrow. "At least not until you're done fixing up the store."

"Thanks." He takes a sip, then looks down at the cup and seems perplexed before he takes another sip. "This is...delicious." He looks up at me.

"I spent all morning personally straining the coffee beans, just for you."

"Is that why the cup says Main Street Café?" He smirks at me.

"Exactly." I beam. A smirk is *so* close to my goal of getting a smile out of him.

He takes a few more gulps of the coffee before tossing the cup in a public trash bin near the sidewalk. I watch as he tucks his hands in his pockets and casually walks back over. We make eye contact and I quickly try to distract myself by unlocking the front door. I push my weight against the door to try to get it to open, but the trim sticks. Not ideal when I'm carrying my own hot beverage in my other hand. The coffee sloshes over the lid as I try to use my body weight to push the door open.

I feel the burn of liquid against my chest and look down to see the mess. My heavy white cashmere sweater now has a large tan stain on the front.

"Shit," I murmur to myself.

I suddenly feel body heat behind me.

"Here, I'll hold your coffee." Donovan reaches around me and takes it from me before I can even react. He then grabs the handle and pushes the door open halfway with little difficulty. "I will have to sand and fix the door for you. Something's sticking in the frame."

Man, a little coffee must go a long way with this guy. He's almost being what I would call *sociable* today.

"Thank you," I tell him as he shuts and opens the door again to test it—it creaks loudly on the hinge.

"I'll fix that, too," he says from directly in front of me. I feel his body warmth still, and it unnerves me to be this close to him.

"Thanks," I whisper as he backs up for me to step inside the shop first.

Once he's followed me in, he quickly goes past me down the hallway to start his work for the day. That conversation would definitely be what I call progress.

At this point, I might as well set our wedding date. Is this spring too soon?

Chapter 12

"Thunderstruck"

Ivy

Three hours later, I'm still at the store checking off stuff that needs to be accomplished. I've already reorganized all of our designer inventory books and sorted new purchase orders. Donovan is in the hallway painting panels of the wood that he replaced, a much-needed repair from years of deterioration. It feels nice to have another body present on the days when the shop is closed. It can get a little lonely for me in this old store, especially with no one to talk to but Barnaby. For some reason, he never talks back.

I am currently in the old storage shed out back, digging around in boxes and trying to see if there's anything worth salvaging to donate before I trash most of the items. It's an absolute dust pit in here and I don't think anyone has even walked in here in the past twenty years.

All I've found so far is broken clown dolls and ripped clown paintings—this place is nightmare fuel.

Fuel would be a good idea actually; I'd rather just light this whole shed on fire instead of cleaning it out.

I can picture it now:

*The song "Thunderstruck" starts playing in the background. I maniacally laugh and walk towards the shed. I kick open the door with my boot—*I'm wearing steel-toe combat boots in this fantasy*—then take a bright red lighter out of my back pocket. I start by lighting a single cardboard box on fire. It spreads, and the first clown doll slowly ignites, then the next and the next. I laugh as the clown heads slowly melt like wax dripping from a candle—a horror movie. Brushing off my hands, I take one final satisfactory glance around the shed, turn my back, and saunter away. As I make my way across the parking lot towards my store, the shed explodes in slow motion behind me—clown doll parts raining down in every direction—right as the chorus of the song plays.*

I don't think I could handle an arson charge, though, so I guess trash bags it is.

Brushing some dust from my hands against the front of my jeans, I stand up straight, ready to head out the door to grab a few more garbage bags. As I step forward, I see a small dark rope hanging down in front of the shed door.

That's weird; I didn't run into it as I walked in here ten minutes ago.

I take a step closer and get ready to grab the rope so I can toss it out of my way, when it moves.

The rope *moves.*

The rope is not a rope after all. It's a big, terrifying snake, and it's now sliding down the wooden ceiling beams, directly in front of me.

I scream at the top of my lungs.

Chapter 13

"Firestarters"

Ivy

What doesn't even seem like five seconds after my initial scream, Donovan busts through the shed door, out of breath and wild-eyed.

"What's wrong?" he demands, his chest visibly moving in and out at a rapid pace.

I struggle to get the words out. "Sn-sn-snake," I tell him, pointing up.

He looks directly above him.

Blinks.

Then he reaches up a single arm and lifts the snake gently around its middle.

The snake coils around his hand comfortably, and Donovan walks out of the shed like this is an everyday event.

What the fuck?

I quickly follow him and watch as he releases the snake into some nearby bushes towards the back of my property. He tucks his hands in his pockets and watches as the snake slithers away, seeming satisfied once it's hidden from sight.

I stare at him dumbfounded as he walks back over towards me.

"What?" he asks.

"You just picked up a snake like it was a sweet little puppy."

Donovan shrugs. "I work with all kinds of creatures daily. We live in the middle of nowhere on a lake, there's never a shortage of wildlife."

"Right," I say, still staring at him, flabbergasted. Why is this turning me on?

He scowls at me. "Don't scream like that, I was worried that there was an emergency."

"There *was* an emergency—a snake."

"That was a harmless little rat snake. It was probably just trying to get out of the cold."

"Oh, let me guess, '*It's more afraid of me than I am of it*,' right?" I mock.

"Exactly." He slides his hands out of his pockets and readjusts his trucker hat. "Well, if you're fine now...I'm going back inside."

"Right, okay." I smooth down my stained sweater. "Yes, I am. Thanks for your help."

He looks at me for a moment longer before he turns and stalks off. The bottom of his hair that hangs below his hat blows slightly in the wind, and I watch as he takes every confident step towards the back entrance.

I know I'm overthinking our every interaction, even though that felt like a knight in shining armor moment—he only came because he heard me scream for help.

But on the other hand, he did just tell me that he was worried, didn't he?

Chapter 14

"Let Me Think About It"

Ivy

"S o, he just manhandled the snake? Like it was a feather?" Jade snorts. "And then walked away like nothing happened?"

"Yeah, that's it." I shrug and bite into a warm slice of pizza.

"Tell us again how he rushed in to save you," Zoe adds with dreamy eyes, squeezing a pillow on my couch in her arms like she's embracing a lover.

We are currently having a staff girls' night and dinner at my apartment, and I just finished telling all the girls about the incident at the shop earlier today.

They are now reading way too far into the events of the day, too, and I'm secretly eating it up. I'm glad I'm not the only person to notice that the moment was slightly swoon-worthy. He did rescue me, after all, even if he was frowning while doing it.

"And he's so hot," Blair says, as she opens my fridge to pull out a bottle of white wine.

"That he is." Jade quickly sits up from her slouched position in the seat across from me at my table. "I have an idea."

"Okay?" I chuckle slightly and take a sip from my water bottle.

"You should sleep with him!" She says it like it's a no-brainer.

Completely taken aback by her idea, I choke on my water. As I cough and sputter, Zoe stares at me, wide-eyed. "Are you okay?"

"Mhmm," I tell her, before coughing a few more times. Then, finally clearing my throat, I add, "I just didn't expect my sex life to be an open forum with my employees."

Blair opens the wine bottle and pours it into four glasses, handing one to each of us before she kicks off her shoes and sits next to Zoe on my couch. "Yeah, definitely a workplace violation in there somewhere."

"Oh, fuck the rules. We are all way more than just coworkers." Jade rolls her eyes. "You showed us your ingrown hair last week, Blair."

"Okay, and? I was concerned." Blair shrugs.

"On your crotch," Jade adds, narrowing her eyes at her.

"I don't regret it one bit." Blair flips her hair over her shoulder before turning towards me. "Write me up for showing my who-haw, Ivy."

"The only thing I'm about to write you up for is referring to your female anatomy as a 'who-haw.'" I laugh. "That's actually a crime."

"Jamie *loves* my *who-haw*." She laughs, and I reach forward to grab a nearby decorative pillow to chuck at her head. Blair ducks and sticks her tongue out at me.

Jamie's her husband; they were high school sweethearts and have been together for over ten years. They basically have a Hallmark movie romance.

Jade groans. "Fire her, that's disgusting," she jokes.

She would never actually mean it for a second, though. We

are much closer than most workplaces, especially considering we have all only known each other for a year. I basically consider the three of them to be my sisters at this point.

We talk about *almost* everything.

"When I first saw him, I thought he was a movie star," Zoe says in her Disney princess way. "He just has this presence about him."

"Yeah, sex," Jade deadpans. "That aura is called arousal."

Zoe blushes—her sweet, innocent heart.

The girls have seen Donovan a few times now because he tends to show up to Vera Bridal early when they are leaving for the day, and the three of them always shoot me suspicious looks.

"There's nothing going on between us." I grab another slice of pizza from the box in front of me. "It's strictly professional."

"It could...not be, though...down the road." Blair grins.

"I don't think I'm his type."

"I'm calling bullshit," Jade snaps. "You're everyone's type. My brother is gay, and he said he would date you."

I hold my hand to my heart. "I'm flattered, I would totally date Mark. Tell him to give me a call sometime."

"I'm being serious, though," Blair says. "I think you should consider asking him out whenever he's done fixing up the shop."

"Or at least sleep with him!" Jade adds.

Trust me—if he acted interested in me at all, I would gladly go on a date or sleep with the man. Not that I would admit it to any of the girls, though.

Chapter 15

"Suicide Messiah"

Ivy

I'm finalizing a few veil orders on my laptop at the front desk when I hear the familiar knock at the door—he's here.

Internally, I'm panicking; I haven't been able to stop thinking about what the girls said to me about trying to date him down the road. Maybe I should just try to flirt with him a little bit and see if he takes the bait.

Closing my laptop quickly, I stand and smooth down my skirt as I head toward the front door.

"Welcome, stranger." I smile as I pull open the door and freeze momentarily when I see his cousin is standing with him.

"You remember Ezra," Donovan says, holding intense eye contact with me. I feel like I'm burning up under his gaze. A cold gust of wind comes through the doorway, pushing my hair back away from my face, but I don't even feel the winter chill.

I want this man.

Ezra clears his throat, and I snap out of my thoughts, realizing he's been holding out his hand for me to shake.

"Good to see you again." He smiles warmly at me and looks around. "This is a cool spot you have here."

"Thanks," I enthusiastically respond to him, taking his large hand in my own. His is rough from probably years of manual labor, but his nails are cut short and clean. "I like it, too. Issues and all."

"He's going to help me with some of the staff bathroom plumbing tonight," Donovan explains, his expression serious. "That's more of his specialty than mine."

"I'm the plumber in the family." Ezra chuckles. "Handling the charter most months, plumbing for the others."

"Is there anything you guys can't do?" I joke. "Thanks for your help, though." I smile at Ezra before turning towards Donovan. "Don't let me get in your way; head on back."

Donovan gives me a single head bob in thanks, and I swear I almost notice his lip twitch a little when he passes me.

The hint of a smile makes me feel confident.

"Hey, I'm going to turn some music on the speakers. I like to listen to something while I clean up from the day. What do you wanna hear, Donovan?"

He stops walking and turns back to face me.

He thinks for a moment. "How about 'Suicide Messiah' by Black Label Society?"

"Oh, of course—that's a Taylor Swift song, right?" I tease.

He gives me a long look before turning around and continuing to walk to the back of the shop.

"That was a joke," I mumble under my breath.

"I know," he responds without looking back. I don't even know how he heard me.

"Also, I wanted to thank you for the other day," I call out after him.

He turns, seemingly exasperated that I'm still speaking to him. "For?"

"The snake rescue. I probably would have had a heart attack if you didn't burst through the door at that minute."

Donovan pauses, then he shrugs slightly. "It was no big deal. Glad I could help." His deep voice seems to rumble down the hallway and up the back of my spine.

I take a breath. "I'd love to get you a little gift as thanks. Snake removal wasn't in your job description." I laugh and add, "What do you like?"

He stares at me again, his eyes dark and piercing. "Let me get back to you on that."

With that, he once again strides away.

I don't even realize that Ezra is standing in the hallway behind me until he walks up next to me. He leans in with a smirk. "Like I told you, he's a little drama queen."

I snort and glance at him before whispering, "I wouldn't call him little *or* dramatic. But he is a man of few expressions."

"He's a teddy bear." Ezra's brows draw together as he looks down at me. "He's just shielded."

"Why?" I blurt out.

Ezra looks down at me, surprised, and shakes his head. "It's not my story to tell."

"You're right. I'm so sorry; that was rude and invasive of me." I cringe inside from my big mouth making things awkward.

"It's okay, don't worry about it, Ivy. Personally, I am an open book." Ezra looks down the hall to where Donovan disappeared into the back room. "My cousin, though, he keeps to himself."

I nod my head in understanding. "Got it. Well, I won't keep you—let me go and turn on that song request for Mr. Anderson." I plaster a smile on my face and turn away rapidly.

Now my head is swimming from the lack of information, and all I want is to know Donovan's story.

Chapter 16

"Outta My Head"

Ivy

Donovan grips my hips and pulls me closer towards him before crashing his lips against mine. His kiss tastes like all my wildest desires, and I need more.

"You're mine," he growls into my mouth. "Don't you forget it." I gasp as his tongue plunges into my mouth, and he claims what's his.

Wow, this is really happening.

He lifts me up in his arms, and I can feel his hard length against my body as I put my hands in his thick, dark hair. He sits me up on the counter and begins to open my legs, giving me a wicked smile as he does—this is all happening so fast.

Wait, too fast.

What is that beeping sound?

I spring up from my pillow suddenly. My chest is heaving as I brush my wild hair that is currently suffocating me away from my face. My body is coated with a layer of sweat, and I'm insanely thirsty. It was just a dream. Just a *dream*. My phone alarm beeps from my nightstand, and I reach over and shut it off aggressively.

Dammit—put me back in.

After my quick workout at the gym in my complex, taking a shower, and putting on a light layer of makeup, I skim through my closet and end up deciding on a bright green sweater and some checkered pants. I know the green sweater always pairs well with my strawberry blonde hair, and I'm hoping Donovan notices, too.

I grab my crossbody bag and take one final look in my bedroom mirror before heading towards my apartment door. As soon as I open it, a strong gust of wind blows me back—I'm not someone who enjoys the cold, which is ironic since I chose to move back to a mountain town where it snows occasionally.

I'm already wishing for warmer weather. The only time cold weather is fun is when it's the holidays, and the only time holidays are fun is when you're in a relationship. Neither of those are true for me right now, so this weather can eff off.

The only thing pushing me out my front door is the thought of a hot coffee from Main Street Café on my way to the shop. This has been my routine for the past year since I pass it on my drive to work: get ready for the day, and then stop there on the way for a little sweet treat and caffeine to start my morning off right.

The first day that I decided to extend the olive branch by getting Donovan one, too, was a good day at the shop. So now I've subconsciously created a habit of it ever since in an attempt to thaw his icy heart.

Today will be no different.

By the time I pull up to Main Street Café, the parking lot is almost empty from the buzz of the morning crowd. Good, a quick line then.

When I get inside, I wave to my favorite barista, Arlet. We have formed a micro-friendship this past year. We don't actually know much about each other, but we've bonded over our love of horror movies. One day she was wearing a Nosferatu tee, and that did me in—friendship formed. Maybe one day we will take this friendship outside the confines of Main Street Café.

"One or two today?" Arlet smiles at me.

"Two." I grin as I walk up towards the counter.

"Man, he must be some handyman if you're buying him coffee every day." She smirks at me. For someone who doesn't know my quirks, she sure figured me out quickly.

"Hey. I don't get him coffee *every* morning. Mostly he works nights."

"And I heard from Blaise on the night shift that you get two coffees at eight p.m. sometimes, too," she continues, eyebrows raised.

"Okay, and? A girl can't stay extra caffeinated? The owners of this place should be thanking me for my twice-a-day business."

"You're right, they should." Arlet snorts before putting her hands in the air. "So you're completely single then?"

"Yes. *Completely* single; there is not a single person of interest in mind," I say, lying to myself.

Usually, I'm blabbering to everyone I know about guys I like. But for some reason, I decide to keep this crush to myself. Maybe because he seems so uninterested, and he's also working for me, so the chances of something happening between us are slim to none.

How do I explain that to other people?

I don't want to get my hopes up or have anyone else involved if I try to ask him out one day and he rejects me.

After I pay Arlet, I walk over and stop at the small corner booth where I usually hide out until my order is ready. The little red velvet booth faces the large street window, and I love to people-watch as they walk by.

It's my guilty pleasure.

I sink into the comfy booth and watch a group of girls walk by—on their way to school, I'm guessing from the uniforms. They are singing a popular Sabrina Carpenter song together loud enough that I can make out the lyrics even through the window. They seem so vibrant and free. It instantly reminds me of myself when I was young. I miss feeling that way with my own friends—the easy fun before real life sets in.

Next, an elderly man and woman walk by together. They walk slowly as they talk and smile at each other. It barely looks like they are making progress, but they don't seem to care about the world around them, like they have nowhere else they would rather be. The man holds the woman's hand tenderly in his own and leads her towards the café entrance.

It's evident that he is only walking somewhat leisurely because that's the pace his wife can handle.

I continue to watch them, thinking about how I want to find that type of love. The patient love that carries you throughout your whole life. The type of love that teaches your children what that word truly means.

The love that remains when looks and health fail.

I'm so deep in my thoughts that I don't even realize a man is standing to my right until he repeats himself.

"Excuse me?" he says again.

I turn my head and make eye contact with a beautiful man. He has golden blond hair that is perfectly styled in a short modern cut. He is very well groomed; that's the first thing I notice. Then, I notice his perfect smile, complete with one dimple on his right cheek. He seriously looks like what you would picture as an *all-American guy*.

He continues to speak. "Hi, these are yours."

I realize he is holding both of my coffees in his hands, but I know for a fact I've never seen him working here, and he doesn't have an apron or nametag on.

"Oh, uh, thank you," I stammer and slide out of the booth to grab my drinks.

When I stand, I look over my shoulder to peek and see if Arlet is paying attention so I can make a *what the fuck* face at her about this wacko guy.

She's nowhere to be seen, though, and the guy keeps talking to me. I blink and take the two coffees from his waiting hands.

"I am here to personally thank you for your business here twice a day." He grins.

"Uh...what?" I can't hold back the strange look I give him.

"You're Main Street Café's best customer, Ivy Penny."

How does this guy know my name? Arlet must be playing a prank on me, asking me if I'm single and then sending a hot guy over to mess with me.

Seeing my creeped-out expression, he chuckles. "I know your name because I own this place." He tucks his hands in his pants pockets casually.

"You don't own this place; a woman does. I've seen her here."

I think back to the gorgeous blonde woman who is sometimes in the café. Last time I saw her, she was doing inventory behind the counter and was also heavily pregnant. I piece two and two together. "Oh! Is she your wife?"

"Cora is my sister. She usually handles everything in-house and I'm more the behind-the-scenes guy." He shrugs his shoulders. "But she just had her baby, so here I am. No longer behind the scenes."

"Oh, that makes sense! Well, nice to meet you." I give him a small friendly smile—this guy is cute but not my type. He seems too charming and clean-cut. I usually like my men looking a little more rugged.

"You know, you're kind of blunt." He laughs, looking down at me. "Just flat out telling me I don't own this place."

"Well, I didn't want a *man* taking credit for a woman's business." I raise my eyebrow. "We businesswomen have to stick together."

"Oh. I see." The man has a playful look on his face now. "And you're also a business owner?"

"Yes."

"Care to elaborate?"

"A bridal store."

"Nice." He looks impressed. "My name's Lee, by the way. Thought you should know since I already know your first and last name..."

"Lee," I repeat. "Well, it was nice to meet you, *Lee*, but I've got to get going."

"To your boyfriend," he blurts out, nodding his head in agreement.

"Wha— No." I'm completely caught off guard by his assumption.

He motions to the two coffees. "Sorry, I just thought..."

The moment grows instantly awkward and he shuffles on his feet.

"No, I'm single."

"Well, in that case—can I have your number?" He stammers across the words, and I can't deny that it's a little endearing.

Lee is conventionally very attractive, so the fact that I'm making him nervous intrigues me.

"Is this how you usually introduce yourself to customers?" I can't hide my smile as I tease him.

"Well, no. I never usually talk to the customers, so I think this is why I'm handling this interaction so horribly." He shifts his weight on his feet again, obviously feeling uneasy, and I give him a small, playful once-over.

"Oh, I see, hmmmm." I pretend to think for a moment, my hands still full with both hot coffees.

I'm battling with myself internally, deciding if I should step away from my regular, broody, bad-boy type to give this boy-next-door kind of guy a try.

If the muscular tattooed guys haven't worked for me in the past, why don't I give this guy a chance? Donovan sure doesn't seem interested.

"How about this?" I finally say. "Write your number on my cup."

Lee breaks into a large smile and takes my coffee from my hand. "Great, let me grab a pen, one second." He walks off quickly behind the café counter.

I see Arlet, who apparently was watching us from the register, hold out a pen and hand it to him with a sly smile.

Now I know I've been set up.

Chapter 17

"Alright, Alright"
Ivy

Shortly after, I pull up to Vera Bridal, feeling a little giddy still from this morning's interaction. Someone is interested in me; maybe not the person I was hoping for originally, based on my dream this morning, but this could be happening for the better. I have always been a—mostly—positive person, and I'm going to lean into that.

Donovan is standing near the front door with a stack of lumber, waiting for me. He has on a heavy Carhartt jacket and work boots; all he needs is an axe and a flannel to complete this mountain man fantasy that I'm quickly daydreaming up.

I step out of my car with an armful of lace swatches in a box and the two coffees teetering in the other. Seeing my full hands, he quickly walks forward and reaches to take the coffees from me.

"Thank you." I let out a relieved breath. "That could have been another coffee-spilling catastrophe."

"No problem." Donovan nods. "It's getting chilly out, huh?"

Is he sparking up a conversation with me right now? I must

still be asleep. He usually only speaks caveman—grunting and scowling.

I look up at him. "Yeah, I wonder if we will get snow this year. I would love it for the holidays; the only time snow is acceptable is for Christmas."

"I forgot that's soon."

"Yeah?" I laugh. "Happens the same time every year."

Donovan grunts a response. Oh look, the caveman is back.

"You're not a big talker, are you?" I snort as I unlock the door, pushing it open easily since Donovan has fixed it.

"Nope."

Once I go inside, I sit all the swatches down on the front desk as he follows me in and hands me one of the coffees.

"Thank you," I tell him.

"Thank you for the coffee every day."

I tip my head and give him a small smile. "Of course, you deserve it. You've been working so hard around here."

"It's my job." He brushes off the compliment before he turns to head back outside to grab the lumber from the sidewalk.

A moment later he steps back through the doorframe with a quizzical look on his face. He looks like he wants to say something to me.

"Uh..."

"Yes?"

"There's a phone number on my cup."

Shit.

I slap my forehead and rush over to grab it from him. I completely forgot about Lee the second I laid eyes on Donovan —just like that.

"I'm so sorry." I laugh. "That's mine."

I can feel his eyes on me as I quickly grab the cup from his large, warm hand.

"Whose number is it?" His voice is deep and low.

"Oh, just a guy I met this morning." I chuckle, hoping it comes off as playful as I try to lighten his intensity in this moment.

"Are you going to call him?"

"Oh, uh...I think so?" I bite the inside of my cheek and look away. I would rather be anywhere else than this moment right now; it's extremely awkward.

I know that he is still looking down at me; I can feel his gaze roaming over me, but I refuse to meet his eyes again.

He seems like he has something else to say but instead just backs away and heads through the front door to get the rest of the wood. As soon as he is gone, the room feels like it's grown exponentially, and I let out a relieved breath.

Why is he questioning me about the number? He has made it obvious that he has no interest in me and has had nothing but biting responses for every conversation we have had.

Donovan steps back inside and walks past me with the lumber under one arm. He grabs the other coffee cup off of my desk—the one without the number.

I quickly move out of his way so I don't block his path and pretend to have a huge interest in the pleating on a pair of curtains by the window.

Convincing, Ivy, I think to myself.

I keep "inspecting" the curtains until I hear that he is all the way down the hall, and the staff bathroom door shuts firmly.

I think he really bought my acting; I was a maple tree in my elementary school play, so I know how to perform.

Busying myself with work for the next few hours, I don't even realize that the sun is starting to go down outside until Donovan is standing in front of me, clearing his throat.

I look up from my laptop. "Done for the day?"

"Yes."

"Well, thanks for the work today. I will see you tomorrow at six p.m., right?" I smile at him.

"Yes."

I look back down at my laptop, thinking the conversation has ended, but Donovan continues to tower above my desk.

I meet his eyes once more. "All good?"

"I'm bringing the coffee tomorrow."

"What?"

"I am going to get the coffee for us tomorrow."

"Oh, okay." I give a slight shrug. "Well then, thanks in advance."

He seems satisfied with that response and nods once in goodbye before walking out the door.

After he leaves, I shut my laptop and can't help but grin to myself; something about today obviously got under his skin.

Is the impassive and grumpy Donovan Anderson actually *jealous*?

Chapter 18

"Ready To Go"

Ivy

Two weeks later

That Tuesday, Donovan *did* bring me coffee. The next day he did the same. And then the next day after that, and every single day since. He brings it from my favorite coffee shop each day, the one that Olive and I have spent years going to together, Violet's Cup.

I was suspicious at first, wondering if Hunter or Olive possibly told him that I love that place, but Donovan explained to me one night that he passes it on his way into town.

That night opened up the chance for a conversation, so I also found out other details about him, like the fact that he drives over an hour to come work at my shop every day because he lives on Onilley Lake. I should have put two and two together since he and Ezra own a fishing charter, but I completely forgot. I almost felt flattered for a moment thinking about the fact that he drives all the way here every day, whether it's early or late, until I remembered he's getting paid.

The more I see him, though, the more I continue to like

73

him. I seriously can't help it—the crumbles of information that I find out about him just make me want to learn more.

I'm living in a state of delusion currently—and I'm gladly hiding it from my friends at this point.

I haven't reached out to Lee since that day at the coffee shop, and I do feel slightly guilty about it. I told him he could give me his number, and to just never reach out isn't very nice. And to make matters worse, since Donovan has been bringing me coffee, it really seems like I'm avoiding him and the coffee shop now. I got too in my head about potentially going out with him, and I feel like too much time has passed for me to contact him now without it being strange.

So I'm shocked when I pull into the Vera Bridal parking lot and see an unknown car in a spot near the entrance. Even more surprised when I park in my usual spot and see a tall, handsome blond man get out of the car with a bouquet of flowers and walk towards me.

I roll down my window.

"Hello, Lee." I'm unable to hide my grin; he looks so cute today.

He bites his lower lip with his teeth and gives me a half smile—the single dimple is on full display right now.

"Hi, Ivy. It's good to see you."

"Yeah, you, too." I turn off my car and step out. "Are you in the market for a wedding dress?"

"No. Just the woman who sells them."

"That's a bold statement."

He hands me the bouquet of flowers he is carrying, and I accept it. It's a wildflower bouquet, a rare sight in the winter months.

"Well, I felt like I needed to make a bold gesture...since you have been avoiding me." Lee gives me a modest smirk. There's that charm.

I cross my arms; the bouquet gets shoved against my left shoulder.

"I have not been *avoiding* you. My handyman has been bringing me coffee every day recently." I shrug. "Sorry, but I will gladly take a free beverage if someone brings it to me."

"Man, that sounds like some great service." Lee laughs. "Who is your handyman?"

"Donov—" I start to say, when a voice I have come to know and desire cuts me off.

"I am."

I follow the sound coming from behind me and turn to see Donovan walking towards us from his truck. He is in head to toe black—a stark contrast from Lee's light-blue North Face jacket and khaki pants.

Donovan's face looks shadowy and severe as he strides towards us. I see him glance at my flowers, and a look of annoyance momentarily passes across his features.

Oh great, he's extra irritable today.

I turn back to Lee, ready to give him a smile in apology for Donovan's bad attitude, when I notice he doesn't even seem fazed.

"Well, nice to meet you." Lee smiles and reaches out a hand towards Donovan to shake. "A friend of Ivy's is a friend of mine."

Donovan steps from around me and briskly shakes Lee's hand.

"And you are?" he asks.

Lee clears his throat. "Sorry, I'm Lee." He flexes the fingers on his right hand. "You've got quite the handshake. I think you were about to snap my pinky."

I laugh at his joke and expect Donovan to do the same, but he just stands there, staring Lee down.

This is incredibly awkward, and it needs to end right now.

"Donovan. If you could give us a moment alone, that would be great." I hand him my door key. "You can let yourself in, thanks."

He meets my eyes and looks down at me with a serious expression. "I have your coffee in the truck."

"Okay. Thank you," I squeak out as he takes my key.

"From now on, come to me," Lee tells Donovan. "I will give you two both coffee—on the house."

"You seriously don't have to do that," I say quickly, but Lee holds his hand up.

"You've been a great customer. I can spare some coffee... maybe even a muffin if you agree to go out with me."

Hearing this, Donovan steps past me and walks over to the door. He unlocks it quickly and walks inside, completely ignoring Lee's kind offer.

Lee looks at me wide-eyed, then at the shut door, and murmurs, "I can see why you have him come work when you are closed. He's not exactly the face of customer service."

The comment causes me to burst out laughing. "He really is grouchy, but he does great work. He should add 'does not play well with others' to his business contract."

We stare at each other for a moment, both smiling and completely silent. It feels comfortable—like a place I have been before.

"And if you're wondering how I knew you were closed today and where your bridal shop was...I might have found your store website." Lee winces. "I'm hoping this grand gesture and my honesty are endearing and romantic, instead of creepy and horrifying."

I chuckle, looking down at my flowers with a blush. "It's romantic," I respond quietly.

Lee claps his hands together. "Great, so...would you like to go out with me?"

I pretend to think about it before grinning and saying, "Yes, that sounds great."

"How about tonight?"

"Tonight?"

"Yes." He looks friendly and relaxed—unlike that broody jerk inside.

Why am I even thinking of that jerk right now?

This is how it should feel: easy. Lee feels like a safe option.

"Sure," I say. "I'll go out with you tonight."

"Fantastic." He smiles. "Do you want me to pick you up here?"

"No, I'll drive myself."

"Okay. How does Tova's sound at six p.m.?"

"That sounds incredible," I gush. "I love that place."

"Okay, I'm glad. Well, I'll see you later then, Ivy." He gives me a large smile and a final tilt of his head in goodbye before stepping off the curb and heading to his car.

I've got a date tonight for the first time in over a year.

Chapter 19

"Good Enemy"

Ivy

When I walk in the shop a moment later, I don't expect to see Donovan waiting for me—but he is. His large body is stiffly seated against the cream couch near the entrance and he stands when he sees me.

"Who was that nerd?"

"Nerd?" I scoff. "What are you, a nineties teen movie bully?"

"He had a clip-on phone holder on his belt."

"No, he did not." I cross my arms in frustration.

I can't believe the one time he decides to spark up a conversation with me, *this* is what it's about.

"So he's the one that put the number on your coffee cup?"

"Yes."

"And then he just showed up here?" Donovan glares.

"Yes."

"And you're not uncomfortable with that?"

"No."

"Are you going to go out with him?

"Yes."

"A complete stranger?" Donovan scowls.

"You're a stranger to me, too, basically," I snap back. "And I am alone here with you nonstop."

"It's different."

"Is it?" I stand my ground.

"Forget about it, Ivy."

"Okay. I will."

He looks disappointed. "Whatever." He shakes his head. "It's your bad choice to make."

Donovan turns and begins to walk away down the hall before I can respond. "My truck is unlocked if you want to grab your coffee."

The nerve of this guy.

"Bad choice? How about *good* choice?" I yell out after him. "And I don't want your cranky coffee." *That will show him.*

So much for being professional.

Chapter 20

"10,000 Emerald Pools"

Ivy

D onovan and I avoid each other for the rest of the day like the plague. I can't believe he had the nerve to question me about agreeing to go on a date with Lee when he has been nothing but closed off towards me.

If he is interested, he should have asked me out.

I'm done trying to get his attention.

We both said a quick, monotone goodbye to each other before parting ways at five p.m. His attitude is not my issue. I try to shake away the thoughts of how he pissed me off today with his questioning and turn my attention to tonight.

I'm currently rushing back to my apartment so I can get ready. Lee deserves to have a pleasant first date with me; I don't want my sour feelings from the encounter earlier to ruin my first time going on a date in practically *forever*.

Stopping at a red light, I glance down at my phone and turn on some music to get me pumped up. "The Sharpest Lives" by My Chemical Romance blasts through my speakers, and I start to scream along with the lyrics.

Before I know it, I'm home and running up the stone staircase to my apartment complex two at a time. I purposely chose a living space near my shop so I can make it back and forth within fifteen minutes. I used to live on the other side of town in a real piece-of-shit complex, so I'm happy to be here now.

I unlock my deep blue front door, and my chain of keys jingles loudly as I twist the handle. I have about ten keys on the ring, and I don't remember what half of them go to, but I'm too scared to toss them out—knowing I will need the key the day after the trash goes out.

In less than thirty minutes I'm walking back out my front door, looking and feeling like a new woman. I changed into a pair of body-hugging black flare jeans, a light pink off-the-shoulder sweater that stops right below my navel, and gold jewelry.

My long hair is pulled back with a claw clip, leaving a few loose strands framing my face in a way that hopefully comes off as nonchalant and effortless.

Once I pull into the parking lot of Tora's, I see that the car Lee was in earlier—a dark blue Nissan—is already here. I'm right on time, so I appreciate his punctuality.

One point for Lee.

Lee's head pops up next to my car window a moment later, and he waves to me with a large grin. His hair is perfectly styled, like both times I have seen him previously, not a single strand out of place. He has on a forest-green collared button-up and khakis that fit him like a glove—I swear this man probably gets his underwear tailored.

I begin to open my door, and he steps aside to open it the remainder of the way, reaching his right hand out to help me stand.

I take it and thank him as I slide out of my driver's seat— point two, Lee.

81

"Hi, Ivy. You look striking," he tells me, giving me a quick once over.

"Thank you." I smile and mentally give myself a pat on the back. I reach back into the car and grab my keys, purse, and phone.

"Want me to carry your bag?" Lee reaches out his hand, and I see an expensive gold watch shimmer on his wrist.

Wow, this man must have money; he's wearing a Rolex. I would have never expected that from his humble personality and the simple Nissan he drives.

I grew up with money, though, too. Except my parents didn't usually spend it on items like designer brands; they were more of the "vacationing" type of wealthy that always spent their money on experiences rather than objects.

"Yes, I would love that," I chuckle as I hand him my pink purse, and he slings it over his arm. A man without fragile masculinity—point three, Lee.

He's raking them in quickly.

"Well, let's get out of this cold." He holds out his arm, and I take it. He leads me towards the entrance, an expansive space with shrubbery and a set of red double doors. Lee takes a step ahead of me and opens it. I graciously nod my head to him; someone really taught him manners as a boy.

A bored-looking teenage hostess greets us at the front, and Lee gives her our reservation name. I try to suppress a giggle as I see her strangely eye my bag on Lee's arm. Taking notice of her staring and my failure at quiet laughter, he speaks up.

"Do you like my bag?" Lee asks her. "I was trying to add some color to my outfit today. I didn't know if I should go with pink or blue, though. Did I make the right choice?"

She looks flustered for a second but quickly recovers. "Oh yeah," she deadpans. "Great choice."

"Good, because I really want to impress my date." He glances back at me and smiles.

"Oh, I'm impressed," I tell him. "Actually, I have a purse *just* like that one."

"You don't say." Lee smiles at me, and we just gaze at each other, lost in the moment and the small joke we are sharing.

The hostess clears her throat. "You two can follow me now."

Lee rotates back towards her. "Sorry! Fantastic."

She leads us down a hallway filled with black and white photos that lets us out into the large dining hall. The room is packed, and the sound of soft guitar is heard over the noise of guest chatter and silverware clinking against plates. I inhale deeply and smell fresh bread and herbs; my mouth waters.

The girl stops in front of a small corner table, then sets down the menus before turning to face us. She hurriedly says, "Enjoy," without looking at Lee, and walks off.

I lean in towards Lee. "I think you made her uncomfortable," I snort.

He shrugs. "A six-foot-two man in khakis should be able to carry a pink purse without getting a weird look. That's her problem."

"Oh, you just had to casually slide your height in there, huh?" I tease.

"Are you impressed?" He laughs.

He pulls out my chair, and I take a seat. Point four.

"Everyone is taller than me, so I'm not *that* charmed by your height."

"You *are* pretty short," he jokes. "I think you could fit in my pocket."

"That's why I work out." I pull up a sleeve of my sweater and flex my arm playfully. "No one is kidnapping me with these bad boys."

83

Lee raises his eyebrows. "I'm glad to know you will be able to defend my honor if needed...because I think the hostess has an issue with me now."

I laugh, and a young server walks over to our table, momentarily stopping our conversation to take our drink orders. I get a glass of red wine, and Lee gets a local beer on tap.

"So, tell me about yourself," he says as soon as the server walks away.

"Geez, right to it." I laugh, straightening. "Okay, let's see..."

"Actually, start with three things you hate. It's way more fun to bond over hates than similarities."

"You're so right." I bite the inside of my cheek, deep in thought for a second, then I clap my hands together. "Okay. I hate the smell of gorgonzola cheese, when dentists try to talk to you when you have a mouth full of crap, and romance books with love triangles."

"Interesting," Lee responds. "I don't think I've ever had gorgonzola cheese, so you don't have to worry about the smell of it when you're around me, and I, too, hate when dentists talk to me with my mouth full of tools. Look at that, we have so much in common! Although I think *that* particular dentist hate might be universal."

Our server sets our drinks in front of us, and I take a small sip before Lee continues to talk.

"Why do you hate romance books with love triangles?" he asks. "That's an oddly specific thing to hate."

"Easy, I hate when the main character doesn't choose the person I wanted them to be with." I push a loose strand of my hair that has fallen in my face back towards my claw clip.

"Isn't that kind of like life, though? We can't choose who's right for someone else. It's their journey; all we can do is sit back and witness."

I bite at my lower lip. "Well, aren't you a thinker," I tease.

Lee shrugs. "It's true. We can't change the way other people are or what they like. We can only better ourselves."

I think of Donovan suddenly, his features passing over my mind in a split second. I've been thoroughly enjoying myself and haven't thought about him all night, but suddenly here he is, distracting me.

I swat away his image like the annoyingly sexy gnat it is.

"So," I quickly say, "what about you? What do you hate?"

"Coffee."

"*Coffee?!*"

"Yeah, I hate it." Lee smiles, his friendly eyes creasing in the corners.

"You're messing with me."

"No, I truly hate it. I actually don't even drink caffeine usually."

"Oh, okay. So you're an alien," I tell him matter-of-factly.

He shakes his head and laughs. "I usually just like water."

"How does a *water drinker* end up owning a coffee shop?"

"Because a *water drinker* wants to make his sister's dream come true."

"Well, shit, never mind. That's sweet."

"I know." Lee leans in and whispers playfully, "What can I say? I'm a sweet guy."

Yes, he is.

The rest of our date continues to go on without a hitch; Lee really is charming and easygoing. His eyes illuminate as he tells me a funny story about a new hire accidentally dumping salt in yesterday's muffins instead of sugar, and Lee almost vomiting when he tried one because it was so bad. He said the poor girl's face was horrified until Arlet discovered it was so awful because the ingredients were wrong.

Everything he tells me makes me smile or laugh; I think this is the best first date I have ever been on. As we walk back out to the parking lot, I decide I'm going to kiss him.

This date would be incredible if I could end it with a nice kiss.

We step over towards my car, and I lean against it, bouncing slightly to keep myself warm. Lee looks down at me and scoots a little closer.

"Cold?"

"Yes."

"May I?" He holds out his arms, and I nod before walking into their embrace. His body is solid and warm. His cologne smells like an ocean breeze, and I lean into his hold.

"I had a really good time tonight," Lee tells me in a low voice.

"Me too."

"Let's do it again."

"I agree."

"Can I kiss you?" His voice is even softer now.

I tilt my head up to meet his blue eyes. "Yes."

Relief washes over his features for half a second, and he leans his head down to get closer. I stand on my tippy toes to meet his awaiting lips.

The kiss is warm and soft, sweet.

Just like Lee.

He pulls away, a large smile on his face now. "Alright well, I'll call you."

I nod my head and tell him goodbye as he opens my car's driver's side door for me.

Driving home, I'm happy and content. It was a good night and I'm excited to get together with Lee again. He really seems to be a nice guy, exactly the type of guy I should be dating— kindhearted and funny.

Donovan's beautiful, carved face pops into my head suddenly with a smirk. *"You just keep telling yourself that, sweetheart."*

Chapter 21

"Romance"

Ivy

One week later

I've gone out with Lee two more times since our first date. We went to an ice cream shop on our second date and to the movies on our third. Both times were enjoyable and full of laughter, exactly what I wanted for the holiday season. He asked me to get together tonight, but since it's Christmas Eve, I felt like that would be a little too serious—we have only been on a few dates. So I made other plans to go watch the local Clairesville holiday parade with Summer and Eddie.

Lee surprised me by dropping off some roses at the shop this afternoon with a card. We are supposed to be closed today, which he knows, but Donovan insisted on working, saying he "didn't want to get behind on his schedule," so I'm here to let him in.

I bought Lee a gift a few days ago, a Hydro Flask, since he loves drinking water—and basically only water. He chuckled as he opened it today, telling me that I "get him."

I *also* got Donovan a gift. I'm not exactly sure why I

thought it was a good idea, but when he mentioned to me that he wanted to work this week because he likes to stay busy— after I told him to take it off for the holiday—Donovan told me Ezra is traveling to visit his parents and they have no other family in town. I guess I felt sorry for him.

Hearing that he would be all alone made me pity him, so I had to buy him something. I know he would be annoyed if he knew I felt bad for him, but the thought of his sexy, grumpy self waking up on Christmas without receiving a gift *and* being all alone was too much for me to bear.

So, I bought him a beanie.

Ten minutes later Donovan knocks on the front door, and I walk out from one of the nearby fitting rooms to greet him. We have been doing this awkward dance around each other since the day that Lee first asked me out in front of him. Donovan hasn't brought up anything about it again, which is the way it should be since he's literally here to just do handy work, not to give me love life advice, but it has still felt different.

I'm trying to ignore the pull I feel towards him when he's near and tell myself that it's just my toxic dating history trying to make an appearance again.

Dragging the handle open, his large stature greets me in the doorway. When I take him in, I lose my breath. He is wearing a dark green flannel and black pants; his hair is pulled away from his face, and it makes his chiseled jawline even more severe than previously. I also smell cologne, which I have never smelled on him before. He obviously has put a little extra effort into his appearance today.

I'm at a rare loss for words.

He looks down at me and smirks slightly. I instantly feel like he can read my thoughts. I move out of the way for him to walk through the doorway. He takes two steps past me before setting his toolbox on the floor.

"Merry Christmas," I say in a less than confident voice, still eyeing him as he walks past me. "You're fancy today."

"Oh yeah? I just came from this thing I go to."

"A thing?"

"Just like a group I'm in." He looks around at the wall in front of him. "We had a little Christmas party."

"You're so mysterious." I shake my head. "Anyway, I got you something."

Donovan turns towards me. "Oh yeah?"

"Yeah." I walk over to the desk and pull out a small green wrapped package with a gold bow. I extend my arm to him, and he steps towards me to grab it. "You can open it tomorrow, or now if you want."

"I'll open it now." His voice is soft, which is something I've never heard from him.

I watch his expression closely as he tears open the paper slowly until the beanie is revealed. He looks down at it in his hands, and I see his eyes warm slightly. He lifts it up and meets my gaze.

"Thanks for this, it's really kind of you to get me a gift. You didn't have to do that."

I shrug my shoulders. "I know, I just wanted to say thanks for all your hard work. It was nothing really."

Donovan still looks at me, but this time his expression has lowered slightly to my fitted red dress. His gaze pans over my exposed legs and the curve of my waist. Realizing what he's doing, he snaps his eyes up quickly to meet my own.

"Not nothing," he responds in a quiet voice.

I bite at the inside of my cheek, feeling like there's so much more I want to say to him. Why am I never completely able to express my desires to him?

Donovan luckily speaks up first this time for once. "Well, I guess I'll be getting to work then." He places the beanie on his head. "What do you think?"

"Very handsome." I grin at him.

"Good." His eyes hold an intensity that I would almost think was longing if it belonged to someone else.

I feel like I'm physically burning under his stare.

I speak up now. "I also like your hair like that, too," I motion towards him. "It really shows off your features."

Donovan's face twists slightly. "My features?"

"Yeah."

"What about them?"

"I think you know you have a nice face to look at," I snort.

"A nice face?" He cocks an eyebrow.

"Yes." I cross my arms. "I'm pretty sure you're well aware of how handsome people find you."

He takes a step towards me.

"Do I?"

He smirks. He's messing with me now.

"Yes. I think you do."

"Well, what if I don't care if *people* find me attractive? Maybe there's only one person I want to find me attractive."

He strides even closer to me, and I almost take a step back as he continues to talk. "So do you?"

"Do I what?"

"Do you find me attractive?"

I slap my hands against my sides. "Of course I do, Donovan; I'm not blind."

He pauses, takes off the beanie, sets it aside on the desk, and then says in a low whisper, "Say my name again."

I look up at him, feeling confused by what's happening and extremely turned on. "*Donovan?*"

The warmth of his body seems to surround me, and I feel

drunk off his scent. I so badly want to kiss this man; I feel an unexplainable pull towards him.

"Hmm." He stares down at me with a wicked expression.

"I know I've told you before that you're not much of a talker, but I don't get you. I can never read you," I blurt out in frustration.

"I don't express myself well, I know that." Then a *smile* breaks from his lips. "I'm so much better with my mouth than with my words, Ivy."

I gasp at his statement and the fact that I just saw Donovan Anderson smile for the first time.

Suddenly feeling bold, I say the thing that I've wanted to for weeks. "Then show me."

Chapter 22

"The Summoning"

Donovan

Fuck it.

93

Chapter 23

"Dark Matter"

Ivy

Instantly Donovan's mouth is on mine, and he kisses me with a fury that rivals my own need for him. I feel *everything* in our first kiss.

I accept his tongue in my mouth and stand on the tips of my toes trying to get closer to him. Noticing what I'm doing, he lifts me into his arms and pulls my legs apart so I straddle him. My tight dress has now risen up so much that it's bunched around my stomach, my thong completely on display.

Donovan pulls away from my lips and draws his body back slightly so he can glance down at my black lace underwear.

He groans before looking back up at me. "Damn, Ivy."

His left hand roams up and down my butt and hips as his other arm continues to hold me up; my name sounds so sensual on his lips.

Thank god I wore cute underwear today. Tis the season for sex.

"Kiss me," I whisper, and he instantly meets my demand.

His mouth tastes like all my sinful desires—the man that isn't supposed to be what you want but still is regardless.

He continues to explore my body with his hands, and I can feel his length hardening between my straddled legs, straining inside of his pants. It causes the already overpowering ache inside of me to grow. I haven't slept with anyone in so long, and I *really* want to sleep with him right now.

"I want you," I moan into his mouth.

He answers me with a growl, holding me up with a single arm, as he pulls down my dress and begins to cup my breast.

"What about your boyfriend?" he whispers against my ear.

"I don't have a boyfriend," I respond with a moan as he kisses down my neck. "I'm just dating."

Donovan moves his kisses down my chest, and I bury my face in his shoulder as I let out another moan.

"Now," I tell him. "I want you *now*."

"Fuck," he grunts and pulls away. He looks down at me, his eyes burning with familiar dark intensity. "Okay."

"Back room," I tell him quickly.

He walks with me down the hallway, still in his hold. The short walk feels never-ending in this moment; my body aches to be filled with him. Donovan reaches the door and pushes it open with his shoe.

"There," I command him, pointing to a small couch that sits in the middle of the room. He gently lays me down on it before standing back up to begin undoing his belt. I yank my dress off over my head and watch as he takes off his boots, followed by his pants and flannel.

My mouth waters as I slowly scan my eyes across his toned body. Hard abs mix with muscle and a deep V at his pelvis that goes exactly where I want to be.

I begin a slow clap.

"Uh, what?" His expression is instantly confused, and he looks down at himself.

"Congrats, sir. You are, in fact, one fine specimen, and I

think you were truly carved by the gods themselves; it's actually unfair."

Donovan lets out a quick snort at my compliment before instantly turning into a predator again. He walks towards me and leans down over me, kissing me sensually. I lay my body flat to make room for him on the much-too-small couch as our mouths continue to touch and he lies over me. I'm instantly consumed with his weight and intoxicating scent.

He pulls away from the kiss, breathing heavily. I stare into his shadowy eyes as he begins to touch me more intimately, the lust causing them to fall half-lidded. Donovan delicately trails his hand from my breast to my navel, then my crotch, stopping between my legs.

He pulls away and kneels over me; I groan from the lack of his touch, and he smiles wickedly.

"Enough of the teasing," I beg him.

"But it's so fun to see you flustered."

"Of course the only smile I get from you is when you're torturing me." I roll my eyes.

"Is this torture?" He leans down, still looking into my eyes and puts my left breast in his mouth. I tilt my head back from the pleasure, another moan escaping my lips.

Donovan leans forward and lightly kisses down the side of my face before whispering into my ear, "I'm going to take off your panties now."

"Okay," I whimper.

He pulls my thong down painstakingly slowly. The sensation of lace material sliding down my thighs causes shivers to go through me.

The anticipation is killing me.

Donovan gives me one final kiss before moving his body down mine.

"I have a Christmas gift for you, too." He lowers his face in front of my center, and I can feel his warm breath against me. He gives me a cocky smirk. "Do you want it now or later?"

"Now," I say breathlessly. "*Right now.*"

That's all he needs to hear; he buries his head between my thighs. I'm instantly overcome by the sensation. I squirm deliciously as he licks me, and he pulls my legs apart farther, refusing to let me hide from the pleasure.

After a few minutes of raking my hands through his hair, it's all becoming too much and I want to feel him—the fullness of him.

"Take off your boxers," I tell him.

He lifts his head from between my legs. "I don't have a condom."

"It's fine," I rush out. "I'm on birth control."

His chest heaves up and down rapidly as he looks at me; it seems like he's taking a moment to think. The moment seems like an absolute eternity as I lie bare in front of him.

Finally, he stands and pulls off his underwear. His length is at once released from his boxers, and I reach out to touch him.

Donovan grunts, "Fuck."

I open my legs wider as he kneels between them again on the couch. We make eye contact, and he slides into me slowly. The moment is so wildly intimate that I feel lightheaded. Never in a million years did I think I would be having sex with him today.

I get used to the fullness of him and shift my hips to match his slow pumping rhythm. We maintain eye contact as he picks up the pace—I refuse to close my eyes for a moment and miss any of his expressions. He looks so vulnerable right now, so open. His face is consumed by lust and desire for *me*.

I never want this moment to end, but I'm close. I feel the deep ache building in my core, begging for release.

"I'm going to come," I breathe out.

He increases the speed of his thrusts even more, somehow going even deeper, exactly to the spot that sends me over the edge.

My core spasms around his length, and he throws his head back as he finishes with me. The final thrusts make me feel like I'm soaring, like I'm falling backwards.

No, wait...I'm *actually* falling backwards.

"Oh, shit!" Donovan exclaims suddenly as he grabs the back of my head to catch my fall, and we both go down to the floor.

We broke the fucking couch.

Chapter 24

"Two of Hearts"

Ivy

Two weeks later

"New couch?" Jade asks from the other end of our phone call.

"Yup...just felt like we needed a change since there are renovations going on." I turn away from the rack of clothing I'm currently looking at to browse a lower shelf of the store. "You know, after that nasty old one randomly broke the other week, I thought, why not?"

"Yeah, we all know it was Barnaby," Jade snorts. "It's nice, though. I like the dark purple shade."

"You're right, Barnaby was probably the culprit... Or maybe it's the fact that the couch has been in the shop for many years, probably before any of us were born. I always thought all it would take was one movement on it and—poof—broken."

"I sat on that crusty ancient thing all the time, it seemed super sturdy to me."

I quickly change the subject. "Anyway, can you go through

and schedule pick-up appointments for the brides? I left you a list somewhere on the desk."

Then I hear her heels click down the Vera Bridal hallway to the front desk, followed by the slight crinkle of paper. "Found it. Yup, I'll get on that."

"Thank you." I rest my phone on my shoulder and pick up a bikini bottom that wouldn't even fit half of my anatomy in it; bless the women that can wear this.

"There are only a few appointments this afternoon, so it's an easy day. Is Donovan coming by?"

The mention of his name snaps me back to attention immediately. "Uh, I'm not sure, probably. Why? Did he call and say he wasn't?"

Jade lets out a puff of breath. "Ha...are you okay?"

"Yes," I respond a little too quickly. The truth is I've been in a state of chaos since I slept with him on Christmas Eve. As soon as we finished and broke the damn couch, things got so awkward.

Donovan helped me up after we had sex, and we both put our clothes on in silence. I tried to joke around with him a few times, but he was instantly unsmiling again and told me that he's "not looking for anything serious." That made things ten times weirder. Does he think I would call a spur of the moment hookup at my place of business serious?

He has made it pretty obvious he isn't interested in me like that.

Donovan has never asked me on a date or even hinted about wanting to go out sometime—I know what that was. Just sex. *Great sex.*

I hate feeling like he has the power, though, because I would sleep with him again if I had the chance, without a second thought.

So like the mature woman I am, I've been hiding from him

as much as possible ever since that night. I texted him the day after Christmas that my schedule was going to be insane starting in January, so I just left him a key to let himself in the shop from now on.

His only response back to me was, "Ok." If he has caught on that I'm dodging him, he doesn't seem bothered in the slightest.

This is now a situation that I've never had to deal with before in my industry. Believe it or not, I've never slept with someone I've sold a wedding dress to. I know I need to put on my big girl panties because I will have to face him again to discuss everything workwise as he's finishing up. He should be done within the next week or two, it seems; there are only minor projects left still.

"Hello? You still there?"

"Shit, sorry, Jade." I pick up a red bikini that says "sexy" across the chest—"SE" on one side and "XY" on the other—and get ready to call it quits. "I'm struggling to find stuff for Summer's bachelorette trip."

"Yeah, I can imagine it's hard to find flip flops and bikinis when it's thirty-eight degrees outside and we live in Tennessee. I don't know why you waited till the last second to get a swimsuit."

"Because I assumed I would be able to find the bikini I own, and it's disappeared somewhere in my apartment. I basically tore apart my room yesterday—no luck." I push my hair away from my face, feeling overheated in my winter jacket. "Every swimsuit I've found requires a deep waxing and a prayer to stay in place."

"You're hot. Get one of those."

"I really don't want to," I groan.

"Also, this might be your sign that you need to clean your closet..."

"I will do no such thing; I have a method to my madness. I know where all my stuff is in the clutter."

"Except for your bikini."

"Right, exactly." I never go in the water, so a swimsuit isn't high on my priority list. "I'm going to go, Jade. I need to focus on this task."

"Alright. I'll text you if anything needs your attention."

"Okay, thanks."

"Get the skimpy one."

"*Bye,* Jade."

We hang up, and I turn back towards the string bathing suits; there are literally no other options here, and we leave for the bachelorette in five days. The choice has been made for me; I will be showing it all. I grab a neon green suit and walk to the counter of the small store.

A wispy woman in her mid-forties stands behind the counter with an overly bright smile as I hand her the dental floss suit.

"Great choice," she exclaims. "We just got new swimwear in last week, so you were in luck. This will look great on you."

"Thanks, I'm going to Florida for my friend's bachelorette party."

"Well, won't that be a blast!" the woman responds, her voice raising an octave with excitement—she nails this customer service thing. I wonder if she would ever want to sell wedding dresses.

I take my credit card out of my wallet and smile as I hand it to her. "Yup, excited to get away from the cold and get a tan."

She bags the "swimsuit"—that I could fold into the size of a tissue and slip in my pocket—and pushes it towards me. I thank her and walk outside, instantly kissed by the icy breeze.

I pull my jacket closer to my chest and get ready to head towards my car when I hear my name being called. I turn and see a familiar handsome face looking at me from across the road.

Lee.

His eyes crinkle with a smile as he quickly crosses the street to walk up to me. I stand in place waiting for him. We have texted on and off since the night I slept with Donovan, but this is my first time seeing him in person. I feel mildly guilty, even though I know I shouldn't. We aren't exclusive, and for all I know, he could be dating other women. We owe each other no commitment at this point.

But nonetheless, I feel weird.

"Well, if it isn't the most beautiful woman in the world," Lee greets me with a coy smile.

"Well, if it isn't the charmer," I laugh.

"Doing some shopping?" He curiously looks behind me to the sex shop that I just exited.

"Yeah, trying to find a swimsuit... Apparently they aren't in season right now." I glance around us. "Shocking, I know."

"My sister always complains about the lack of clothing stores in Clairesville."

"It's really a problem. Who wants to travel forty-five minutes to find a department store?"

"Horrible." Lee shakes his head playfully.

"Yeah, well, at least now all my shopping is done." I hold up the bag. "Now I can pack."

"Oh yeah, I completely forgot you're going out of town this weekend."

"Will you miss me?" I tease him.

"Of course, when will you be back?"

"Sunday."

"Get dinner with me before you leave."

"Okay, I will." I grin.

Lee smiles and leans down to kiss me. The kiss is tender

and warm—his tongue touches against my lips lightly, and I open my mouth to deepen our contact.

I wasn't expecting this from him, especially in public; the moment is hotter than I thought it would be.

"Get a room," a gruff voice shouts from my left.

I open my eyes to see an elderly lady giving us a disgusted look and eyeing the sex shop behind us.

I recognize her instantly as one of the ladies that gave me a dirty look the day I was looking at the chapel with Summer.

"Oh, I remember *you*." She narrows her eyes at me and then gives Lee a once-over before throwing her scarf over her shoulder and walking away.

"Geez, who was that?" Lee laughs.

"Never seen the woman in my life."

Chapter 25

"Milkshake"

Ivy

Two days later, I'm waiting in the Main Street Café stockroom for Lee to finish having a staff meeting so we can go on our date. I told him I would meet him here after I left Vera Bridal, and we decided we would just do something casual tonight, like grab dinner and see a movie.

I peek out when I hear laughter and can't help but smile when I see Lee standing in front of the staff, talking animatedly. He has completely been embracing the role of working in-house running the café since his sister has been gone on maternity leave. He has such a tender heart; I'm glad the staff is showing him respect and that they are bonding.

Lee glances at me and winks, mouthing, "Five more minutes."

I nod and step backwards to hide in the stockroom, letting him focus on the meeting.

Seeing a stack of recipe books labeled on the shelf, I get curious and lean up on my toes to grab one. I skim through bakery recipes, scanning the ingredients and trying to take a mental snapshot so I can attempt to replicate an easy one at some point—I can't bake to save my life.

Give me chicken and sides, I can make you a five course meal. Give me flour and eggs, you get burnt concrete.

A few more minutes pass, and a particularly thick notebook labeled "Lee" on the outside catches my attention. I grab it and flip it open, hoping for some juicy insight, and I am quickly let down when I realize it's just his inventory book.

Biting my lower lip with my teeth, I skim to a page towards the back of the notebook and grab a pen out of my purse so I can write a little note for him to find one day.

You're amazing and I'm so lucky to know you.
I hope something good happens to you today.

Reading over the message, I add one more thing at the end: "Your Smiley." Lee has started calling me that as a nickname, and I have taken fondly to it. I told him that I only seem so smiley around him because he brings it out of me.

The sound of footsteps shuffling from the main lobby alerts me that the meeting has probably ended, so I quickly close Lee's notebook, setting it up on the shelf, to leave the surprise for another day.

"Are you ready to go, Smiley?" Lee steps into the stockroom doorway.

"You bet."

"You know, I kind of liked you hiding back in here while I did 'business.' It was like a sexy little secret," Lee teases and winks at me.

"Oh yes, didn't you know I'm your mistress of the night?"

"Well, mistress, I'm starving. Let's go get some burgers?"

"Burgers it is. You also owe your mistress a milkshake."

"Only if she gives me a kiss."

"I guess that can be arranged." I smirk. "But it better come with whipped cream and a cherry."

Lee's expression turns serious. "Come here."

I walk over to him and he takes my hand, pulling me in close to him.

Lee cups my face. "You know, you're so damn beautiful."

I look down at my shoes. "Thank you." I can feel a blush forming on my cheeks and Lee leans down, kissing my forehead gently.

His hands move to my chin and he tips it up, forcing me to meet his hungry gaze. His eyes are swirling with longing right now and I can't take it.

I bring my lips to his and he immediately melts into the kiss, placing both his hands in my hair and massaging my scalp as our lips continue to graze each other's. The contact deepens and I start to ache for his touch, wanting more than I'm currently getting.

I pull back from him, breathing against his mouth. "Is anyone else here?"

"No," Lee pants. "Just us. Everyone left." His eyes search my own like he is trying to puzzle together what I want.

I nod and lean back in to feel his touch again.

"Can I make you feel good?" Lee asks.

"Yes," I whisper, incredibly turned on now.

Lee brings his hands down in front of my jeans and slowly begins to unbutton them. He slides his hands into them, rubbing around the outside of my underwear before intaking a breath when he feels my wetness through them.

"I'm flattered," he says, laughing, and I can't hide the blush that creeps up on my face again.

Lee pulls my jeans down farther so they are around my thighs and slides his hand into my underwear before he begins to slowly tease me. I focus on his hand, watching it as it moves up and down in my panties. I'm visually stimulated from watching and physically stimulated from the pleasuring sensation that's currently building in me.

Lee adds another finger, and I bite down on my lip, unable to hold back my orgasm at this point. I moan and convulse around his fingers.

"Let go, Ivy," he whispers into my ear as the final shocks spasm through my body.

Lee slowly removes his fingers from me and gently pulls my pants back up. I'm still breathing through the release, unable to speak or help him with my pants.

Lee pulls up the zipper of my jeans and grins. "Well, I've surely worked up an appetite."

I nod in response as he continues to speak.

"Also, Ivy, I'm only getting you a cherry on your milkshake..." He grins, holding up his fingers. "Because it looks like you already got cream."

Flabbergasted, I reach over and chuck my purse at him.

Chapter 26

"Claws"

Ivy

Friday

Olive opens her car trunk and I slide my black suitcase next to hers and Summer's. This week went by in a blink, and thankfully, everything was completely professional when I did have to discuss the final renovations with Donovan at the shop yesterday. He didn't once bring up our hookup, other than to try and give me money for the new couch. I told him to not worry about it, that I didn't even buy the couch we had previously in that room.

I let Donovan know I would be out of town this weekend, so if he had any issues, he would need to reach me by phone. He shrugged and told me he was actually unable to come to the shop this weekend anyway, because he had something going on. Then Donovan told me he would finish the job next week.

The sooner he gets done at the shop, the easier it will be for me to remove him from my head.

I slam the trunk and slide into the backseat of Olive's small SUV.

"You know what I miss?"

"What?" Olive looks at me through the rearview mirror as Summer types away on her phone in the passenger seat.

"Your purple car."

Olive groans. "Oh god, *Barney*. That thing was a piece of shit."

I laugh, remembering the name she gave her car. "Yeah, but it did get you laid."

"That's true!" Summer chirps while still looking at her phone.

One night when Olive's car broke down, her husband, Hunter—who wasn't even her boyfriend back then—came to help her in the rain, and they ended up sleeping together for the first time.

"Yeah and then I pushed him away for months like an idiot! Not that great of a memory," Olive snorts.

"Shhhhh." Summer playfully smooths down her hair. "It all worked out in the end, buttercup."

I laugh and look out the window. "Are we getting Leena?"

"She's going to meet us at the airport. She had a work thing," Olive tells me as she backs out of the parking spot at my apartment.

Leena is Eddie's twin sister and a blast to hang out with. She's just like Eddie, but funnier and prettier. I can't wait to have a whole weekend of girl time.

Summer's fingers continue to click across her phone at rapid speed.

"What are you typing up there? The constitution?" I joke.

"I'm texting Eddie," she says, laughing.

"Are you guys going to be able to handle a whole weekend without each other?" Olive teases.

Summer rolls her eyes. "Ha, ha." Then she changes the

subject. "Let's hear this bachelorette playlist, Olive. It's a long ride to the airport."

"On it." Olive hands her phone back to me. I open her playlists to find the one she made for our trip and hit shuffle.

"Claws" by The Haunt plays through the speakers, and Summer cranks the volume up louder as she starts singing.

"I added all of your favorite songs," Olive shouts over the music to Summer, as I pull a pack of Airheads out of my purse and reach forward to hand them to her.

"Yay!" she shrieks. "You guys get me."

Two hours and forty-three songs later, we pull up to the small beige airport and park. We quickly get our suitcases out of the car and head towards the entrance sign that's illuminated, but missing the "E." The airport is rundown in appearance, but it's the closest one to us, and the planes are absolutely fine; it's just not the prettiest building.

Leena is waiting for us inside, and we all hug and begin to catch up when Summer suddenly clears her throat and stops our conversation.

"Guys...I have something to tell you. Don't be mad at me."

"What?" We all look at each other, confused.

"Surprise!" someone shouts, and I turn to see Eddie walking up from behind us.

Not just Eddie, though; Wes, Hunter, Eddie's cousin Marcus, Ezra, and *Donovan* stand behind him.

I instantly make eye contact with Donovan—a pathetic moth to his flame. He holds my gaze and tips his head in greeting slightly. I give him a once-over before forcing my stare away to greet everyone else.

Well, now I know what Donovan is doing this weekend.

Chapter 27

"Whiskey Fever"

Ivy

"Again, please don't be mad at me," Summer pleads with us girls, as the now *large* group of us stands in a circle. "We just decided we really wanted to do a joint bachelor/bachelorette weekend."

"It was my idea, and very last minute, I might add," Eddie pipes in. "So blame me."

"Did you know about this?" Olive points an accusatory finger at Hunter, who walks over and takes her in his arms.

"No." He kisses her on the forehead. "Eddie told us we were going to Atlantic City, like I told you. He just broke the news to us in the parking lot. I would never lie to you." He kisses the tip of her nose.

I'm unable to keep from glancing at Donovan, who is watching their public display of affection. I wonder what it would be like to be in his arms like that, to be that carefree and comfortable with him. It seems impossible because he's "not that type of guy," apparently.

"The flights?" Leena asks.

"I handled it all," Eddie tells her. Of course he did; he's a tech genius. He probably changed everything over in fifteen minutes one-handed while working out.

"You ruined our girls' weekend." Leena crosses her arms with a frown.

"I promise we will still do all of our girl stuff, and the guys aren't even staying at the same hotel as us! We will just meet up for some dinners and clubbing."

Leena still looks frustrated and Eddie gives her a "don't you start" look.

I can feel things starting to go off the rails, and I plaster a smile on my face, not wanting to upset Summer since she's the bride. "It's whatever you want. This is to celebrate you guys, and if you want to do it together, then fuck yeah, let's do it together."

"I agree," Wes chimes in. "We are here to celebrate you two...and get *fucked up!*"

I roll my eyes as Wes and Marcus fist bump—he's such a textbook party boy, and it looks like he has found a young apprentice on this trip.

Summer reaches over and squeezes my hand gratefully before mouthing, "Thank you." I squeeze her hand back. This weekend isn't about us; it's about celebrating them.

"Well, let's get on our flight then, I'm ready for some sunshine and tequila." Olive grins, and takes Hunter's hand. They walk towards the counter to check in.

Donovan's eyes are on me and when I meet his gaze he quickly looks away and follows the group as they head towards the counter.

Eddie gently touches my arm to hold me back for a second.

"Hey, Ivy, is there any way you would switch seats with me on the flight so I could sit with Summer? She's been stressed about a big case that just got presented to her yesterday and was in tears to me before bed, ready to cancel the whole trip. I changed the tickets in the middle of the night after she fell asleep and presented the idea to her in the morning, convincing her to enjoy the weekend and set work aside. I told her I would be by her side to make sure she has a great time, and I just want to comfort her because I know she will try to work on her laptop the whole flight, stressed out."

"Oh my gosh, I had no idea." I glance in front of us to see Summer standing against a wall typing away on her phone again. "Of course, Eddie. You sit with your bride."

"Awesome, thank you, Ivy. I'm in seat 42C."

Chapter 28

"You Can't Hurry Love"

Ivy

Scooting awkwardly through the walkway of the plane, I finally find my row and slide into the aisle seat that was originally Eddie's. There's a small woman with tight grey curls who has got to be at least eighty years old seated at the window, and I give her a soft smile and head bob before making myself comfortable in my seat. I grab my AirPods out of my tote and slide them into my ears, hoping I can just fall asleep for the short flight. I close my eyes and tap my fingers against my thighs as "Cut My Hair" by Dear Seattle blasts from my headphones.

Unexpectedly, I feel a large hand gently pat my shoulder. My eyes shoot open to see Donovan's muscular forearm pull away from me.

"Sorry, I'm next to you." He motions to the middle seat. "42B."

Of course he is.

I pull my headphones out and bunch my legs up to my chest to let his gargantuan form pass by me, and he awkwardly settles into the cramped middle seat.

115

The elderly woman at the window seat is staring at Donovan with wide eyes, and I know he notices. I expect him to scowl at her or act annoyed, but instead he turns to her.

"Sorry about smooshing you in the corner, ma'am." Donovan tries to stretch out his legs slightly, but his knees bump the seat in front of him. "The middle seat was a last-second ticket for me."

The woman seems pleased instantly and smiles brightly at him. The smile makes her appear years younger. "That's okay. I feel safe next to someone like you."

"Someone like me?" Donovan asks her, the confusion evident on his features.

She leans in even closer to him and whispers, "Yes. The *air marshal*."

He quickly tries to correct her. "Oh, I'm not the air—"

She winks. "It's okay. I know you can't say anything."

Donovan starts to try and protest, but the old lady seems to be having none of it. Having apparently made up her mind, she just winks again before turning forward and clicking through the TV on the headrest in front of her. She puts in headphones as she turns on the news, and Donovan sits there with his mouth slightly agape. I try to suppress a giggle and it causes my shoulders to shake violently.

Donovan takes notice and turns to me and mouths, "Not funny."

"You're right," I say under my breath. "Hilarious."

"It's not," he tries to insist sternly, but I can see a light-heartedness in his face that I'm not used to. The difference makes me grin, and his eyes dart down to my mouth. They linger on my lips for a moment until the flight attendant comes by to do the final aisle check, which causes him to quickly snap out of whatever he was thinking. He almost turns robotic; his frame is now statuesque as he faces straight ahead, his eyes on the cockpit. It's always whiplash being around him.

The plane begins to taxi on the runway.

"So, you were supposed to sit next to Eddie?" I ask.

"I guess." Donovan still looks straight ahead as he speaks. "He got the tickets last minute, he said. So we are all spread throughout the plane."

"Well, sorry I'm not Eddie," I joke.

He just shrugs in response. "It's fine."

"And you're a groomsman in the wedding?"

"Yes."

"I didn't know you were in the wedding." I raise a brow. "That's fun."

Donovan nods but continues to keep his eyes forward; his body is still more rigid than usual. Stiff.

"Are you...okay?"

"Yeah."

I look down to see his leg tapping against the floor aggressively—the only part of him that's moving.

"No, you're not," I counter.

Donovan turns to look at me. "What?"

"You're not okay. What's wrong?"

He frowns at me but ends up speaking anyway. "Fine." Donovan leans his head closer to my ear and whispers, "I kind of...don't like flying."

"You don't like flying?" I repeat back.

"Yeah."

The sound of the captain's garbled speech sounds out through the speakers as he begins to say the usual pilot spiel before takeoff.

Donovan tenses even more next to me as he continues to speak. "I mean, did you see this airport? It's falling apart."

"It's fine, I've flown out of here a thousand times."

"You have?"

"Yup."

His chest heaves as the plane begins to pick up speed.

"When is the last time you flew?" I ask him loudly so he can hear my voice as the engine noise continues to increase.

"Never."

"Never?" I turn towards him.

"Never."

I can't hold back my shock. "So it's not that you don't like it. You've never done it."

"Because I don't like it."

"Got it."

The plane turns so we are now at the final runway before takeoff. It's when we suddenly stop so the engine can build up speed that I see the fear that he's trying to hide in his eyes. I quickly try to think of a way to distract him and remember I have music. I pick my AirPods out of my lap and hand one to him.

"Here, listen with me. It helps."

Donovan takes the single left headphone from me without a second thought, and I place the other one in my right ear.

The plane starts to move forward as "You Can't Hurry Love" by The Supremes starts to play on my phone and Donovan closes his eyes. This probably isn't the type of music he listens to, but at least it will distract him for now.

Our speed increases down the landing strip, and the front wheels begin to lift off the ground; I glance up at Donovan again to make sure he's okay.

He has his eyes squeezed shut as tightly as possible. He looks like he's in physical pain—his knuckles are turning white from gripping the armrests so aggressively.

I can't help but smile, though, as I see him mouth every single word of the song as we lift off into the air.

Chapter 29

"Licky"

Ivy

By the time we arrived in Florida, Donovan seemed to have gotten used to being in the air. He only kept his eyes shut for the first thirty minutes of the flight, and after I ordered a coffee for him from the flight attendant, I swear he almost was at ease with me.

Now that we have landed, passengers are slowly beginning to exit the rows in front of us, and I see people from our group making their way off the plane. I felt like I was in this bubble for a moment with Donovan in our row, alone—it was us on a trip, as a couple—but back to reality now. He reaches over and hands me back my left headphone.

"Thank you for the music."

"Of course. Hopefully I made your first flight a little less scary."

"You did." He holds my gaze, and it looks like he wants to say more when we hear someone call out his name from behind us.

"Donovan! Your first flight cherry is popped!" Wes yells.

"Oh my god." I hear Leena groan from a few rows in front of us, and Olive peers back and rolls her eyes.

A family nearby gives Wes a dirty look, then glares at Donovan.

Donovan clears his throat, obviously embarrassed. I smile up at him and try to make the moment less uncomfortable.

"He was a champ," I say loudly back to Wes. "I was such a baby all flight, and he made me feel better."

Ezra stands up from a seat two rows behind us and starts to grab a bag from the overhead compartment. I didn't even realize he was so close to us. After he grabs his black bag, he gives us both a look. A suspicious look.

What was that about?

After we finally exit the plane, the men and women part into groups, and all the girls make our way over to where Summer is waiting for us. She somehow has pulled a giant wad of T-shirts out of thin air, even though we were just on the same flight.

"What are these?" Olive gestures to the shirts.

"Oh nothing, just some *custom* shirts I had made for our girls' weekend."

"I'm scared," Olive responds.

"I hope mine says 'I do anal'," I joke.

"Oh even better." Summer smirks while digging through the shirts and finding the one that is apparently mine. "Here."

I take the shirt from her hands and open it up to read *I'm 5 feet tall and ready for 5 more inches.*

My mouth hangs open.

Olive reads the words behind me. "Summer!" she gasps.

Summer shrugs. "I had to match Ivy's freak."

"I love it." I toss the shirt over my yoga pants and sweatshirt without a second thought.

"I am *not* wearing a penis shirt," Olive tells her.

"Don't worry," Summer says, laughing, "your shirt is... sweet." She hands it over to Olive, and I have a feeling it's anything but.

I read the words across the purple T-shirt and cackle.

Found my Hunter, and now I'm gathering his seed.

"Do you get it?" Summer grins wickedly.

"Yeah, I think we all do," Olive snorts. "You're lucky this is your weekend." She slides the shirt on as well.

"What a good sport," Leena teases. "Alright, shirt me."

Summer tosses her a pink shirt that says *Best tits in Tennessee.*

I let out a sigh. "I do agree."

Leena laughs. "This isn't awkward at all to wear on a trip with my brother."

"Again, don't worry. The boys don't exist right now." Summer pretends to shoo away the men who are standing twenty feet away. "They are going on their way, and so are we. We'll meet up for dinner tomorrow night. This is our time now."

"Well, where's your shirt?" I ask.

Summer smiles and yanks off her cream sweater. "I thought you'd never ask." Her bright blue T-shirt is now on full display.

It reads *I'm a lawyer.*

Olive scoffs. "Not fair! Yours isn't even bad."

"Wait for it," Summer says, and begins to walk away.

On the back of her shirt it says:

...which means I can get you off in more ways than one.

Chapter 30

"Venus"

Ivy

Once we get to The Pink Palm Tree, our hotel, the party really begins. Before we can even take a step into the lobby, a well-dressed man with curly pink hair is pressing a round of tequila shots into our hands. He doesn't even blink twice at our crude shirts and introduces himself as Nolan, the manager, before giving us a tour of the grounds.

Everything is pink and animal print, the perfect amount of cheesy and retro. We are all silent as we take everything in as Nolan leads us towards a long hallway; a pink disco ball hangs from the ceiling, and an indoor fake palm tree with silver and neon green bulbs dangling from it leans against a doorway. He opens the door and leads us outside to what appears to be a courtyard. We instantly see the expansive pool, decked out with pink flamingo chairs and a dolphin statue in the center of the water that shoots water out its mouth every few seconds.

Summer is buzzing with excitement and cheerily suggests that we should all get our bikinis on once we check in so we can go to the pool. We gladly agree; I wonder what it's like living somewhere where it's eighty degrees in January. My hotness potential would be so much higher if I lived somewhere that I could lie out at the pool all year long.

After Nolan's tour ends, he leads us back to the front where the counter is located. We check in at the front desk with a woman wearing cat-eye-shaped glasses and a plaid suit. She has a strong Irish accent and sounds like she's singing as she points us in the direction of the elevators to head up to our rooms.

Once we get our key cards, we step into the elevator to ride up to the third floor. Of course, the interior of the elevator is a base-to-ceiling pink checkered print. The song "Venus" by Bananarama plays through a ceiling speaker, and Leena sings along.

"This place is so cool! Kitschy!" Summer smiles at us. "Thank you guys for planning this weekend all for me."

"It was no big deal." Olive shrugs and looks at me. "Ivy did most of the work."

Leena chimes in, "Yeah, my literal only job was to find the penis straws."

"Well, way to ruin the surprise!" I joke.

"Well, *I have a surprise.*" Olive grins and yanks a bottle of tequila out of her bag.

"Where did you get that?"

"I may have asked Nolan to set it aside for us."

"Thank god," I say. "I need some liquid courage before I put on this bikini."

"*You?*" Summer blurts out. "Never. You're the most confident person I know, and you work out all the time."

"Confident? Yes. Ready to show my labia at the pool? Not so much."

"On that note." Olive laughs. "Here's our floor."

The door opens up slowly, and we all step off and head down a narrow foyer to our rooms. Leena and Summer are sharing the bridal suite, and Olive and I are sharing a honeymoon suite down the hall—it was all we could find in a tourist town on less than a month's notice. It said online that the room only has one bed, but that won't be a big deal since Olive and I have been friends since childhood.

I grab our room key and find the pink door with the number 4418 labeled in purple swirls above the trim.

"We're here," I turn and tell Olive, who is currently pulling both of our suitcases.

I push the pink door open and click on the lights. I stop suddenly and stand in place, taking in the honeymoon suite, and Olive slams into my back by accident.

"Ooof, sorry," she grunts.

"Holy shit. Look at our room," I respond.

Olive glances around and bursts out laughing. "This place is *insane*." She continues to laugh and pulls her phone out of her back pocket. "I have to send a picture to Hunter."

Insane is the right word.

The suite is bright red with a circular cheetah-print bed on a *rotating* platform. There are red curtains with cherries painted all over them and the words "Sex Bomb" on a neon sign above the window.

"Who designed this room? Axel Rose?" I snort.

"I feel like this room is full of sperm."

"And other bodily fluids..." I walk over to the bedside table and pick up a bottle of complimentary lubricant and raise my eyebrows at Olive. "You should stay here with Hunter... not me."

"No way." She shuts the idea down immediately. "This is our girls' trip."

"I guarantee you that Summer is going to end up with Eddie tonight after a few drinks, and Leena couldn't care less.

She has a man. Also, you guys never went on a honeymoon... and this room is definitely for *that*."

I pull open the bedside drawer and whisper under my breath, "You've got to be kidding me."

"What?" Olive asks.

I lift a black whip and red fuzzy handcuffs out and toss them at her. She squeals and ducks out of the way.

I laugh and cross my arms. "It's decided. I'm not sleeping here tonight with you. Sorry, but I want this room to get put to use...so Hunter it is."

Olive turns and sees a black record player on a glass table in the corner.

"Ooo, music!" She jogs over and sets the needle on the record.

"Fuck the Pain Away" by The Peaches starts to play, and Olive turns back to me, stunned.

"Hunter," I tell her, eyebrow raised.

"Hunter," she agrees.

Chapter 31

"Blow My Mind"

Ivy

T hirty minutes later, we are lying poolside with Summer and Leena and have already discussed the plan for Hunter to take over my room with Olive. Everyone agrees that they deserve this little getaway for the two nights we are here. They both work so much since they run their own businesses—Olive's bar and Hunter's videography—that there's little time in their lives for travel together.

Hunter, just like Olive, repeatedly told me over the phone that I didn't have to switch with him, but I insisted. He eventually accepted my offer graciously. He's going to drop off his room key shortly. Summer told me where the guys are staying, and I'm grateful when I find out their hotel is only two buildings away, so I won't be far from here at all.

I no longer feel insecure about my suit thanks to the two more shots I downed in our room before heading out. Lee Face-Timed me while I was still up in the room and was laughing his ass off when I gave him the tour around the sixteen hundred square feet of sex.

We have not been fully intimate yet, but it's not from the

lack of me wanting to; he just hasn't made the first move, other than that moment in the coffee shop. I was hoping that he'd make a bigger attempt later on that night—my interest was absolutely piqued—but he just ended the night with a simple kiss.

I adjust my body on the beach chair that I'm currently lounging across, ready to get some sun on my back, when I see a familiar tall and tan pair walking up. The Anderson boys.

Ezra gives me a broad, cheeky smile when we make eye contact.

"I come bearing gifts," he shouts out, holding up a room key. "Well, a gift."

"Where's Hunter?" Olive sits up in her chair quickly. "Is he okay?"

"Perfectly fine." Ezra tries to hold back a smirk. "He will be here shortly. He saw an old couple sharing an ice cream cone on a bench on the way over and struck up a conversation with them. When they told him they were celebrating their sixty-year wedding anniversary, he asked if he could interview them for his YouTube channel."

Olive grins. "Of course he did."

"Such a romantic." Summer smiles.

I playfully roll my eyes and mock her. "*Of course he did.*"

"Don't be jealous," Olive says, tossing the container of sunscreen next to her at me.

I duck, and it lands past me on the ground, right in front of Donovan's feet. I instinctively stand up to grab the bottle and completely forget how tiny my swimsuit is until I see his eyes widen as he looks at me.

"Daaaamnnn, Ivy!" Ezra says. "I didn't know you had abs! Not fair, they are better than mine!"

"She works out every morning," Leena chimes in. "She makes the rest of us appear *very* lazy."

Donovan looks away quickly, suddenly finding immense interest in a dragonfly skimming the water. He knows that I have abs. I push the thought away, not wanting to daydream about his undressed body right now.

I turn to Ezra. "When you're short like me, you've got to have some pack behind your punch to feel safe."

"Yeah, I can't say I know what it feels like to be a woman, but I would probably share the same sentiment if I were in your shoes."

Donovan reaches out his hand and gives me the bottle of sunscreen—I didn't even see him grab it.

"Thanks." I can't hold back a small grin. I feel like I haven't seen him in weeks, even though we just shared a flight this morning.

He holds my gaze and nods before stepping back to stand near Ezra. My phone chimes loudly and I turn back to my lounge chair so I can read the text.

Lee: *I forgot to tell you on FaceTime that a toddler dumped her mom's coffee on my shoes this morning, and I tripped over a pallet of sugar. So, that's how it's going back in Tennessee... fantastic.*

I smile and type back: *Oh no! Don't tell me it was your favorite pair of loafers?*

Text bubbles appear instantly.

Lee: *I feel like you're teasing me, but I will answer anyway. No, it was not my beloved pair of penny loafers. You should respect my reliable choice in footwear, especially when they share your last name.*

Me: *Oh, I absolutely do. It's quite sexy that you have bought shoes you can wear now and when you're 80; Ivy Penny approves.*

Lee: *Exactly. I'm glad you understand.*

I laugh and look up from my phone, not realizing Donovan and Ezra are both looking at me.

"Don't mind her." Summer smiles, sliding into the seat next to me. "She's just texting her future *boyfriend*."

I quickly set my phone down. "You don't know that, Summer," I murmur.

"What's his name again? David?"

"Lee," Donovan says, still eyeing me.

"Yes! Lee, that's it." She cracks open a bottle of water and takes a sip, then turns to Donovan. "So you've met him?"

"Yes." Donovan puts his hands in his pockets. "For a few minutes."

"He seems super sweet," Olive adds. "And a looker. I got to meet him on FaceTime earlier."

I want this conversation to end immediately.

I feel like I'm betraying Lee by being with Donovan on this trip, even though I didn't know he would be here. Lee doesn't know that there is more to our relationship than just him working at the shop. He doesn't know that we are intertwined in the same group now, which complicates things.

Hunter steps through the courtyard door and makes his way over, camera in hand.

"Got some great footage of Mavis and Walter." He grins.

"Oh, you're on first-name basis already!" Olive laughs and stands to kiss him.

"You know it, babe." He cups her chin and kisses her lovingly.

"Go upstairs and enjoy that room, Hot Dog. Please," I snort. "It's built for sex."

Hunter turns and looks at me with sincerity lining his features. "Thanks, Ivy. You are a great friend to both of us."

I brush off the comment. "Of course."

"We can help you move your bags over to our hotel whenever you're ready," Ezra tells me.

"Don't worry, I've got it." I flex my arm teasingly. "Muscles, remember?"

Ezra chuckles. "Right, *muscle mami*."

"I'll move them for you," Donovan says. His face is serious, and it's obvious he isn't going to take no for an answer.

"Uhhh...okay, sure. Thanks, Donovan."

Olive grabs our room key from her bag and walks it over to him.

"Room 4418."

Donovan takes the key in his left hand. "What color is your suitcase?"

"It's black with a purple tag." He nods, beginning to walk away, and I quickly add, "You can't miss it; it's right next to the forty-eight-ounce bottle of lube and the nipple clamps."

He pauses.

"She's kidding," Olive tells him. "At least, I think she is. We haven't found nipple clamps yet..."

Chapter 32

"Daydreamer"

Ivy

After hours at the pool, my skin has a pink tint to it as we head off to our planned dinner reservations. We decided to keep tonight as a girls' night and do a dinner with the group tomorrow.

I showered and got ready in my new room at Dunes, the men's swanky, modern hotel. I have a feeling this place is extremely expensive to get at the last second; Eddie paid for all of their rooms apparently, since he switched the plans. He definitely disbursed a lot of money to spend some extra time with Summer this weekend.

Olive, Leena, and I have on dresses in various shades of blue to surprise Summer since it's her wedding color, and she's wearing a white strapless pantsuit. Her vibrant dark red hair bounces against her shoulders as we walk down a crowded strip of beach restaurants, with her leading the way. She always looks effortlessly cool and ethereal. If you told me Summer was secretly a fairy, I would believe you.

"There!" I point as our destination comes into view—a

black building with a large patio overlooking the Atlantic Ocean.

"Ivy searched for the best crab cakes in town, and according to the internet, apparently this place has them," Olive tells the others.

"Is Seagull Bay known for their crab cakes?" Summer laughs.

"Probably not," I deadpan. "But I couldn't find any gator tail, so I'm sorry to disappoint."

"Do people actually eat alligators here?!" Leena's eyes grow into saucers.

"I'm sure. It's Florida, after all," I joke.

"The armpit of the United States," Olive adds.

Two shirtless, tanned men carrying surfboards walk by us and quickly step off the path to get out of our way. They smile at us before continuing on.

"But what a well-kept-up armpit," I say, turning back to get a final glance at them.

"You're horny," Summer snorts.

"Always."

"I'm shocked you haven't slept with Lee yet." Olive raises an eyebrow at me—she knows how important that aspect of a relationship has always been to me.

I shrug. "We're taking things slower. He doesn't seem like that... He's just a polite, sweet guy." I leave out the story about the infamous milkshake; somethings are better left private, I've decided. I love that he showed me that goofy side of himself—I didn't expect it and it felt like something that he doesn't bring out often, so I want to keep it to myself.

I know the girls would crack up if I told them, though.

"That's a change from your normal type," Leena says.

"I'm trying to be better," I tell her. "Less *toxic*."

"Well, we like you just the way you are," Olive says. "Don't lose your sparkle completely."

"My sparkle was mental illness and shattering wind-shields."

"Yes, yes it was." Olive laughs.

We walk up to the glass double doors and head inside to bloat ourselves on shellfish and cocktails. All I can think about the whole time is how I'm ready for the next phase of our night to begin.

Chapter 33

_____

"Head Over Heels"

Lee

Reaching above my head, I stack a final box of espresso beans on the top shelf of the stockroom with a grunt. Who knew working in a coffee shop would be such a workout every day? Ivy has briefly mentioned to me that she enjoys working out, and I don't have the heart to tell her that I *hate* the gym.

I like Ivy so much, though, that I would go to the gym every day if she invited me—I would pick up any hobby she asked me to.

Arlet keeps calling me a *simp*, whatever that means. I told her the first time she said it that "yes, I am *simp-ly* mad about Ivy," and she snorted, saying, "Point proven."

"I heard you split your pants today, boss," a familiar young and rough voice says from the doorway behind me. It's Blaise, our customers' favorite and most requested barista. Not sure if it's because women and men both love him or if it's because he actually makes good drinks. He's one of our employees who has been around since Cora and I opened this place.

"News travels fast around here, huh?" I look at him and

brush my hands against my legs to clear away some dust. "That's why I'm hiding out back here."

"You can thank the group chat for that." He smiles and shakes his head—his neon green buzzed hair looks like a high-lighter against his tan skin.

"Group chat?" I ask.

"Oh, shit..." He looks guilty and scratches at the back of his neck. "Sorry, Lee. Yeah...all of the employees have a group chat."

"But not with me?" I pretend to be hurt but I'm not actu-ally bothered—I'm glad our employees are close enough to talk outside of work.

"I can put up a vote in the group to see if they want to add you," Blaise sheepishly adds.

"No, no. I wouldn't want to impose where I'm not wanted," I joke. "I'm sure you guys would be making fun of me regularly for how much I hate coffee in the chat, and I don't feel like defending myself daily."

"We mostly just send *Love Island* gossip and memes."

"What's *Love Island*?" I ask.

Blaise's eyes bulge. "Yeah, I don't think you would win the vote to join the chat with that one."

"I listened to a really good podcast about bridge develop-ment the other day. I can send it to you if you want."

"Oh, look at that, my service just got cut off indefinitely." Blaise lifts his phone. "Sorry, boss, wouldn't be able to receive it."

"Ha-ha," I deadpan. "You're missing out. *The Bridge Boys* are an exhilarating listen."

"If I ever want to get Millie to sleep, I'll look them up," Blaise jokes.

He's a single father of a three-year-old daughter, Millie, and always prioritizes her. He first walked into Main Street Café when we were in the hiring process, stressed out because he found out his girlfriend was pregnant and he didn't have a stable paycheck. The relationship didn't last; they were young and dumb, Blaise always says, but his dedication to his child has never wavered.

"I saved a cookie for her from morning shift. I know you said she likes the butterfly sprinkle ones," I say. "It's next to the computer in the office."

"Thanks, man. She'll love that." Blaise taps his hand against the door frame. "How's life going for you? Still talking to that girl you met here?"

"Wow, you guys really do talk in the group chat."

He shrugs. "Arlet was proud of herself for facilitating."

"Yeah, I owe her one. Ivy's out of town right now, but we've been texting."

"When does she get back?"

"Her flight is on Sunday. She rode with some friends to the airport so she's kind of on their timeline for when she gets back into Clairesville."

"Forgreen Airport?" Blaise asks; it's the closest airport to our town, even though it's still over two hours away.

"Yup."

"I can tell you really like her."

"Oh, yeah?" I ask him.

"You just seem more cheerful recently. I know we all appreciate your good mood around here."

I laugh. "I don't think I was ever in an unpleasant mood before, was I?"

"No, not a bad mood." Blaise chuckles. "Just more reserved."

"Yeah, she brings a fun side out of me, I suppose." I push an empty box to the corner of the room. "I miss her," I admit. "And

I don't want to text her too much and bother her when she's having fun with her friends."

"You should surprise her and pick her up from the airport, then."

I blink. I didn't even consider that. "You think?"

"Yeah." Blaise shrugs. "Women love grand gestures and surprises. You are dating after all—show her you'll put in effort for her."

"You're right."

"Go get your woman! And maybe get some new pants before then." He laughs and walks out of the stockroom.

I guess wearing an apron backwards to cover my split pants wasn't as good of an idea as I originally thought.

Chapter 34

"Pour Some Sugar On Me"

Ivy

W e leave the restaurant a few hours later and do a little bit of tourist shopping before heading back to The Pink Palm Tree. Summer has a slight buzz going, which I'm grateful for because the next point of our night is something she will need a few drinks for.

Olive and I look at each other and smirk as we lead the girls up the elevator to Summer and Leena's room. When Leena unlocks the door, I snort.

Their room is adorable.

A plush baby pink carpet on the floor, a white couch, an elegant floral glass chandelier hanging above a couch in the center of the room, and pink lace curtains lining the windows. There are two doors on either side of the room, both with a light pink paisley wallpaper on them, that I assume lead to the bedrooms.

This room makes ours look like a sex dungeon.

Summer kicks off her heels and jumps onto the couch, letting out a big sigh. "Today was a blast; thank you, guys."

"Oh, the night isn't over yet." Olive smiles. "You have

about"—she glances at a clock on the wall—"fifteen minutes until the next event begins."

Summer stops in the middle of putting her vibrant curls up into a ponytail. "Oh god. Should I be afraid?"

"Absolutely." I snicker. "Afraid to have your wildest dreams come true."

Leena leans down and hands Summer a glass of chardonnay with a penis straw. "Here."

Summer looks at the straw, rolls her eyes, and drinks out of it anyway. "I don't usually drink my wine with a straw."

"When in Rome," Olive jokes and sits down on the couch next to her.

There's a sudden knock at the door, and I clap my hands together in excitement as I head to it.

He's early.

I yank the door open and jump as the man greets me on the other side with a loud,

"AAAAAAUUUAAAAAUUUAAAA."

The girls all whip their heads in my direction as I step out of the way and welcome him in.

"You're perfect." I smirk.

As soon as he is inside the pink doorway, Olive lets out a squeal, and Leena claps wildly.

"You've got to be fucking kidding me." Summer shakes her head, but she can't hide the excitement in her eyes. She quickly looks up and down at the deep V of his abs that leads to a small cloth covering his junk.

"Yes. It's exactly what you think. I got you a *George of the Jungle* impersonator for your bachelorette." I grin.

Leena looks between Summer and the man. "Do you love that movie or something?"

Olive chimes in, "You could say that," and nudges Summer's shoulder. "It was her sexual awakening."

I turn to the guy and sigh. "Wasn't it all of ours?"

He nods, a stringy brown strand of his wig sliding in front of his eyes; he blows it away. "So I've heard." He sets down the portable speaker he was carrying in his hand on a side table and stands waiting for my cue.

"Music?" Summer looks around at us nervously.

I nod to the man and give him a thumbs-up.

He plugs his phone in and clicks on a song. "Pour Some Sugar On Me" by Def Leppard begins to play and I watch Summer's eyes bulge as the man grabs a chair from the table and places it in front of us.

"I know it's winter right now, but I've been dying for *Summer*," the knock-off George of the Jungle loudly states as he takes her hands and guides her to the seat.

Olive, Leena, and I squeal and laugh, kicking our feet and leaning into each other, watching as Summer's eyes grow into saucers when she looks over at me.

"Oh yeah, tiny detail I didn't add. He's not just an impersonator... He's a dancer, too."

With that, he yanks off his tiny loincloth to reveal a shiny red thong.

Chapter 35

"Do It For Me"

Ivy

Two hours later the suite looks like it's been ransacked. Summer's suitcase is strewn around the room from an impromptu drunken fashion show we had after the exotic dancer, who we found out is named Garrett, left.

Leena is face-down asleep on the plush carpet, and Summer is snoring lightly from the couch. Olive yawns from her spot on the floor and crawls over to grab her heels.

"I would say it was a successful night," she says, smiling at me.

"We did it."

"I'm ready to head over to the room; the guys should be back. Come with me, and I will have Hunter walk you home."

"He doesn't have to. You guys just relax."

"No, I won't be able to go to sleep unless I know you have made it back safe."

"Okay, fine."

I grab my phone and pull down my paisley blue dress that has ridden up my thighs annoyingly all night. Olive waits for me at the door, and we head down the hallway to the honeymoon suite.

Olive knocks twice, and within seconds Hunter opens the door. When he takes in our appearances, his eyes widen.

"Wow, good night?" he asks, chuckling.

"Oh yeah, Hot Dog, it was a blast." I smile.

"Yes, it was." Olive kisses him on the cheek, and he moves aside so we can step into the room. "Are you okay with walking Ivy back to her hotel?"

"I totally would, but he offered to," Hunter says and nudges his head towards a chair behind us, where I turn and see Donovan sitting stiffly.

"I'll take you." Donovan springs up quickly.

Olive gives me a surprised look and then turns to him. "Great! Thanks, Donovan."

"I'm sure he can fill you in on our night on the walk back." Hunter laughs, and surprisingly Donovan chuckles, too.

"I can't wait to hear about this," Olive tells Hunter.

I stand in one spot, still not uttering a single word or reacting to his random presence at three a.m. in the *sex bomb* room.

"Are you ready to go?" he asks me.

I nod and follow him to the door like a suddenly needy puppy. My slight buzz isn't helping the trance he has over me—I stare up at him as we make our way to the elevator, and he pushes the down arrow.

Donovan looks over at me and tilts his head in greeting, his energy relaxed and friendly as he tucks his hands into his pants pockets.

I want to have sex with him.

I quickly push the thought out of my head—no.

He looks so good in those black pants and button-up, Ivy.

"You're quiet tonight."

You could just give him a quick hug in the elevator and see if he makes a move.

"Hello?" Donovan waves a hand gently in front of my face. "You okay?"

"Shit, sorry. Yes." I shift my weight on my feet. "I'm just tired, it's been a long day of travel and then partying."

The elevator dings, and we both go in, him letting me take the lead.

"Do It For Me" by Rosenfeld is playing as we stand in the elevator, and I can't hold back my snort.

"You've got to be fucking kidding me," I say under my breath.

"What?" Donovan pushes the ground-level button and turns to face me.

"Nothing."

The elevator begins to descend and we just awkwardly stand in silence as the lyrics sing out.

"Holy shit, this is some crazy music for a hotel elevator." Donovan laughs.

"Is it?" I pretend to listen for the first time. "I didn't even notice." I tilt my head. "Wow, you're right. *So dirty.*"

The elevator doors open slowly—oh, thank god—and I step out into the lobby. It's dark everywhere with only one lone light on behind the front counter. A man in a staff shirt reading a book looks up from his leaned-back position.

"Have a good night," he sleepily tells us before looking back down and continuing his chapter.

"You guys should really do something about that elevator music," I say quickly as I tipsily follow Donovan out the door.

Once we are outside, I note how the air has grown crisp since hours ago when I arrived here with the girls; I hug myself.

"I thought Florida was supposed to be warm."

"I think it's hot during the day and drops at night during

the winter," Donovan says. "At least that's what our waiter told us. Here."

I look over to see that he is unbuttoning his shirt. "What are you doing?"

"Take my shirt."

"Then you'll be cold."

"I don't mind. I'd rather be cold than you."

He holds his shirt out to me, and I slide it around my arms. It's short-sleeved but way warmer than just having on a spaghetti strap dress. His masculine scent surrounds and hugs me as I walk.

"Thank you."

"No problem," Donovan murmurs.

We walk in silence for a few minutes before I can't handle the lack of conversation and break it.

"So, what did you guys do tonight?"

"Well, first we went to dinner at a really cool burger bar on the beach."

"Burger bar on the beach," I repeat. "Try saying that three times fast."

Donovan chuckles. "Yeah, kind of a tongue twister."

"And then what did you do?"

He pauses walking and looks at me before saying. "And then we went to a strip club."

I stop and glance at him. "Okay?" I laugh. "What's so wild about that? We had an exotic dancer come to the room."

"Well...we thought it was a gentleman's club..." Donovan raises an eyebrow, his expression almost sheepish. "But, it turns out it was a gentleman's club for *gentlemen*."

I can't hold back my laughter. "You guys went to a gay strip club?"

"Yes."

"Why didn't you just leave?"

Donovan starts walking slowly, and I follow next to him. "We didn't know what to do. Everyone in there was so nice and kept buying Eddie drinks to celebrate, so we stayed. We had a lot of fun, actually."

The thought of six straight men spending a bachelor party at a male revue is too much for me to picture.

I love it.

I continue to laugh. "I wish I was there."

"Well, if I ever go back to Clams, I'll bring you."

"Hey! That's where Garrett works!"

"Garrett?" Donovan asks.

"Our dancer tonight—he was great. I can see how Clams would be a confusing name for a male strip club, though."

"Right." Donovan chuckles. "Wes was very apologetic. He's the one that found the place."

"Oh, well it all makes sense now. He just wanted an excuse to get up on stage and strip."

We stop walking again and laugh at that, both of us knowing Wes's personality all too well. Donovan stares at me as our laughter dies down, and his expression turns serious.

"I'm glad we are getting to see each other on this trip. I know it isn't what you planned with your friends...but I'm having a good time."

My heart beats faster.

"Me too," I tell him, and look down at my heels—the vulnerability in his confession makes me feel surprisingly bashful.

"Sorry if it was weird that I was waiting in the room for you." Donovan kicks a stray rock with the toe of his boot. "All the other guys had been drinking pretty heavily and were going to continue to bar hop. Hunter was ready to call it a night, and I just wanted to make sure you got back to the hotel safe, so I told Hunter I would come wait for you."

I nod. "Well thanks for not drinking too much so you could responsibly walk with me." I smile up at him.

"It was no different than any other night out. I don't drink."

"You don't?" I'm stunned to hear this. I could have sworn he was drinking the night I first met him at Olive's bar—but looking back now, he never had a beverage in his hand.

"Nope."

"Oh, that's cool," I quickly tell him; inside I'm dying to know if there's a story behind his decision but also don't want to pry.

Donovan takes the final four steps to the front door of our hotel and opens it for me. I step around him and try not to ogle him too much as the muscles in his arms flex as he holds it.

"You're on the sixth floor like Marcus and Eddie, right?"

"Right."

We take the small staircase up to the hallway of elevators and step into an open one. This elevator luckily only has jazz playing—with him shirtless, I think my ovaries would fall out if there was anything else playing right now.

My composure is wearing thin.

Five minutes later, he follows me to the outside of my door. I turn back to face him. Should I invite him in? I don't know what the right decision is, and it could be the drinks in my system, but I convince myself that yes, I should invite him in. I sway slightly on my feet and lean against the door for assistance, ready to ask him, when he speaks before I can get the words out.

"Alright, well, goodnight, Ivy. I'm in room 1116 on the next floor up if you need anything."

I blink. "Oh, okay, sure. Goodnight, Donovan, thank you for walking with me."

Now's obviously not the right time; I must be reading the cues wrong.

He gives me one last smile and waits, then glances at the key card in my hand. I realize he is making sure that I get in my room okay—ever the gentleman—so I quickly hold the card up to the sensor and turn the knob once it clicks green.

"Bye," I add before shutting the door.

Panting against the shut door, I slide down onto the floor of the room and realize that I'm still wearing his shirt. I bring the collar to my nose and inhale his scent—woodsy and spicy with a hint of tobacco, I'm guessing from the strip club.

My feet ache with a pounding now that I'm settled on the ground, and I kick my heels off. They smack against a small cabinet to my right—oops—and I vow to check the spot for marks in the morning. I'm too tired right now.

I grab my clutch and take my phone out of the small zippered pocket. Seeing that I have four missed text notifications, I unlock my screen. The first two are from Jade and Zoe —just general stuff about orders at Vera Bridal; I will have to call them tomorrow morning. The third text is from my mother, a picture from their current trip in Peru. The photo is of my dad throwing up in a bucket and my mom smiling beside him, giving the camera a thumbs-up. They must be doing ayahuasca again.

The final text is one I'm not prepared to see right now. My head is already spinning from the alcohol I've consumed tonight and the inhalation of Donovan's cologne.

It's a text from Lee.

I've been thinking about you all day, beautiful. I can't wait for you to get back. I have a great date planned for us.

Fuck.

Chapter 36

"Knock On Wood"

Ivy

Saturday morning was spent at the beach with the girls and margaritas. My shoulders and arms are tomato red after hours in the brutal Florida sun, but I'm keeping my fingers crossed that it will eventually turn into a tan.

Now back at my room, I'm trying to decide between a hot pink fitted polka dot dress or a swanky black dress that stops at the knee and has a back so low, underwear has to be skipped. I pick up my phone and FaceTime Olive. She answers seconds into the first ring with her hair up in a towel and a toothbrush in her mouth, wearing a teal strapless top sans pants.

We are getting ready to go out to dinner with everyone tonight; apparently Eddie has a surprise for us all. I gladly let him change the plans for dinner because all we had planned was to go to a popular boardwalk restaurant. When Eddie told us we would need to get dressed up for his surprise, my curiosity was piqued.

"What are you wearing tonight?" I ask her.

Olive spits out her mouthful of toothpaste. "Gold dress."

"The silky one?"

"Yup," she murmurs before resuming her brushing.

"That's sexy. Okay, my backless dress it is then."

Olive nods and responds with jumbled speech while she scrubs her front teeth. "Wofv hft."

"What?"

She spits out the paste. "Love that."

I laugh. "Okay, I'll be at The Pink Palm Tree in an hour to meet you guys."

She sets down her toothbrush and pulls the towel off her head, the dark strands falling in her eyes. "Walk over with the boys."

I shake my head. "It's fine."

"Hunter already told them to wait for you in the lobby to walk over."

"Ugh, of course Hot Dog did. Tell him I said thank you for always being so thoughtful."

"You're welcome!" Hunter cheerily adds from somewhere behind Olive's phone.

"You know you shouldn't be eavesdropping on our calls," I pretend to scold him.

"I'll spank him later as punishment." Olive giggles and looks above the screen, wiggling her eyebrows.

"That's what I like to hear! Put that room to good use." I hear Hunter laugh. "Alright, I'm hanging up now."

I end the call and stare at my reflection on my phone screen once it goes black. I can't help the jealousy that makes its ugly appearance every once in a while. It's difficult seeing my friends so happy with men that will move heaven and earth for them while I'm still at square one—dating.

Shit, speaking of, I completely forgot to text Lee back last night. Maybe this is why I'm single: *does not text well with others*.

I open up my messages and shoot a quick message back to him.

Hi! So sorry I left you on read last night; I had a few drinks and was exhausted. I literally opened your message and then fell asleep by the front door of my room. I hope you are having a good day, and I would love to hear about this date.

He responds while I'm in the shower.

Glad to hear you are having a good time on the bachelorette. I passed out by the front door on my 21st birthday. (Look how much we have in common... It's unfathomable. Try not to fall in love with me.) Also, I can't tell you about the date. It's a surprise.

I laugh at his message and respond.

You're funny. Give me a clue about the date.

He texts back seconds later.

Wood.

I roll my eyes at his lack of explanation and decide to poke at him, bring his silly side out.

Yours? Or someone else's?

Text bubbles appear and then go away.

I chuckle to myself and set back down my phone so I can focus on getting ready. I curl my hair in long cascading waves, trying to channel my inner Aquamarine, and apply a dark wine lipstick color. By the time I finish applying my mascara, Lee has texted me back.

If you want my wood, I'll give you my wood.

Oh shit. I bite my lower lip as I type back my response.

Well, show me next time you see me.

There's an abrupt knock on the door that causes me to jump. I check the time on my phone: 7 p.m. I didn't realize it had already been a whole hour.

"Coming!" I quickly shout. I slide my dress on and shimmy

it into place before grabbing my heels and my black clutch. After one final look in the mirror, I head to my door.

I pull it open, and Marcus, Eddie's cousin, is waiting on the other side.

"Wow, Ivy. You look great."

I push my hair off my shoulders lightheartedly and look down. "What? This old thing?"

Marcus laughs, and his smile illuminates his whole face. He looks a lot like Eddie, just ten years younger. "The other guys are headed downstairs now. Mind if I escort you to the elevator?"

"You flirt," I tease him. "Won't your current situationship get upset?"

He puts his index finger over his mouth and makes a "shhhh" sound.

He holds out his arm for me to take, and I let him lead me towards the elevator.

"So, I heard you guys went skateboarding today?" I ask, making conversation.

"Yeah," Marcus responds. "We had a blast."

"I didn't even know you guys brought boards."

"We didn't." Marcus smiles. "We just went to a nearby skate shop and bought boards. Since Wes is pro, they gave us free wheels and everything in exchange for him to post a picture at the shop and sign a deck."

"What? That's awesome!"

We step up in front of the silver elevator door, and he pushes the down arrow. I stare at our faces in the metal reflection.

"Yeah, it was super cool. We skated for a few hours, and when we were done, we handed the boards over to some younger kids to keep."

"You guys probably made their month."

"Yeah, for sure. They were stoked."

The door dings and slides open quickly.

One tense and handsome face stands inside—Donovan. He's wearing a white dress shirt with the sleeves rolled up to expose his tattooed arms, and the top few buttons are open. He has on black pants, and his hair is pulled back into a low ponytail.

Oh my god.

Thank god I'm not wearing underwear right now because they would have *dropped*.

Chapter 37

"Bring Me To Life"

Ivy

Once the whole group is gathered in the lobby of The Pink Palm Tree, Eddie informs us that we need to leave right away to make it to the surprise on time. Summer tries to pry clues out of him, but he just kisses her on the forehead and tells her she will find out very soon.

We are all buzzing with excitement as we walk down the main strip of restaurants and shops. There's a chorus of our heels clicking against the pavement rapidly as Eddie leads the way in front of us, looking back to smile at the group every few minutes.

Everyone is dressed up, the men in button-downs or casual suit jackets and the women in dresses. Well, *almost* everyone. Wes is underdressed—and I wouldn't expect anything else from him. He's wearing a printed floral shirt unbuttoned all the way and a gold chain, accompanied by some cut-off jeans that he told us all are his "slutty" shorts. His long blond hair is blowing behind him, and he is saying hello to everyone as we pass. He looks like a local.

Summer and Leena are singing a horrible a cappella cover

153

of "Bring Me To Life" by Evanescence. Summer's singing the female vocals, and Leena is lowering her voice as dramatically as possible to sing the male backup. Everyone is laughing; even Donovan cracks a smile. Hunter takes a small vintage video camera out of Olive's purse and begins to record us all—I already know he's going to make a highlight reel for their rehearsal dinner.

Eddie halts suddenly in front of a tiny hole-in-the-wall shop. I blink in surprise and stop walking along with the group. The exterior is a bland tan stucco that is barely visible because there are overgrown vines climbing up the front wall. A tiny sign hangs on the blue door, but I can't make out the words. The place looks vacant and extremely run-down. It's a shack, to be honest.

"We're here!"

We all stare at each other confused. I glance at the two formal businesses standing on either side of the small building: a luxury purse store and a cake boutique.

"Babe?" Summer questions.

"Are you fucking with us?" Leena points at Eddie and snorts.

"Come on." Eddie grins and confidently leads us to the entrance. The blue wooden door is so low that Eddie actually has to duck as he steps into the place. I turn back to face Olive and give her a *what the hell is this?* look. She shrugs her shoulders and nudges me forward. Ezra and Donovan step in behind us, both having to crouch down some as well.

When we step inside, the first thing I notice is that there's a strong smell of coconut and the place is dimly lit. There is a woman with platinum blonde hair sitting behind a tall beige desk that almost takes up the whole interior—we are crammed together like sardines as she greets us.

"Hi! Is this Eddie's group?" She smiles, her voice

containing a strong vocal fry. I notice a tall candle to her right. "Warm coconut breeze"—that's the smell.

"This is us!" Eddie cheerily says from the front of our pack.

I look at the wall to my left and see there are dozens of framed photographs lining it, showing famous celebrities standing with a charter crew in front of a yacht.

Oh no.

"Alright, great. Well, follow me this way." The woman stands from her spot, and I see she is wearing an all-white outfit —either she is about to commit us all to an asylum, or she's about to take us to a boat.

Shit. Shit. Shit.

We awkwardly walk in a single-file line, with me taking the rear, to a thick black door with a glowing exit sign above it. She opens it and lets us step through one at a time. I can't see past everyone to check what's on the other side of the door, but I start to feel anxious.

"Watch your step, sweetheart; hold onto the railing." She smiles at me, and I thank her as I step across the threshold of the exit.

What I see is the most breathtaking view of the ocean—but also, my worst fears have come true.

Eddie booked us a yacht.

Chapter 38

"Can You Feel My Heart"

Donovan

I walk down the wooden staircase onto the dock in awe—I had no idea Eddie planned something this sick for our night. There's a giant eighty-foot yacht sitting on a private dock in front of us. I'm stoked. Even though I get to be on the water almost every single day during our charter season, the feeling of going on a boat never gets old for me. It's something I love, and I don't love many things.

Ezra walks up behind me and claps me on the back. "Man, we really need to step up Anderson Charter. We *need* a yacht like this."

"Yeah, maybe one day. We have to run about five hundred thousand more charters a year to be able to afford *that*." I gesture my head towards the luxury yacht.

Eddie walks over with Summer holding onto his arm and shakes a man's hand, who I assume is the captain.

"Sorry about that entrance, everyone; we like to maintain a low profile to keep the paparazzi away from some of our guests." The captain smiles at all of us.

156

Eddie laughs. "Yeah, the group lost faith in me for a moment, I think."

"Have you had any rockstars on this yacht?" Wes chimes in.

"*The Grand Dame* has had many celebrities of all calibers on it," the captain tells Wes.

"Any of the Osbournes? How about Metallica? Ooo! I bet Fred Durst. Just blink if I'm right."

The captain just looks at Wes, a customer service grin still plastered on his face. "I cannot say."

"You blinked! I'm right, man, this is awesome!" Wes holds up his hands.

"I think he was just blinking like a normal human to lubricate his eyes." Summer looks at Wes and rolls her eyes. "Sorry about him," she tells the captain.

The captain chuckles. "No problem. If you will all follow me this way, I will introduce you to our chief stew, Carrie."

Carrie begins to talk to us about the boat and our dinner cruise for tonight as a young woman hands out glasses of champagne on a tray to each of us. I politely decline, and she hands one to Hunter, who is standing to my right. He thanks her but seems distracted as he glances behind him. I follow his line of sight and realize that Ivy and Olive aren't standing with the group.

They are standing near the top of the wooden steps above the dock. Olive is rubbing her hands up and down Ivy's arms, and Ivy appears to be shaking.

What's wrong?

I clear my throat and turn to Hunter. "Everything okay?"

"Oh, I hope so." He looks back at his wife quickly and then leans into me. "Ivy is terrified of the water."

What? When we first met, she said she wanted to go on Anderson Charter this spring.

I gulp. "She is?"

"Yeah," he continues in a low tone, "she won't go in anything except a shallow pool sometimes. Olive said for as long as she's known her, it's been like that."

"I had no idea." I stare at the girls again; Olive appears to be talking quickly while Ivy shakes her head *no*.

Hunter looks also. "I think Olive is trying to tell her she will stay with her. She wouldn't leave her alone while everyone else goes out."

"And if Olive stays, I'm assuming you won't want to go either, right?"

"Right, I'm not going to do something like this without my wife; I would just be wishing she was with me the whole time."

Carrie the chief stew is done talking with the group, and I see Eddie and Summer head onto the yacht with Marcus following close behind. Ezra takes Leena's hand to help her step onto the boat next. I have a decision to make.

"Does everyone know she's scared of the water?" I ask Hunter.

"I don't think so—she never brings it up. I just know because of Olive. Ivy would probably be embarrassed and would feel like a burden if she were to mention it now."

"You go; I'll stay with her."

"No way, man," Hunter tells me.

"I go on boats *all the time*." I smirk, trying to act like I don't care. "I'm going to send Olive over. Just tell the group I'm not feeling well and that Ivy offered to go with me back to the hotel."

"Are you sure?"

"Absolutely."

I back away then—not giving him the option to argue any other outcome—and begin to walk towards the steps. The girls don't even notice me until I'm a few feet below them on the wooden staircase.

"Oh, hi, Donovan." Olive smiles. "I'm feeling a little tired, and I think Ivy is going to hel—"

I hold up a hand and interject before Olive can finish the lie. "I wasn't really feeling going on the water tonight; we had a long day of skating, and I'm burnt out, to be honest." I chuckle. "I was just thinking about hitting that taco truck we passed on the walk here, grabbing some food, and going back to the hotel."

Olive perks up. "Oh! Oh, that's perfect; she's tired, too." She turns to Ivy and gestures to the walkway. "Aren't you, Ivy? You should go back with him."

I suppress a laugh because Olive can't even keep her story straight as she's trying to keep her friend's fear a secret.

Ivy looks ghostly pale as we meet eyes. "Okay," she tells me in a small, hoarse voice. "I'll go with you."

"Great." I clap my hands together. "Hope you're in the mood for tacos."

Ivy nods slowly. "Yeah, sure."

She still seems shaken but tells Olive to have fun and quickly starts to walk up the path back towards the little building. I go up the final steps to follow her when Olive reaches out and takes my arm.

"I know you're lying, but thanks."

"I know you were lying, too," I tell her.

"I've never heard you say you were tired of being on the water."

I shrug and slide my hands in my pockets. "Today, I am."

She glances back at Ivy, who is almost to the door now, and turns back to face me with a quizzical look. "Interesting."

"What?"

"Nothing." She smiles. "Bye, Donovan." Then she turns and heads down the steps.

Chapter 39

"Take Me"
Ivy

Struggling to pull open the heavy black door because my anxiety has left me trembling, I force myself to take a deep breath, trying to calm down, and give it a final pull. It opens, and I quickly make my way back into the cramped space. The woman at the desk stands abruptly, obviously surprised to see me. "Everything okay?"

"Yes," I tell her without stopping. "Just forgot to...to feed my fish," I say breathlessly and push through the front door.

"Oh, okay," she says from behind me, confusion laced in every word. If I wasn't about to have a panic attack right now, I would find this situation hilarious.

I start to walk down the street when I hear Donovan yell out from behind me, "Wait up!"

Stopping myself, I try to breathe deeply again, but the air feels tight in my lungs. I clutch my chest for a second and then turn to face him as he jogs up towards me. I've never seen this man run after *anything*. I didn't actually think we were going to spend time together tonight; I just thought he wanted to go back to his room.

"Sorry," I exhale sharply.

"Aren't we getting food?" he asks me, and looks at my shaking hands.

I tuck them behind my back. "You *actually* want to go get food together right now?"

"Yeah, of course." He takes a step closer to me. "I thought that was the plan."

"Well..." I look away from him, staring at the people around us.

Donovan eyes me, waiting for my response.

"Okay," I agree. "Let's get food."

He gives me a smile, and I try to grin back, but I think my efforts fail because I am still trembling and uneasy on my feet.

"Okay," he repeats. "Let's go."

He slowly begins to walk down the sidewalk, and I follow him. He slows even more to match my pace, so we are now next to each other.

"Do you want to get the taco truck or something else?"

"Ummm..." My mind still feels like it's swirling around in chaos; I can't get a coherent answer out. "I don't want to make any decisions right now." I try to give him a small laugh, but it comes out sounding like a nervous croak.

"Okay, I'll take the reins then. We are going to get tacos, and then we will walk around some. Sound good?"

"Yes."

He glances down at me. "You alright?"

I shrug in response.

"Do you want to talk about it?"

I shake my head.

He looks ahead, and suddenly a small smirk plays on his lips.

"What?" I ask.

"Oh, nothing. I just never thought I'd see the day where you would have nothing to say."

Asshole.

"You're an asshole!" I fling my hands up in the air. "I'm obviously upset."

"Maybe I like riling you up."

"That's rude," I snap back.

"Maybe I think it's sexy when you get sassy with me." He turns to face me.

I stop walking and cross my arms. "So you're trying to rile me up so you can get a hard-on? Gross."

His voice lowers. "I already had one when I saw you step into the elevator in that dress."

Oh shit.

I roll my eyes at him and pretend not to care about what he just admitted, but I *so* care. "Let's go; I'm hungry."

He laughs loudly. "Right."

Beginning to quickly walk away from him down the sidewalk, I scoff, and I hear him chuckle from behind me—prick. My every step is laced with annoyance for him. It's the fact that he always gets under my skin, and I let him; the fact that I have so much desire to be around him, and he just likes to toy with me.

The next ten minutes between us are completely in silence, the only sound the chatter of the tourists around us and soft music coming from inside shops we pass. My mind is now occupied with his mention of my dress and calling my attitude sexy. The compliments are a mosquito in my ear refusing to be swatted away.

It's not until we get up to the taco truck and he begins to order that I realize I completely drifted from my thoughts of anxiety about the boat as soon as he baited me.

Donovan distracted me.

I glance over now and stare at him as he talks to the man inside the food truck. His serious face is intent on the conversation the cashier is having with him—like whatever he is being told is the most important thing in the world. The man is old and speaks slowly, but Donovan doesn't seem to mind and gives him a simple head bob in understanding. He says one final thing before paying for both of our tacos—he insisted—and once the man has turned around to start cooking, he slides a twenty-dollar bill into the tip jar.

For the first time, I see him in a whole new light.

Chapter 40

"The Killing Moon"

Ivy

By the time we get our food and are taking our last bites, it's past ten p.m. The crowd walking around us as we sit on the curb has changed from families to the drunken nightlife scene in the past thirty minutes. I thought I would feel exhausted at this point after my anxiety attack, but I feel surprisingly refreshed and ready to continue exploring.

"Can I ask you a question?" Donovan speaks.

"Sure." I take the final bite of my crunchy chicken taco, the tangy, spicy sauce exploding in my taste buds.

"Why did you want to go on our fishing charter if you're afraid of the water?"

I set down my taco on the wrapper in my lap. "I think my exact words were '*see*' your guys' charter. Not that I wanted to go on the boat."

Donovan shakes his head. "Huh. I guess that is what you said."

I laugh. "Yup, I don't really do the whole ocean, lake, or river thing." I look up at the sky and stare at the moon. "How did you know?"

"I could just tell because one of my younger sisters has anxiety."

I look at him, surprised. "I didn't know you have sisters."

"Yeah, I have two."

"Are they in town?"

"Nope." Donovan straightens out his legs in front of him on the curb. "Do you want to tell me why?"

"Why, what?"

He stares intently at me. "The water."

I gaze into his dark eyes. "You promise you won't laugh at me?"

His face turns serious. "I promise."

"Okay." I exhale a long breath. "Well, when I was a little kid, my parents took me on a boat when we went on a trip to Michigan. They decided they wanted to go on a fishing excursion—which is insane because my parents don't even eat fish. Everything was great, and once the boat ride finished the captain said we could swim along the edge of the lake. I was really scared, but my mom reassured me it was fine to go in the water, so I did, even though I was unsure."

I glance over at Donovan and he nods to encourage me to continue talking.

"After a little while I started to get more comfortable and have fun. I was splashing around and playing—I even made friends with another girl my age in the lake. We were playing mermaids, but her older brother wouldn't stop pushing her in the lake, and she was getting upset, so I told him to stop it or I was going to tell his mom." I laugh. "I know, I was a total narc, which really pissed the kid off, so he walked over and pushed me as hard as he could into the water. I didn't expect it, so my mouth was wide open when I went in, and it caused me to swallow a big gulp of nasty lake water."

"Geez." Donovan shakes his head. "That kid was a little shit."

"That's not even the worst part. When I inhaled, I swallowed something in the water, like a little minnow. It was horrible; I could feel it slithering down my throat, and it felt like it was stuck forever. I was absolutely traumatized because not only had I just swallowed a living animal, but I also was terrified to tell my parents what happened. I thought I would get in trouble because they don't eat fish—I was only six when it happened. So for years and years I just kept this secret, thinking I had a fish living inside my stomach, eating half of my food and growing, and I was scared that if I went back in water, it would come out of my mouth to be free." I pick my last bite of taco back up. "So that's why I'm scared of the water."

Donovan stares at me with his mouth wide open in shock; the corner of his lip twitches slightly.

"You said you wouldn't laugh." I eye him.

"I'm not laughing—that just might be the most insane story I've ever heard. In a nonjudgmental way, of course."

"That's why no one knows that I'm afraid," I say. "Because I know they will think the fear is silly and stupid, especially for a thirty-year-old woman to still carry."

"I don't think it's stupid. You're allowed to have fears, even if other people don't understand them."

I take my final bite and nod. "I know."

"I just want to make sure of something." Donovan glances at the food truck and then back at me. "You know that you don't have a fish living inside you now, right?"

I burst out laughing. "Yes, of course, the fear now is more of a 'don't want to swim in water that I can't see through or have the chance of falling in water I can't see through' panic. The anxiety of going back in the water takes my breath away. I only go in pools."

"But you planned a bachelorette to Florida, which is surrounded by beach," he says, chuckling.

"Exactly."

We look at each other, both still smiling until Donovan breaks the silence.

"You want to walk around some?" he asks me and stands to throw away his empty taco wrapper.

He reaches out his hand and gestures to take my trash as well.

"Oh, thanks." I hand it over and brush my hands against each other. "You read my mind. I would love to explore some more."

"Alright, well, you decide which way."

"Let's go down that street." I point to a narrow road off to our left that has a few eclectic-looking shops. One of them has a 24-hour sign flashing. "I want to go *there*."

Donovan snorts when he sees the shop I'm pointing at. "You want to get our fortunes told?"

"Absolutely, I've never done it." I stand up.

"I don't believe that crap."

"Okay, you don't have to. Appease me, then."

Donovan stares down at me, and I put on my best puppy dog eyes. He groans. "Okay, fine. I'm not going to enjoy it, though."

"Even better," I joke. "By the way, I think we have officially hit you saying more than five thousand words to me. You're almost a certified yapper."

"Ha-ha, funny," he deadpans. "I talk when I want to."

"I talk all the time."

"Oh, *I know*."

We cross the busy street and make our way to a blaring lilac shop that looks like it also doubles as a home. The front door is black with the moon and stars painted all over it. *Ms. Elsa's*

Crystal Readings is written on the glass window in weather-worn stickers.

"I feel like this lady is probably asleep," Donovan murmurs to me.

Before I can even knock, the door flies open. "WELCOME!"

I let out a yelp in surprise.

A woman, who I'm assuming is Ms. Elsa, stands in front of us in a bright pink muumuu with her grey hair up in tight curlers.

"How did you kno—" Donovan begins to ask.

"Ms. Elsa knows everything!" the woman responds with wide eyes and a Broadway-worthy, haunting voice. "Follow me, and I will tell you your fate."

I clap my hands together in excitement and start to follow her in the door. "Yay!"

Donovan shakes his head, making his distaste for the situation obvious before reluctantly following me in. He shuts the door behind him and scowls.

The smell of cats and incense hits me like a freight train the second we walk in, but I keep following her. Two cats run down the hallway past us, and I see a stairwell to my left that has four more cats lounging on it. Donovan sneezes repeatedly behind me; I turn back to see him itching at his eyes with his palms. Is he allergic to cats? Tomatoes and cats?

Random.

Ms. Elsa turns to the right at the end of the hall and leads us into a tiny room, no larger than a closet, with a small round table in the center and a large crystal ball on top. There are two plastic chairs, one on either side of the table, and a mound of pillows on the floor. The room contains no windows but does have some yellow lights twisted up around the ceiling.

Ms. Elsa sits on one side of the table. "You will go first." She points at Donovan.

"Oh, no. Let her go; I'm just with her."

"No. Ms. Elsa says you will go first, now sit down, immediately." She points at the chair across from her, like a mother scolding a child.

Donovan stares her down before complying and doing as she told him to. His shoulders sink like he lost a battle. He sneezes. I have to stifle a laugh as I lean against the doorframe behind the two of them.

"Now, I shall begin." She places her hands over the crystal ball dramatically and closes her eyes before quickly pulling her hands back. "For a small price of forty dollars a person."

Donovan scoffs and starts to stand up. "No way."

"I'll pay," I chime in and take out my wallet. "Do you take cards?"

Donovan gives me a cross look, but I ignore him as she responds.

"Of course." Ms. Elsa snorts, whips a credit card reader out from under her muumuu, and tells me, "Just tap here."

Where was she keeping that thing?

I pay and step back towards the wall.

"Now, I may begin." Ms. Elsa holds her hands over the crystal ball and closes her eyes. It might be the placebo effect, but I swear the room is vibrating with energy. "I see many things in your future," she tells Donovan. "I see a family, I see hard work, I see money. But most of all, I see you saving someone's life!" Her eyes shoot open, and she looks at him dramatically, scooting in closer as she speaks. "I see your life flashing before your eyes and someone saving you, as well. Someone coming to your rescue when you least expect it, and you will come to theirs in return."

She places her hands in her lap then and looks at him.

"That's it?" Donovan blandly asks.

"Yes. Now up! It's your turn, darling." She looks at me.

Donovan scoffs as he stands, obviously annoyed. I gladly move into his seat.

"I'm ready," I tell her cheerily. "I've never done this before."

"Well, Ms. Elsa is happy to do this for you then," she says before closing her eyes and placing her hands on the crystal ball.

She makes a pained face and quickly pulls them back.

"What's wrong?" I ask her.

Ms. Elsa shakes her head slowly. "I see heartbreak in your future."

"Heartbreak?" I repeat.

"Heartbreak." She nods slowly.

"Oh no..." I sadly reply. "That's all?"

She stares back at me. "That's your future."

I begin to sink down into my seat when Donovan startles me by speaking up. "This is bullshit," he tells her. "We're leaving."

He takes my hand and pulls me up out of the chair.

Before Ms. Elsa can even respond, Donovan is quickly leading me down the hallway.

"You're a fraud," he shouts as he leads me towards the front door. He opens it for me to step through and starts to follow but appears to change his mind.

He turns back, leans inside, and yells one final thing. "And this place smells like cat piss!"

Chapter 41

"Heads Will Roll"

Ivy

"Well...that was interesting?" I awkwardly laugh as we stand down the street from the shop. *What if what she said is true?* What if I'm destined for nothing but heartbreak in my future? That's all I've known in the past, so it wouldn't be far-fetched if that was my future, too.

"Stop."

I look up at Donovan. "What?"

"Stop. I can tell you're spiraling and overthinking everything that *fraud* just said to you."

"I believe her." I shrug my shoulders. "If Barnaby is real, then so are psychics."

"Who is Barnaby?" Donovan's eyebrows crease as he looks down at me.

"The ghost of Vera Bridal."

He rolls his eyes. "You've got to be kidding me. You don't have a ghost at the store."

"I do, and I'm surprised he hasn't introduced himself to you; he's the one that brought down the shelves."

171

"No. Them being held up by crumbling drywall and not getting put up correctly with enough nails brought them down."

"Well, it's because Barnaby loosened the nails, so tomatoes, toe-my-toes."

"What?"

I look up at him, confused. "Tomatoes, toe-my-toes?"

"You know that's not the expression, right?" Donovan stares at me incredulously.

"Yes, it is? I've been saying it all my life."

"It's tomatoes, *tow-mah-toes*."

"No way, you're wrong. Someone would have corrected me by now if that was the expression."

Donovan begins to laugh and doesn't stop—I've never heard him laugh like this.

"What?"

"It's nothing bad. You're just unlike anyone I've ever met before."

"Okay," I respond and touch my hair, unsure if he means it in a good way or bad. "Thanks, I guess?"

He eyes me for a moment in silence. "If there was anything in the world you could do right now, what would you want it to be?"

"Hmmm." I look around and then glance back at him. "I want to go dancing."

"Okay, let's go."

I quirk an eyebrow. "You are going to go dancing with me?"

"I'm not sure yet if I'll dance...but I'll go."

"You have to dance to at least one song." I cross my arms in conclusion. "Or, I'm not going."

"Okay, fine, Ivy. I will dance a *little*."

"There's a club over by The Pink Palm Tree; I saw it advertised when I was planning the trip. Do you wanna go there?"

"Sure."

We make it to the club, Disco Dee's, in less than ten minutes, but we have heard the booming music for the past five, luring us to our destination. There is a long line outside, and I start to walk towards it when Donovan takes my arm.

"Come on." Donovan motions towards the entrance.

"There's a line." I point to the very obvious crowd of thirty people waiting in front of us.

"We aren't waiting. Watch this."

Donovan walks up to the bouncer and says something. The guy looks at him and then points to the line. They talk back and forth for a minute, and then Donovan stalks back to me.

"He said we have to wait in line."

I snort. "No shit. What did you say to him?"

Donovan shrugs. "I just asked him if we could go in."

I burst out laughing. "And you thought that would work?"

He just stares at me. "I've never been to a club. It's not my scene." Donovan looks at the line ahead and lets out a grunt in annoyance. "We are going to be here awhile."

"I have an idea; follow me."

I walk up to the doorman with Donovan following a few feet behind me. The guy has a handlebar mustache and an early Justin Bieber swoop to his hair—this will be a piece of cake.

"Sir!" I step in front of him quickly and widen my eyes. "My friend, she just got her period in the bathroom. It's a mess. I mean, a *mess*—it's a stage five period."

The bouncer's face pales a little. "What's that?"

"If you don't know...you don't want to. *Trust me*."

I turn and point back behind me to Donovan. "My boyfriend was trying to help me get in so I could get to her without being graphic, but here we are. We have to get in

173

there." I reach into my small clutch and pull a tampon out of it. "*Now*."

The doorman quickly nods and hands me two wristbands before stepping out of the way. "Of course. Go on in."

I turn around and hand one to Donovan. "Come on, sweetie."

He follows me through the club doors; the music is a million times louder now that we are in the building. Smoke and vibrant disco lights are flashing in front of us.

Donovan leans down to shout in my ear as we walk down a narrow red hallway. "What the hell is a stage five period?"

I turn and shout back, "I made it up."

"Didn't anyone ever tell you it's bad to lie?"

"What are you going to do? Punish me?" I flutter my eyelids playfully and then turn away before he can answer.

The hallway ends and leads out into a giant space, full of dancing and drunken people. A rainbow disco ball hangs from the ceiling and reflects on the crowd, and there's a smoke machine that has made everyone's lower halves invisible. Two beach balls are currently being tossed around the crowd, and a remix of "Heads Will Roll" blasts—this is my heaven.

I grab Donovan's hand and pull him into the mass of people.

He stands awkwardly still like a statue behind me as I bounce around and yell out the lyrics, dancing my heart out. I try to get him to join in for the next few songs, but he wants nothing to do with it, just shaking his head swiftly and putting his hands in his pockets.

The DJ's deep and sultry voice sounds out through the club suddenly. "I thought we should slow it down for a second. Bring the lights down." The lights in the club dim, and the disco lights are shut off, replaced with silver flashing lights.

"Let's make it sexy."

Chapter 42

"Dark"

Ivy

The crowd cheers out in approval as he says, "This is the final song of the night, ladies and gentlemen. 'Dark' by WesGhost."

A deep, haunting melody starts to play and I get ready to turn to Donovan and tell him we can go. I don't plan on awkwardly grinding in front of him while he stands behind me stiff as a board.

Before I can say anything, he leans down and whispers in my ear, "Dance with me."

I face him and look into his eyes with a question in my own. He nods to me before he runs his hand down my right arm gently, caressing it. My breath intakes as I watch and subconsciously feel myself lean into his touch. The delicate movement feels so sensual in this setting, so strangely intimate.

No one knows us here; it's just us.

He takes the sides of my hips and turns me back around before pulling me in close—my bare back is now resting up against his body. His heartbeat feels like it's pulsing through me as the lights flash, and I feel a fire burn through me from his touch.

I begin to sway my hips against his body; the size difference between us is more visible than ever now as I dance against him. My heels give me a few inches of height, but he still towers over me. I press into him more as I move my hips, rocking them against him to the beat. He moves against me as well, surprisingly fluid, and I feel myself getting turned on.

Donovan must sense it, too, because his touch against my hips becomes more desperate. He removes one hand from my hip and cups my chin, turning my head with his index finger and thumb so I'm now looking up at him.

I hold eye contact with him and continue to move against him, feeling his hard length stretch against his pants. His eyes are dark with hunger now, and it turns me on more knowing that hunger is for me.

Rotating my body to face him, I continue to move as I lower my hand to rest against his crotch. His expression looks almost pained as he watches me begin to stroke up and down on the outside of his pants. I haven't had a drop of alcohol tonight, but I feel absolutely intoxicated in this moment.

Who cares if he only wants sex or something casual?

I just want him. *Right now.*

Donovan's eyes are half hooded as he continues to watch me stroke him. He leans down and whispers in my right ear, "I need you."

I look at him, biting my lower lip, and nod before motioning my head towards the front exit.

That's all the confirmation that he needed to see, apparently. As if a rubber band has snapped, Donovan immediately takes my hand and pulls me away from the crowd.

He goes in the opposite direction of the front door, taking me down a dark hallway that seems to lead to the bathrooms.

"I'm not waiting; I want you now," he tells me.

My legs are ready to give out from my own want for him, and I bite down on my lip harder to quell the need.

He bangs on a graffiti-streaked door with a restroom sign on it, and when no one responds, he opens it quickly.

It's a single bathroom with a dark green tinted light and black walls, but before I can even look around fully, his lips are on mine.

He kisses me deeply, furiously pinning me up against the wall as I whimper into his mouth. I lift my arms to untie the top of my dress as he kisses down my neck, and when it quickly drops to reveal that I have nothing on underneath, Donovan backs up to look at me. I'm standing completely nude except for my heels, and he drinks my body in.

"Shit, you wore no underwear, baby. Was that for me?"

I say nothing as he drops to his knees in front of me and begins to lick me. My legs shake, ready to give out as he moves his tongue against me, paying attention to my most sensitive spots like he already knows what I like. My legs start to close together instinctively; the sensation is too much, too good—my knees buckling.

Donovan refuses to let me give in, opening my legs wider and pinning them up against the wall as he holds me up by his sheer strength now. His tongue quickens, and I can't hold back the orgasm that's been building inside. I yell out, grabbing his hair with both hands, as my body convulses around him.

When I finally stop moving, the moment feels deliciously long; Donovan pulls back his face from my center and gives me a feral grin.

"Hope you're ready for me, baby."

He stands and yanks down his pants, his length springing out to greet me—the nickname "Big Dick Donovan" instantly pops into my head.

I bet he would like that one.

He pulls my body closer. "You're so fucking sexy."

He turns me, and I moan as he cups my breasts with his large hands. My body is consumed with want for him again; I've never felt a passion like this before. I crave him inside me.

I bend over in invitation, and he kisses up my back before entering me slowly. His strokes are teasing and gentle. I put my hands against the wall and thrust myself against him, telling him I need more.

"Oh, you want it rough, baby girl? I guess I do need to punish you for your white lie."

"Yes," I breathe out and bite my lower lip. "Now," I whimper.

He answers me by plunging the entirety of his length into me, the sensation instantly causing me to scream out.

"Go ahead, sing as loud as you want. Show everyone how much you want me."

I'm unable to keep quiet as he continues to pound into me. The noises coming out of my mouth are unrecognizable, animalistic.

I feel my core heating. I continue to hold my hands against the wall to match his aggressive thrusts.

"Come for me," he commands. I can hear a smile in his voice as he orders me.

My inner muscles spasm as I come undone, screaming out his name as I finish.

His release quickly follows, and I love the sensation as he fills me.

Donovan holds my hips as he gently pulls out before turning me and kissing me deeply on the lips. We are both panting, the electricity between us undeniable. His cum drips down my legs as his tongue swirls in my mouth, but I couldn't care less. This man just gave me exactly what I wanted.

I fucking love Florida.

Chapter 43

"*I Wanna Be Your Dog*"
Donovan

Last night ended up being a blast. Who would have thought I would have more fun in a club than on a yacht? Not me—especially *sober* me. I had to have Ivy last night; she looked so fucking beautiful, and the more I'm around her, the more I need her, I can't help it.

After our hookup in the bathroom, I walked her back to her hotel room. I would have slept in her room if she invited me, but she didn't. Instead, I went back to mine and touched myself to the thought of when she dropped her dress, the surprise of nothing underneath. The look on her face when—

"Donovan?" Ezra repeats.

I open my eyes and turn to my cousin. "Huh?"

"Damn, dude." He laughs. "Did you take a horse tranquilizer? You must really not be feeling good; you've been out of it from the second we got on the plane. We're here."

I blink twice and look around us, shocked that we are already back in Tennessee. I was so wrapped up in thoughts of Ivy that I didn't focus on the flight.

Ezra unhooks his seatbelt from next to me and stands.

180

Eddie, Wes, Marcus, and Hunter are all one row ahead of us and have started to shuffle down the aisle already.

We were unable to get a last-minute flight back with all the women, which was a bummer after last night's developments. Eddie *did* get us all first-class tickets though, which was a positive experience compared to being crushed in the middle seat.

I wish I had the chance to get a glimpse of Ivy before we left. I was hoping to catch her at breakfast, but she wasn't in the lobby. I even passed the hotel gym in case she was there working out, but I didn't see her.

Ezra tosses me my backpack from the overhead bin. I nod. "Thanks."

I follow him off the plane, and we walk over to the group of guys. Wes has sunglasses on and is rubbing at his temple with a wince, and Marcus has a green tint to his appearance. Everyone seemed to have a wild time on the boat.

When they asked me earlier what I did last night, I just told them I grabbed food with Ivy and we went back to the hotel. I'm not one to air out my business—especially when it involves someone in the same wedding party as me, and it's *Ivy*.

"Eddie, Marcus, and Wes are going to ride with me," Hunter tells us. "That way you guys can just head back to Onilley Lake and not have to take a detour."

"Alright, sounds good," Ezra says to him. "Donovan and I drove separately because he 'can't stand how slow I drive' when we go long distances."

"You drive like a grandpa," I respond.

"You would, too, if you'd had more than ten speeding tickets. I learned my lesson."

"I don't believe it," Eddie snorts. "You used to drag race in the lot next to the skate park."

"Times change." Ezra shrugs. "I was sick of being on a first-name basis with the Clairesville police."

"Excuse me." Marcus runs off suddenly, tossing down his backpack before he begins to throw up in a nearby trash can.

We all turn away from him, giving him his privacy with the can.

"Gnarly." Wes laughs. "Poor kid."

"I told him that twelve tequila shots was too much," Eddie says.

"He's twenty-one; this is his time for fuck-ups," Ezra states.

"Like twelve speeding tickets," Hunter jokes.

"Exactly." Ezra laughs.

"Do you know when the girls' plane lands?" I ask Eddie, trying to appear nonchalant as I say it.

Ezra turns to me and gives me a strange look, but no one else seems to notice.

Eddie unzips his backpack and grabs a stick of gum out of a pack. "I think about forty-five minutes." He hands it to Marcus, who has now joined the group again.

"Can we go? I need about sixty hours of sleep," Marcus groans, clutching his stomach.

"Agreed." Wes shakes his head and then winces from the obvious pounding the movement caused.

We all walk to baggage claim to retrieve our bags. By the time we have found them thirty minutes later, and Marcus has run off outside to puke again, I have made a decision.

When everyone starts to walk out to the parking lot, I tell them I'm going to run to the bathroom and not to wait up for me.

I head to the men's restroom and rest my bag on the counter before taking my deodorant and cologne out of it so I can try and freshen up quickly. I smell my shirt first. The strong scent of diesel and sweat lingers on it. I dig through my bag and find a white cotton tee—I usually keep a spare shirt for after I skate or work in my backpack. I switch shirts quickly and glance at my watch.

The girls' plane has landed by now, and they are probably headed to get their suitcases at baggage claim.

When I see Ivy, I'm going to ask her if I can give her a ride to her apartment. I just want to spend some more time with her, ask her some questions about herself, and let her know I'm interested in more than sex.

If the other girls are around, I will make up an excuse about needing to talk to her about the renovations to make things easy on her—I don't know how she feels about me, but it's obvious that we aren't telling anyone about what's happening between us.

What *is* happening between us?

I grab my backpack and walk out of the men's bathroom, ready to head back towards baggage claim. Once I round the corner, I see Ivy standing next to Olive with both of their backs facing me. I decide to wait until she's done to go talk to her.

I can't hold back my smile as I watch her; she's grabbing Summer's and Leena's bags for them off the conveyer belt before they get the opportunity.

My smile is immediately wiped from my face a moment later when I see a blond man walk up behind Ivy with a bouquet of flowers.

Lee.

I watch in dismay as he taps her on the back, and she spins around; her expression is instantly ecstatic as she sees who is standing behind her. She jumps into his arms and gives him a tight hug.

Quickly stepping back around the corner to hide, I walk in the other direction, not wanting to appear creepy.

If they saw me now, it would just be embarrassing.

I obviously read things between us wrong this weekend.

Chapter 44

"Save Me Some Sunshine"

Ivy

"Lee! What are you doing here?" I brush down my T-shirt as he stares back at me—perfectly put together, like always—with a handful of daisies.

I'm shocked to see him right now, hours away from town.

"Hi, Smiley, I missed you." He grins. "I thought I would surprise my girl; is that okay?"

"*My girl?*" Leena coos from next to us. "That's adorable."

"I'm excited to finally meet you, Lee. I might have questioned Ivy the whole car ride to the airport about you. She's being so secretive." Summer winks.

Lee smiles, and I turn to introduce him to the girls. "Summer, Leena, and...Olive is over there getting a soda." I point in her direction, where she's currently pounding on a vending machine.

"I think the machine took her dollar," Lee says, laughing, his golden hair catching in the light that shines through the airport windows.

"You look like Captain America," Leena tells him.

"Really? I've never heard that before."

184

"Leena compares everyone's appearance to superheroes because her boyfriend looks like Peter Parker." I grin.

"And who are you?" Lee looks down at me, eyebrow raised playfully.

Leena speaks up before I can. "Why, she's *Poison Ivy*, of course."

"I should have known," Lee replies, nudging my side.

I tilt my head down and smell the daisies Lee brought me, a small blush on my cheeks.

Olive walks up behind us. "That damn machine took my dollar!" She does a double take when she sees Lee. "Holy crap, Lee? When did you get here?"

"Hey, Olive." He gives her a large, genuine smile. "It's great to meet you in person."

"Did you come to pick up Ivy?" she asks him.

Lee turns to me, his single dimple on full display from his lighthearted grin. "Well, that's up to her."

I look at the girls and then down at my flowers again—he always brings me flowers. I don't think I will ever be able to look at a bouquet for the rest of my life without thinking of Lee. He may or may not be conditioning me like Pavlov's dog.

Summer speaks up. "Don't worry about riding back with us. Eddie and I switched up your plans enough this weekend already. You deserve this surprise."

Lee gives me a confused look. "Plan switch-up?"

"I will fill you in, in the car, I guess," I tell him with a chuckle.

"Which bag is yours?"

I point to a black suitcase with a Bob's Burgers sticker on it. "That one."

"Hey! I like that show." Lee smiles. Of course he does; he might be the perfect guy. "Are you ready to head out?"

"Yup." I turn to my friends to tell them goodbye. Leena

185

gives me a giant hug, promising to send me the trip photos later, and Summer whispers in my ear that Lee is so cute.

Lee picks up my bag and takes my empty hand in his own before leading me towards the parking lot.

"Wait!" Olive runs up behind us, and I turn quickly to see what's wrong. "I just need to tell Ivy something really quick," she tells Lee.

He nods and points to his car in the lot; he's right in the front row. "I'll give you two some privacy. Just meet me at the car when you're done." He grins at me.

"Thanks, Lee," I say and watch as he continues to the car with my bag before turning back to Olive. "What's up?"

"Do you want to go with him?" she asks.

"What? Of course. Why wouldn't I?"

Olive shrugs and leans in. "I just didn't know if something happened between you and Donovan this weekend."

I don't know how to answer this question.

Olive is my best friend, but I promised myself a few years ago that I wasn't going to involve any of my friends in the ups and downs of my love life until I was really sure about someone. Now they all know about Lee because of my lack of self-control and him showing up here. I really don't want to make things any messier at this point by telling them I'm also hooking up with someone who happens to be in the same wedding party.

Especially when that guy made it clear he only wants a hookup, that he's "not the relationship type"—I don't need other people's opinions right now. I love Olive to death, but she has seen all my bad relationships in the past, so I know she can't help but be a little biased when I tell her about someone new. Not to mention, two someones.

"Nope, not really," I lie; the words taste bitter as I say them.

When I figure out what's going on with my love life, I will let her in.

I'm more embarrassed than anything that all my friends have relationships and I am still floating around trying to find myself.

Olive eyes me; I know she doesn't believe me—that's thanks to years of knowing each other—but she doesn't pry anymore.

"Okay, I just want you happy. You can tell me anything." She leans forward and hugs me.

This makes me feel even shittier.

Olive pulls back and looks above my shoulder at Lee's car. "He's looking over here like a worried puppy. You better get going," she teases with a laugh.

I peer over my shoulder at him, and he quickly looks away, pretending to busy himself with something on his dash. I grin. "Alright, I'll text you tonight. Love you."

Olive turns to head back inside to meet the other girls. "Love ya!"

I walk over to Lee's car, where he's listening to music with all the windows down. Once I slide into the passenger seat, he turns it down and smiles at me. "So, how sleepy are you?"

I glance at the clock; it's noon. "Not tired at all."

"Perfect, because we are heading to our date right now."

I look down at my T-shirt and leggings. "Uhhhh...how casual is the date? Because I'm dressed for the gym."

"Very casual."

"Well, okay, let's go then."

Lee lets out an enthusiastic "whoop, whoop" before backing out of the parking spot. I watch as Summer exits the airport and gives me a big wave. I return the gesture and blow her a kiss.

"Do you want to drive in silence or talk?" he asks me. "I don't know what your preference for a long drive is."

I look over at him. "What do *you* think I like to do?"

He chuckles. "I'm going to assume talk."

"Correct. It would pain me to shut up for that long."

"Okay, well let's see..." He scratches the back of his neck, thinking. "Tell me the story of how you decided to open a bridal store."

I spend the next ten minutes explaining to him about how I've worked in bridal stores for the last ten years, and when I moved back here from Atlanta, I had a plan to open my own.

"I was nervous about getting approved for a loan to open the shop, especially since I wasn't great with money when I was younger... I was kind of a party girl." I chuckle, waiting for his reaction to that.

"I would think so," he says, shrugging. "I think you're the life of the party."

I brush my hand against his arm. "You flatter me." His dimple pops in response as I continue to talk. "So when I got approved for the loan, I just found a shop in the budget I was approved for and went from there."

"That's awesome."

"I'm also super lucky because my parents bought most of the furniture for my shop to support my dream."

"That's amazing that they did that for you."

I nod in agreement and then clap my hands against my thighs. "Can I ask you one thing?"

"Sure." Lee glances at me.

"The Rolex."

He looks at his expensive watch and laughs. "Yeah, I know. Not very practical." He winks at me. "Not very me, but it was a gift from my parents when I graduated college, and it makes me feel closer to them when I wear it. I also didn't have the heart to tell them it's too flashy for me."

"Aw, that's really sweet. What are your parents like?"

"Kind, reserved, quiet. They are getting old now, so they don't get out much. I go to visit them every week or two."

"Where do they live?"

"The edge of Clairesville."

I look out my window and watch the clouds pass by us as we drive. "So, how did you end up owning a coffee shop when you're anti-coffee?"

"Don't make fun of me..."

"I might..."

"Well, when my sister and I turned eighteen, we both got an inheritance from my grandpa. I have always been pretty logical and practical, so I told my sister we needed to use the money to start a business together. She hated the idea; she wanted to blow her money on a trip to Ibiza and a Porsche." Lee laughs.

"As any eighteen-year-old girl with a sudden bout of money would," I say.

"Right. But I talked to her over and over again about it and eventually wore her down. I promised if she would just hold on to the money until we were out of college, she could decide what our business would be. She agreed to do that, and the day she graduated, she decided on a coffee shop."

"I love that," I tell him. "What's your sister's name again?"

"Cora."

I blink. "And you guys didn't name it Cora's Coffee why?"

"Hmm," he says. "I never even thought of that. We just thought Main Street sounded legit."

"It does, don't get me wrong. Cora's Coffee is just cute."

"I'll take that up with the boss." Lee chuckles.

"You better." I laugh. "I'm just busting your balls. Don't change your business name."

Lee stops at a red light and looks at me for a long time.

"What?" I ask.

189

"Nothing, I just love seeing you laugh. You're always a ray of sunshine to be around. My Smiley."

"Thank you," I respond, looking down at my shoes, feeling suddenly shy.

These are the compliments that mean a lot to me. It's one thing to talk about my body—to desire me. It's a whole other thing to talk about my heart—to compliment my soul.

"So, let's hear about this bachelorette trip." He winks at me.

Chapter 45

"One Headlight"

Ivy

Almost two hours later, Lee pulls his car into a small store parking lot that's surrounded by trees. I glance to my left where there is a sign that reads: Ruby Antiques & Customs.

"What are we doing here?" I turn to Lee. His bright eyes catch in the golden light that shines in from the car window as he looks at me—he's basically a human Ken doll.

"Doing a little chopping and shopping."

"What the hell does that mean?" I laugh.

"It's a surprise." He reaches into his back seat and grabs a grey zip-up jacket. "Here, it's cold out. You'll need this."

"Are we going hiking or something?" I joke.

"Yes, kind of."

"No shit, okay." I wasn't expecting a hiking date when he said the *wood* clue to me over text, but I'm down for the adventure.

I pull the jacket around my body and slide my arms in. It smells like expensive cologne with a hint of coffee beans. He steps outside the driver's side, and I follow, stuffing my hands

191

into the jacket pockets when I'm hit with the cold Tennessee air. I feel a tissue inside the right one and something that seems to be ChapStick in the left. Such a practical man.

Lee reaches out for my hand. "Ready?"

"Sure." I turn to look at the shop. "Are we allowed to just park here to go hiking?"

"Yeah, there's a reason. You'll see."

I let him lead me around the side of the antique store to a tree-lined path with a wooden sign directing two different ways.

"Which way?" he asks.

"Hmmmm, let's go left."

"Sounds good."

We walk for the next few minutes in comfortable silence—only the sound of our shoes crunching fallen leaves and our own breathing accompany us. This moment is so peaceful, exactly what I needed right now after a wild weekend.

Lee leads me to a clearing in the trees; it seems like he knows this area well.

He lets go of my hand and spreads his arms out wide. "Pick your favorite one."

"My favorite what?"

"Tree." He smiles down at me.

I look at the forest surrounding us and laugh. "I'm going to be honest, they all kind of look the same."

"Well, see if one calls out to you."

"Okay..." I eye him curiously, but step away to get a closer look at the trees.

They are all similar from a distance, but as I step closer, I see shades of dark brown to light tan bark varying from one tree to the next. I turn and look at another tree to my right. This one is a deep shade of brown with a knot directly in the center of it that almost resembles a smiley face.

"This one!" I exclaim, turning to Lee with sudden excitement. "It smiles."

"Well, isn't that perfect for you?" He shakes his head in disbelief with a laugh and pulls a red band of twine out from his vest pocket.

He walks up next to me and begins to wrap the twine around the tree trunk, finishing off by tying it in a knot. He steps back and turns his head at an angle. "You're right. It does look like a smiley face."

He takes my hand again in his and begins to lead me away, back towards the direction we just hiked.

I turn back and look at the tree. "That's it?"

"For now." Lee grins.

I stop walking. "Okay, spill the beans, please."

Lee looks down at me and leans in closer, cupping my chin with his thumb. "I'm going to have the tree made into a table for your shop."

"You are?!" I blink, shocked and excited.

"Yeah, I wanted to give you something custom that no one else has. Something special, like you."

I'm overcome with his thoughtfulness. His constant generosity. His sweetness.

"How did you even get this idea?"

"My dad's best friend owns that shop. He owns this land and makes custom headboards, chairs, mantles—whatever someone wants." Lee shrugs. "I thought it would be cool to do a new table for your front desk."

"More than cool," I breathe out.

I reach up on my tippy toes and kiss him deeply. His kiss in response is warm, tender, and welcoming—like Lee.

"Thank you," I say against his lips.

"It might take a little while because he does all the work

193

himself and wood engraves designs into the furniture by hand... but it will be worth it when you receive it, I promise."

"This is the best surprise," I tell him, looking up into his eyes. "You're so thoughtful, Lee."

He nods and leans down to lay his forehead against my own. "Ivy, there's something I've been wanting to ask you."

I freeze. *Oh no.*

I listen as he clears his throat, seeming suddenly nervous.

He pulls his head away from mine and takes my face in his hands. "I was wondering if you would like to be my girlfriend, Ivy?"

My heart races—I'm not ready.

I bite my lower lip and look away.

Lee seems to pick up on this cue. "Too soon?"

"I'm sorry, Lee." I shake my head. "I just don't know if I'm ready to be in a relationship yet. Can I have some time to think about it?"

He doesn't even skip a beat. "Of course. Take all the time you need."

"I really like you, I do, but..."

Lee holds up his right hand. "Seriously, Ivy. You don't need to explain yourself to me. I will be here whenever you're ready."

I nod as he reaches down and squeezes my hand with his own, his reassurance that we are good. That it's *fine.*

He's such a good guy, and I *do* really like him—so why do I feel so unsure?

The answer swims around in my head: Donovan Anderson.

Chapter 46

"A Dangerous Meeting"

Ivy

Friday

The date with Lee ended up being more than I expected. I enjoyed myself, and every time I'm around him I feel my heart softening more and more, my feelings for him growing. He's an incredible guy—exactly who I should be head over heels for. I should commit myself to him, take myself off the market, and spend the rest of my life with a man like Lee.

Should.

I can't help the fire running through my veins when I see Donovan, though. The feeling is like no other. I crave it. The constant need to capture his attention—it never leaves me.

I was disappointed when he left me a voicemail on Monday saying he wasn't feeling well and that he wouldn't be able to come in this week. I've been worried about him ever since. If I knew where he lived on the lake, I would have dropped off some soup. I was tempted to text Olive and ask her for his address but decided against it when I thought about the barrage of questions from her that would follow.

Donovan was supposed to finish up the final renovations around the shop this week, and that makes me more nervous than anything, a pit in my stomach knowing that our time together is coming to an end. That I need to talk to him about what's going on between us, because I might not see him again after the wedding.

Something in me thought that after our time in Florida, maybe things had changed in his eyes, maybe he would ask me out on an official date—but nothing has happened. No texts and also no responses. I sent him a message yesterday asking him how he was doing and haven't heard back.

However, I did receive a text from Ezra, asking me if it was okay if he came by and finished up the last of the plumbing tasks this morning. I told him that would be amazing but rolled my eyes as I typed, knowing that he must have gotten my phone number from Donovan—I thought he was done being a grumpy asshole towards me.

Now that the tile has been finished by Donovan in the main bathroom, all Ezra has to do is switch out the toilet, which he said would only take thirty minutes. We don't have any bridal appointments till late afternoon today, so it works out.

I shut my computer lid and walk back to see his progress. Ezra has already been here for twenty minutes, so I know he must almost be done. Jade peeks her head out of the staff room and gestures towards the bathroom mouthing, "He's so fucking hot."

I laugh and mouth back, "Single."

She does a silent cheer before disappearing back into the staff room.

Knocking on the doorframe as I enter the bathroom, I see Ezra bent over on the ground.

When he hears my entrance, he smiles sheepishly and turns down the metal song on his phone. "Sorry, was my music too loud?"

Ezra's floppy dark hair is wrapped up in a black bandana, and he's wearing a short-sleeved motorcycle tee with rips in it.

"Not at all." I shake my head. "Just checking in to make sure it's going okay."

"Yup." He smiles, standing up. "I'm done. Just got to clean up my stuff."

"Wow, you're quick."

Ezra smirks. "With some things."

"I'm going to ignore that," I pretend to scold him.

He throws his head back and laughs before leaning down to grab his tools.

I bite the inside of my cheek, wondering if I want to ask about Donovan or not. I decide that my curiosity is getting the best of me and do. "Hey, uh...how's Donovan feeling?"

Ezra looks confused. "Good, why?"

That ass.

I pretend to be flippant. "Oh, nothing. I just thought he was sick, that's all."

"Oh." Ezra scratches the top of his bandana with his empty hand. "I don't think so? He seems fine this week. He's been fixing up a rundown boat he just bought."

"Hmmm," I respond.

"Yeah, my bad. I thought you told him to take the week off from here or something."

"Nope."

"Oh, well, he's almost done I know, he told me this morning. I'm sure he will be back next week."

I'm incredibly frustrated now. He's purposely avoiding me.

"How about this weather?" Ezra smiles brightly, changing the subject.

Tennessee is having a rare heatwave this week; the temperatures are almost in the '70s which is a welcome change from the chill and snow we usually get around this time of year.

"I love it." I grin, pointing down at my short-sleeved top and skirt.

"We are basically in Florida again," Ezra says, laughing.

I nod in agreement, wishing I could go back in time and relive last weekend.

Ezra continues to speak. "Hey, actually, some of the group are coming out to our place on the lake tomorrow since it's so nice out. We are going to grill out and hang. Do you want to come? I know Summer and Eddie plan on going."

"Oh." I blink. "I actually already have plans with someone tomorrow...this guy I've been kind of seeing."

"What are you guys doing?" Ezra pries. "I didn't even know you were seeing anyone."

I laugh. "Well, you and I haven't had too many personal conversations, Ezra. And we are just going to see a movie."

"Lame, come to our place instead," he jokes. "Then we could grow our friendship, and I can also meet your suitor."

I think this over for a minute. I know Lee wouldn't care about a change of plans, and I didn't schedule myself to come in to Vera tomorrow, so I'm free all day. Also, I kind of want to piss Donovan off after he's given me the cold shoulder all week. The thought of seeing the look on his face if I were to show up at his place after he's been avoiding me is extremely tempting.

I know I'm being petty, but I can't find a fuck to give about it.

It would be nice to hang out with Ezra and the others, too, I quickly tell myself.

"Okay." I nod my head, grinning. "Your place tomorrow."

Chapter 47

"She Rides"

Donovan

"Hey stranger," a familiar female voice says as someone kicks the bottom of my work boot. I scoot out from under my truck and squint against the sun's rays to make out Summer and Eddie staring down at me, smiling.

Summer continues to talk, lifting a small bag in her right hand. "I brought an apple pie. Took me hours."

"Yeah," Eddie snorts. "Hours in the grocery store deciding what flavor to get."

Summer nudges him playfully. "Hey! You blew my cover."

Eddie leans down and kisses her forehead. "I think the price sticker on the lid might be what would have blown your cover anyway, darling."

I stand and brush my hands off on my pants. A bead of sweat drips from my forehead and I brush it away before it reaches my eyes. Today is warm, insanely warm for Tennessee in January.

When Ezra told me he invited the crew out for a boat and

grill day, I agreed that it was a good idea. Who knows when we will next get a few days like this, and I've been itching to take out the twenty-four-foot motorboat that I just fixed up.

I've been a real dick all week, lying to Ivy and telling her I'm sick—not responding to her message trying to check up on me. I threw myself into a project instead, trying to busy my mind with other tasks instead of thinking about her excitement when she saw Lee at the airport.

I'm unable to deny any longer to myself that I'm falling for her, and I hate it. I'm angry with myself. I hate the loss of control. The fear. The sadness I feel when I think of her with another man.

It pisses me off.

What started out as an insane sexual attraction towards her has now led to feelings. Feelings are not something I've ever dealt with while sober. I don't know *how* to deal with feelings when I'm not drinking.

I've purposely stuck to only hookups for the past few years. That's all I wanted with Ivy—something easy. Something simple. I guess that wouldn't be Ivy, though, would it? She's loud and fierce. She's sassy and funny; she's driving me *insane*.

"You doing okay, bud?" Eddie asks.

I clear my throat. "Yeah, why?"

"You just seem kind of out of it." Eddie chuckles. "Dreaming of your new boat, I suppose."

"Yeah, exactly. Dreaming."

"I can't wait to take it out."

"She's running great now." I smile, trying to shake all thoughts of Ivy away. I don't have to worry about seeing her until I go back to Vera Bridal next week.

"What are you working on?" Eddie looks at my truck.

"Just replacing the front axle u-joints," I say.

"I'm going to pretend I know what that is to impress my fiancé." Eddie laughs, turning to gaze at Summer.

"I'm always impressed." Summer leans up to kiss Eddie on his cheek.

"Where do you want us to put this stuff? We've got some chips and veggies in the car, too." Eddie motions back towards his white Audi.

I look down at my dirty hands. "I would help"—I chuckle—"but I'm kind of a mess right now. Just throw it on the counter inside; Ezra's in there."

They both start up the steps of my porch to head inside, and I turn to face the lake, deciding if I want to take a dip to cool off and clean off. I decide it's a good idea and head down towards the sparkling, icy water.

Pulling my T-shirt off over my head and removing my boots, I chuck them onto the loose rock and sand shore before stepping up onto our dock and walking out.

I take a deep breath before diving off the side into the water. The shock of cold almost instantly clears my mind.

As I swim out and do a few laps around the deep, chilly water, my troubles and thoughts begin to dissipate even more. By the time I think about heading back to the shore, I feel almost calm.

When I start to step out of the water, though, I instantly notice the curvy body and breathtaking face I've been obsessing over staring back at me. *Her eyes.* Those piercing blue eyes.

Ivy's here.

I glance to her left to see a tall man stepping out of a Nissan.

And so is Lee.

He walks up and takes her hand in his, waves to me, then says something to her before turning back and smiling at me. I look between the two of them—the comfortable nature they share. I hate that her hand is in his, that he's staring at me with a welcoming smile as Ivy leans into him.

I am suddenly craving a drink more than ever, a feeling I haven't experienced to this magnitude for the past few years.

Chapter 48

"Round and Round"

Ivy

I gulp as Donovan exits the lake like fucking Aquaman in slow motion. Water is dripping down his tanned, tattooed chest, his hair swaying against his shoulders as he steps out of the lake. He doesn't even realize I'm watching him; he's just that hot for no reason.

Never mind, now he's looking at me.

I hear rocks crunch as Lee steps up behind me. "Geez, the guy's a model. He must get lots of women," he jokes.

I force myself to laugh, still not breaking eye contact with Donovan.

Lee takes my hand and waves to him. Donovan walks towards us.

"Hey, man! Nice to see you somewhere other than the bridal shop."

Donovan looks at Lee for a second and nods before his eyes lock back on mine. "Hi, I didn't know you guys were coming."

"Ezra invited us."

"Did he now?" Donovan looks back up towards the house I'm assuming is his. "Hm, okay."

203

"Is that a problem?" I cross my arms, anger starting to grow inside me. Why the hell has he been avoiding me since the trip? "Are you feeling better?"

"No," Donovan responds. "Not a problem. Yes. Feeling better." He bites out the words coldly.

"Great." I scowl.

Lee lets out a nervous chuckle, obviously sensing animosity between us.

"Come on, Lee." I take his arm, leading him away. "Summer texted me already and told us to head inside when we got here."

"Alright." He tilts his head to acknowledge Donovan before following me.

"Everything okay?" Lee whispers in my ear as we walk up a set of stairs to the large wooden porch.

"Fantastic." I smile at him. "Why?"

"You just seemed a little angry back there."

"I'm okay." I squeeze his arm with my hand. "Just a little annoyed that the renovations aren't done yet."

"Oh, okay. Well, he's a nice guy, it seems. I'm sure he'll be done soon."

I plant a smile on my face. "You're right. I guess...I'm just *hangry*," I joke.

"I told you that you could have had another slice of my pizza at lunch." Lee looks down at me and kisses my nose.

"I know, which was very thoughtful of you." I reach up and poke his dimple as he grins. "But I had already taken two of them; I didn't want you to starve." I laugh. "Come on, let me introduce you to everyone."

I glance around the deck to get a quick look at Donovan and Ezra's place. It's filled with stacked tires, chairs, fishing poles, and a few worn-down skateboard decks. Exactly what I would expect from the two of them.

The exterior of the house is a deep brown and has wood siding on the walls, along with a brick garage attached on the left side. Their property is huge, with vast trees spreading out into a forest behind the house and multiple dirt paths that lead off in the distance. The Onilley Lake shore is about twenty feet walking distance away from their porch; it's expansive and very intimidating. I was shocked to see how huge it was when Lee and I drove up.

Lee reaches forward and takes the handle of the double glass sliding door at the end of the porch, opens it, and nudges his head for me to step through. Music blasts from inside the second the door is pulled ajar.

I raise my eyebrows at Lee and he laughs. "Sounds like a party."

Stepping past him and inside the home, I'm greeted with a bear hug from Ezra before I can even take in my surroundings.

"Ivy! My dog! You made it." He smiles, his face slightly flushed from either alcohol or activity. He reaches over and claps Lee on the back next. "Hey, bro, I'm Ezra."

Lee smiles. "Lee."

"Lee, you're very dapper," Ezra jokes.

Wes turns to face us from a tan couch he's lying across in the corner of the room. He walks up and shakes Lee's hand. "Wes," he says, giving Lee a once-over. "You know, you could tell me you're going to be our next president, and I'd believe you."

Lee laughs heartily.

"Can you even name our president now?" Summer snorts, standing from a red barstool in the kitchen directly in front of us to give me a hug in greeting. She reaches over and winks at Lee.

"Of course." Wes crosses his arms. "Tony Hawk."

"Ah yes, President Tony Hawk," Ezra says. "I remember his slogan, '*Grinding for America.*'"

"A guy can dream." Wes shrugs. "First order of business, a skate park in every neighborhood."

"I used to play the Tony Hawk skate game as a kid on my PlayStation," Lee speaks up. "It was my favorite."

I feel a little pride swell in my chest that Lee is so quick to adapt when meeting people. It's all so easy with him.

"My man." Ezra reaches out and daps him up. "I knew Ivy had good taste."

The door slams shut from behind us suddenly, causing me to jump. "Good taste in what?" Donovan says, appearing at my left side, wiping his face with a towel.

"Lee," Summer lightheartedly responds.

Donovan doesn't say anything back, just tilts his head to look down at me. I don't meet his eyes this time.

Ezra clears his throat. "So, I was about to ride the truck to drop the boat at the ramp. Would you guys want to ride with me?"

"Oh, uh..." I start to say, feeling that anxiety bubbling up inside of me again. I knew people would probably want to go on the boat today since the weather is nice, but I didn't prepare myself for what to say if the moment actually came.

I touch my hair with my hands, pulling some of it forward from behind my back so it hugs around my shoulders—security blanket.

Donovan speaks before I can figure out what to say. "I'm driving the boat back to the house; you can ride back with Ezra in the truck if you want to come."

Lee's ears perk up. "Why don't we go on the boat, Ivy?"

Donovan stares at me; I can tell he's almost smug inside, knowing that he knows about my fear of the water but I haven't told Lee. He's reveling in the fact that Lee is in the dark about this.

"I'm going to ride back with Ezra, keep my new buddy company." I turn to Ezra and smack him on the back playfully.

"Thanks, Ivy." Ezra grins and bows his head. His shaggy dark hair slides in front of his eyes and he blows it back with a breath.

I turn to Lee. "But seriously, you go. I want you to."

"I don't want to abandon you on our date," Lee responds with a smile.

Donovan walks past me over to the fridge and yanks it open, grabs a water bottle, and chugs it.

I look back at Lee. "Absence makes the heart grow fonder. I will actually be angry if you don't go." I cross my arms, challenging him. "So go."

Lee chuckles and lifts his hands in surrender. "Alright, I'll go. I haven't been out on Onilley Lake in years—it should be fun."

Summer grabs a handful of chips out of a bowl on the counter. "I'm going out to ride the four-wheelers with Wes and Eddie," she tells me. "Eddie's in the garage putting gas in them now. Want to come with me instead?"

I look down at my flowy teal dress. "I don't think I'm dressed for that. Sorry, I didn't prepare for activities today."

"That's my bad." Ezra smiles sheepishly. "I didn't inform you well. From now on, know that an invite from the Anderson cousins means *Anderson activities*."

"Did you just refer to yourself in the third person out loud?" Donovan scoffs. "Don't include me in that."

Lee and Summer laugh at his comment.

Wes groans. "Ezra, you used to be so cool. What happened, man?"

"That was pretty cringe," I agree.

"My apologies," Ezra says with a grin, before tossing two sets of keys to Summer's awaiting hands. "Eddie has the third set already. After we bring the boat back, I will start grilling, so try not to stay gone too long."

"Noted," she says and smiles at me before walking down a hallway. The sound of a door closing follows a few moments later.

Wes hops up to trail after her.

Ezra clicks off the stereo. "Let's go."

We head out the glass doors, Donovan leading the way down the steps and around the side of their house to a large grey truck with a big boat on a trailer behind it.

"Damn." Lee whistles when he sees it. "She's a beauty."

"Donovan's been fixing her up nonstop all week," Ezra proudly states. "She wasn't like this when she first arrived here, trust me—some serious work was needed. I swear he hasn't slept a minute."

I turn and eye Donovan. So this is what he has been doing all week while he's been avoiding me.

"This will only be her second time on the water," Donovan adds. "I took her out yesterday for a little to make sure she was running okay. Came back and made a few minor adjustments, and she's good now."

Lee walks over, touches the side of the boat, and raises his eyebrows in appreciation. "Nice."

Donovan smirks. "You better keep your hands off my lady without my permission."

What Lee doesn't see is Donovan staring at me with a dark expression the whole time he says those words.

I roll my eyes, tearing them away from his stone-cold expression, and start to walk towards Ezra's truck. I'm sick of his games.

I glance back as Lee pulls his hand away but continues to

stare at the boat in admiration and chuckles. "What's her name? Don't all boats have a name?"

"She doesn't have one yet," Donovan responds.

Ezra has already gotten in the driver's seat and leans out the window. "Ladies get shotgun."

I nod and walk around the front of the vehicle; the loud growl of the truck's engine feels mutual to my own anger stirring inside.

Fuck Donovan, and fuck these mind games he is playing with me.

I grab the handle and pull myself into the truck. Lee, on my heels, gets in the seat behind me, and Donovan gets behind Ezra.

"Let's ride." Ezra puts the truck in drive and turns sharply out of the dirt lot. I squeal as I slide against the window from the rough jerk of the steering wheel. "Sorry," Ezra murmurs.

"Seatbelt," Donovan commands in a low voice.

I look back at him and prepare to shoot him a dirty look when Lee speaks up.

"Good thinking, man." Lee motions to my seatbelt and I roll my eyes as I slide it across my chest before clicking it in the holster, and tightening it at my lap.

Minutes later we pull up in front of a large boat ramp that offers public access to Onilley Lake. Ezra turns the truck around with ease and Donovan jumps out to help him guide it down into the water. They do this so quickly, within two minutes the boat is off the trailer and Ezra is driving back up away from the lake.

Ezra parks next to a small dock to the right of the lake. "Hey, go ahead and hop out if you wanna ride," he tells Lee.

Lee looks at me, his eyes searching for the answer to if I'm still okay with him going or not.

"Go, go!" I wave him on.

209

He smiles boyishly, the excitement of going on the boat radiating off of him. He gets out of the back of the truck and jogs towards Donovan. I watch out the window as Donovan drives the boat near the side dock to pick him up.

Lee stops suddenly and holds up a hand to Donovan. "Be right back!" he shouts.

What is he doing?

I watch as he runs back towards Ezra's truck and stops in front of my window.

"Forgot something." He smiles and tips his head through the window to kiss me deeply. Then he pulls back and taps the doorframe. "I'm good now."

I laugh as he jogs off again and jumps the small space from the dock to Donovan's boat. Donovan looks angry as hell. I can practically see steam rolling off of him.

He gases the engine suddenly, and Lee loses his balance, falling back onto the bench seats on the boat deck. I gasp, and Ezra scoffs next to me, saying, "What the fuck was that?" under his breath.

Donovan looks back at Lee and shouts, "Hold on!"

I blink and watch as Donovan drives off, a wicked smile on his face, and I know for certain that I should have never brought Lee here today.

Chapter 49

"Harder To Breathe"
Ivy

E zra and I chat quietly on the drive back to their house, neither of us bringing up what just happened. Ezra is probably trying to figure out what's going on inside his cousin's head right now, and I know that I will *never* be able to figure that out.

He parks in the same spot his truck was in before and turns off the engine. "I think..." he starts to say and then rubs the back of his neck. He remains quiet; it seems like he is making a decision in his head. Ezra clears his throat and speaks again. "I'm going to start grilling the burgers. You want cheese?"

I shrug but wonder what he was actually going to say. "Who doesn't?"

"You can go hang out on the dock; the guys should be pulling up any minute." He gets out of the driver's seat and murmurs under his breath, "Especially with how fast he was going."

I open my door and climb down from the leather passenger seat to the ground, smoothing my dress quickly as it flutters up from a warm breeze. This weather truly is incredible right now.

I didn't get to take in the beauty of their property earlier with the drama when we first arrived, but this place is picturesque. "Mind if I explore?" I shout to Ezra as he starts towards the house.

"Be my guest," he yells back.

I do a circle, deciding which direction I want to go in. There's a large white garage shed towards the left of Ezra's truck with a four-wheeler missing a wheel sitting outside of it and a few dead plants.

I decide to head in that direction—I'm nosy.

Walking inside through the open garage door, I'm instantly surprised to see that the space is pretty clean. Their house wasn't dirty, but it did look like it's suffered through a few party nights and possibly indoor skateboarding. Who am I to judge, though? I appreciate my mess of belongings.

There's a bunch of fishing equipment spread across black cabinets, and tools line the walls, all perfectly in their spots like puzzle pieces clicked together. There's a grey couch directly across from me against the far wall with a shelf of photos and knickknacks above it.

Don't mind if I do.

Stepping up to the shelf, I smile to myself as I look over photographs of boys that must have been Donovan and Ezra as kids. They are holding up a giant fish together in one and then sitting with a group of guys at the skate park in another.

I recognize Eddie, Wes, and Hunter in the group photo immediately and grin even wider when I see young Donovan, flipping off the camera with his little skater hair covering his eyes and a Black Sabbath T-shirt.

What a little shit, I laugh to myself.

Still a shit.

There are a few books on the shelf, motorcycle magazines,

and a jar full of lures. I get ready to turn when something shiny catches my eye: a coin. I reach out and pick it up.

It's bronze, has a slight weight to it, and has a triangle with words.

One Breath. One Day. One Month. One Year.

It's a sobriety coin, I realize—it must be Donovan's. I suddenly feel guilty about snooping and glance around to make sure no one is watching before setting it back on the shelf quickly.

I walk over to the counter full of fishing poles and pick one up, testing the weight and feel of it.

"Why did you bring him here?" a voice says from the other side of the garage.

I blink and set the fishing pole down on the counter gently.

"Why did you bring him here?" Donovan repeats, this time in a much lower voice.

I hear his boots shuffle against the concrete flooring, the sound getting louder as he approaches me.

I breathe out. "I brought him because Ezra invited us. I told you that."

"You're rubbing it in my face," Donovan snaps back.

I turn quickly to find him less than an inch away from me. "I'm not."

"You're trying to piss me off," he responds.

"What would *you* have to be pissed off about? You blew me off all week."

"For good reason."

"And what's that?" I stare at him, challenging him.

Instead of snapping back with the usual anger he holds so dear, his expression falls. Donovan steps back and grips his hair with his hands. "You're driving me fucking insane, Ivy."

"That makes two of us."

"Do you like me or not?"

I refuse to give him a response after the shit he just pulled following the trip to Florida. I stare up at him, arms crossed, expressionless.

He looks down at me and smirks. "You're not going to answer me are you."

I raise an eyebrow and cock my head to the side.

Donovan bends down and whispers in my ear, "Fine. You know I like you like this."

"Angry?"

"Rebellious."

He leans down over me, placing his arms on either side behind me on the counter. I hold my breath as he lowers his head, his mouth directly in front of mine.

"Where's Lee?" I ask.

"Does it matter?" Donovan responds and plants a small kiss on my lower lip. Then one on my neck. Then one on my ear. He hangs over me for a moment, waiting to see if I will make a move.

This is wrong, so wrong to be this close to him right now, but I can't budge—I'm frozen.

He steps away from me, and I instantly miss his scent, his touch, his warmth.

I touch his arm to stop him from moving any farther away and pull his body closer to mine. I begin kissing him feverishly —the desire pours over with every single touch. The all-encompassing need for him shuts out every other thought in my head.

Donovan pushes the items on the counter out of the way before hoisting me up onto it. He bites my lower lip and groans as I let my tongue dive into his mouth.

His hand roams down between my legs, tracing up the inside of my thigh, and I moan into his lips from the anticipation.

He draws his hand back, pants heavily, and whispers against my lips, "I can't breathe."

"I know," I respond, leaning back in to kiss him—he takes my breath away, too.

"No." He draws back from me, shaking his head. "I"—wheeze—"can't"—wheeze—"*BREATHE.*"

Chapter 50

"Bad Decisions"

Ivy

"Y ou can't breathe?" I look at Donovan, his eyes are wide and he's grasping at his chest. Shit, shit, shit. What is going on?

"EpiPen," he rasps out.

"Where?" I quickly ask.

Donovan points in the direction of his truck.

"Okay, okay." I start to run out of the shed. "I'll be right back!"

My heart is pounding out of my chest as I run to his truck. Where the fuck is Ezra? Where's Lee?

"Lee!" I scream out. "Ezra!"

I continue to scream their names, and Lee comes running around the corner from the deck of the house by the time I make it to Donovan's truck. I pull the handle and throw myself into the truck, quickly digging through all the compartments in search of his EpiPen.

"What's wrong?" Lee asks from behind me, concern in his tone.

"It's Donovan." I throw some papers aside in his glove box. "I think he's having an allergic reaction."

"Oh shit, let me get Ezra. He's inside." Lee runs off back in the direction of their house.

Scrambling as I throw papers and plastic silverware out of the glove box, I finally find the narrow EpiPen in the back of the compartment.

"Thank god," I whisper to myself as I sprint back towards the garage.

Donovan is now standing with his left hand up against the open door and his right against his heaving chest. Pounding gravel sounds from behind me, and by the time I make it to Donovan, Ezra and Lee are right behind me.

I fumble to try and open the cap to the EpiPen, but I'm shaking so violently that I can't get it open. Ezra reaches out and takes it from me, opening it with ease and placing it against Donovan's thigh before forcefully pushing the needle into his skin.

Donovan lets out a deep breath a moment later, his chest rising and falling rapidly as he takes in the air he desperately needs.

My legs collapse under me with relief; I bury my face in my hands and can't stop my body from shaking. The worry of the moment has left me, and now I'm a wreck. Lee bends down and rubs my back, which makes me hate myself in this moment. I don't deserve his sympathy after what I just did.

"Come on," Ezra tells us. "I'm going to take Donovan to the hospital to get checked out. You guys can hang out at the house and wait for the others to get back if you want."

"We'll go with you," Lee speaks up and then turns to Donovan. "Let's make sure you're okay, man. That was scary."

Donovan nods his head and rubs at his neck for a moment

before heading over to his own truck. He shakily gets in the passenger seat, and Ezra jogs to the driver's side.

Lee reaches over and takes my hand, squeezing it as he walks with me to the truck, telling me that everything is going to be okay. I could vomit right now—I'm feeling worse and worse by the minute.

*　*　*

The first fifteen minutes of our drive are in complete silence. I think we are all relieved that Donovan is okay but still on edge until he gets checked out by a doctor. I look out the truck window, remembering what the psychic told us that night about Donovan having a close encounter with death.

"Well, that wasn't fun," Donovan says, with a small, hoarse chuckle. He is still visibly shaking in front of us. Probably a side effect from the adrenaline shot.

Ezra's head turns to look at his cousin. "Yeah, no shit." I catch a glimpse of him in the rearview mirror, and I can see his brow is furrowed. Ezra's been biting his nails aggressively this whole drive—I've never seen him serious like this. He has also been speeding way over the speed limit, but I'm not going to say anything since this is an emergency.

Ezra continues to talk. "What the hell did you eat, dude?"

Donovan shifts in the passenger seat in front of me. "Just my regular: eggs, sausage, toast, and a protein shake. I haven't even had lunch yet."

"You had nothing with tomato?"

"No," Donovan responds.

Lee clears his throat and speaks up. "Ivy and I had some pizza at a pizza shop before we got here. Could us being around you have caused it?"

Fuck.

"No, being near someone usually doesn't trigger the allergy for him. Only if he eats or shares saliva with someone who has, but I don't think he was kissing anyone here," Ezra jokes, but the car seems to grow completely quiet—like everyone is placing that I was the only one with Donovan when this happened to him.

Oh my god, not now.

I put my head down and stare at my dress, refusing to meet Lee's eyes even though I can feel them drilling into the side of my head.

I did this. I caused this to happen to Donovan.

I know this is my fault—and now, so does Lee.

Chapter 51

"Cut Me Loose"

Ivy

"**D**o you even like me?"

"What?" I look away from the ER waiting room TV that's playing a *Seinfeld* rerun and meet eyes with Lee, who is now standing to my right.

He sits down in the chair next to me, holding a cup of coffee, and passes it to me.

I murmur my thanks.

"Do you like me, Ivy? Or are you just wanting to mess around? Because I really like you. I want to be in a relationship with you. You're the only person I'm seeing."

I release a breath. "Lee, can we please just discuss this on the ride back to Clairesville?"

"I just want to know. Should I leave now?"

"No, I don't want you to leave."

"But you're hooking up with him. Right?" Lee responds.

"Not really." I look down at the floor. "Only a few times. Once before Christmas and then once on the bachelorette trip."

Lee shakes his head next to me. "I didn't even know he was

on that trip with you. I feel like an idiot, Ivy, like everyone knew you were with him *and* me...but *me*."

"I'm sorry, Lee." I take in his hurt expression, feeling sick. "No one knew about it, no one does know about it."

"Well, now people are going to know; Ezra definitely figured it out."

"I'm sorry." I can feel myself shrinking. Another bad decision I've made in my dating life, another wrong turn I've taken.

"I mean"—Lee lets out a half laugh—"we aren't exclusive, so you didn't factually do anything wrong. I get why you didn't want to be in a relationship with me though—I can't compete with that guy..."

"Don't say that, Lee." I turn my body towards him and touch his arm. "I really do like you."

"Well, then you need to make a choice, Ivy. I'm sorry if that's unfair of me to say, but I want to be with you, and *only* you. I want a relationship. I'm a grown man who knows what he wants. I'm looking to find my wife, not mess around."

The confidence in that statement alone makes me look at Lee differently. He's what I have never had in a romantic relationship—stability. He's got his life together; he doesn't hesitate.

"You're right," I tell him.

Lee nods his head. "So, just make a choice, please. Sooner rather than later, if I get a say."

I squeeze his arm affectionately. "Thank you."

He smiles, and that dimple I love appears. I finally feel like I can breathe for the first time in hours, so I tip up the cup and take a small sip of the coffee he brought me. It's horrible, and I suppress a gag. I will never get over the fact that he owns a coffee shop and doesn't only hate the drink but also can't make a cup of it to save his life.

"Good?" Lee asks.

"Mhmmm." I nod. Today is not the day to tell him that the drink is like lighter fluid.

"See, I'm getting better."

I let out a laugh and shake my head, but sober up quickly when I see Ezra walking towards us.

Lee and I both stand. Ezra looks between us uncomfortably for a moment before speaking in a low voice. "Ivy...Donovan wants to talk to you."

I wince slightly and look over at Lee. He holds up a hand. "It's fine. Go, Ivy. I'll be waiting for you out here."

"I'm sorry, Lee," I tell him.

"It's fine," he repeats again before sitting back down in the blue waiting room chair.

I hug myself uncomfortably from the cold of the hospital AC and also from not knowing what is in store for me as I follow Ezra through the automatic waiting room door to the sterile ER rooms.

We pass four rooms before Ezra stops in front of one with a curtain pulled and nods to me. "He's in there. I'm going to go get a snack. Give you guys some privacy."

"Okay," I respond.

"I had no idea." Ezra looks down at me and lowers his voice. "I really like you, Ivy...but I'm not sure if you guys are right for each other at this time. He has some demons he needs to figure out. And from how today went down, it seems like you do, too."

I do nothing but lower my head, knowing I deserve the scolding. "I'm sorry about today. I forgot about his allergy."

Ezra shrugs. "I obviously didn't want anything to happen to him today. He's not just my cousin but the closest person to me in the world. It freaked me out, that's all." He glances down at his phone. "I talked to Eddie a few minutes ago; he's going to head this way soon with Summer and Wes to give you and Lee a ride back to his car."

"Okay, thanks, Ezra."

"Donovan's waiting on you; go on in." Ezra gives me a final nod in goodbye and then walks off.

I bite the inside of my cheek as I step forward to the grey printed curtain, exhaling a shaky breath before I pull it to the side and step into the room.

Donovan is sitting in the hospital bed with an expression of boredom on his face. He is wearing a blue patient gown, his large frame is sticking off every side of the bed, and *SpongeBob* is playing loudly on the TV on the wall—if I wasn't so anxious right now, I would find this moment comical.

"Hi," I squeak out.

His gaze shoots from the TV to me, and he hurriedly sits up.

"Hi, Ivy," Donovan says.

"Watching some *SpongeBob*?" I clasp my hands together and sit on the edge of the bed near his feet.

"I guess." He shrugs and looks down at his gown. "How do I look?"

"Like you shouldn't be here, and I'm so sorry, and it's all my fault—"

Donovan cuts me off. "Ivy, it's fine. It wasn't your fault. I made the first move on you."

"I know, but I should have stopped you." I look down at my nails. "What I did today...wasn't fair to you or Lee."

Donovan visibly tenses at the sound of Lee's name. "I wanted to talk to you about that."

"Me too."

"I think..." He sits up farther in the bed. "I think that we are like fire and gasoline together."

I look up into his eyes to find them staring back at me, dark and full of sorrow.

Donovan continues to speak. "I think that if I were with you, it would destroy me, Ivy. I'm not a good guy; Lee is a good guy. Hell, he's a great guy...he's sitting out there *still* here after he found out I was hooking up with you. I know I said that I just wanted to hook up with you...but it's turned into something more complicated now. Things are different; I feel different."

My heart begins to hammer out of my chest at his confession.

He looks away from me. "I have really started to like you these past few months."

"I feel the same way," I say.

Donovan reaches out and touches my hand. "But I think you should be with Lee. He's ready to settle down; I'm not."

I feel like my heart is cracking.

"You don't mean that; you just told me it drives you crazy to see me with him."

"It does, but I will finish up this week at the bridal store, and other than the wedding, we won't have to see each other again. Choose him."

"You're not even giving me a choice," I respond. "You're *telling* me that you're not going to be with me. That it needs to be him."

"I'm doing what's best for you." Donovan leans forward and reaches for me.

I pull back quickly. "You don't get to make that decision for me."

"I don't even live in Clairesville—it would never work between us."

"That's an excuse, and you know it."

"I'm sorry, Ivy." He sits back in the hospital bed and looks away, an expression of boredom on his face again, like I'm wasting his time right now just being in his presence.

His mind is obviously made up.

I feel anger bubbling up inside me now, and I stand quickly. "You make no sense to me. You say you like me, but then make it seem like that's a bad thing?" I throw my hands in the air. "Well then, fuck you, Donovan Anderson. I don't beg for any man. I'll mail you a check and get someone else to finish the job for me."

With that, I walk to the curtain and pull it shut, exiting his room in a huff.

After three steps I realize something, and I quickly open the curtain a foot again and stick my head through. Donovan sits on the bed blinking at me, confused.

I huff. "Again, I'm sorry for almost killing you today from anaphylactic shock. That was really scary, and I hope nothing like that ever happens to you ever again—but aside from that, fuck you still."

Chapter 52

"At Last"

Ivy

Six months later

"Hold still!"

"I'm trying."

"I've almost got it in; don't move." I grunt and let out a breath. "Annnnnd, there." I stand up and clap my hands together in excitement, taking in Summer's wedding gown with the shoes. "I think you needed an eight and a half, not an eight." I laugh.

Summer sticks her heel out from under her dress so she can get a better view of it. "I think you're right, but it's too late now."

"For someone so organized and Type A, you've really taken the back seat when it comes to your wedding. I'm surprised, and might I say a little impressed."

Summer shrugs. "All I care about is that I get to marry Eddie. And I do." She smiles and turns to look at herself in the floor-length mirror.

I walk up behind her and smooth out her veil; the delicate

pearls lining the trim cascade around her dark red curls. "That's right. You do."

Olive opens the door to the bridal suite; her long cerulean bridesmaid gown matches my own but has a strapless neckline, while mine has off-the-shoulder cap sleeves.

"Your date's outside asking for you." Olive grins at me.

I grab some perfume off the counter and spray a small mist for Summer to step through. "Alright, thanks."

"Maybe you're next," Leena says as she lines her lips with a dark mauve shade at a nearby vanity.

"I think *you're* next. What has it been? Five years?" I respond.

"I'm still deciding if I want to get married," Leena says. "Do I want to be a kept woman?" She turns to Summer. "No offense."

"None taken." Summer laughs. "If I was going to back out, I would have done it already."

I take a swig of my glass of champagne. "Be right back, my man needs me. Don't worry, we will find a nice closet to do it in!"

"Ivy! You better not," Summer scolds me. "My great-grandmother is one room over."

I turn to her and raise an eyebrow. "And without her finding a closet, you wouldn't be here either."

Olive bursts out laughing, while Summer rolls her eyes and groans—she knows I'm kidding.

Pushing open the light cream door of the bridal suite, I see my man standing before me. Tall, handsome, and charming. He lets out a breath when he sees me.

"Damn, you look good."

"Thank you, baby." I step up on my toes and kiss him on the lips.

He holds me in his sturdy arms, refusing to let me pull away. "I swear you get more beautiful every single day."

"You're just saying that."

"Because?"

"Because you love me."

"I do love you; you're right. But I thought you were beautiful even before I loved you."

I kiss him deeply again before glancing back to the door. "I've got to go finish helping Summer get ready. I'll see you out there."

"Okay, babe."

I turn away and head back to the bridal suite. Right as I push open the door, Summer laughs. "Uh, Ivy...do you have a Tide pen?"

I blink at the words—a bridal store owner's worst nightmare. "I think in my car...*why?*"

"I may or may not have accidentally tripped while drinking some red wine and spilled a drop on the front of my dress."

I run over to Summer and gasp when I take in her gown. The bodice has an avocado-sized stain shaped like a melting scoop of ice cream down the chest.

"I—I don't think a stain remover pen will help that," I rasp out and look around. "Which one of you bitches brought red wine?!"

Olive and Leena stare back at me and rapidly point to Summer.

"Summer!" I shriek. "I've never seen you drink red wine a day in your life."

"I know," she whines. "But Eddie's great-aunt gifted it to me this morning and said it's a good luck charm to have a glass of it before the ceremony."

"If you're talking about our Great-Aunt Beanie...she's literally been married *four times*," Leena snorts.

"What? I didn't know that." Summer stares at Leena, wide-eyed. "She said it was good luck."

"Maybe 'good luck to not make it down the aisle' given her track record." Leena glances at Summer's dress again.

"Not helping," Olive mutters under her breath to Leena.

Leena seems to realize her mistake and smiles at Summer. "It's fine; it's not even noticeable."

"You think?" Summer looks at her and then me, her brow furrowed.

"I think I'm gonna go find that Tide pen now," I respond.

Olive walks over to Summer. "Everything is going to be okay. Just breathe; we will figure it all out. Here, sit down." Olive yanks a folding chair over from the corner of the room and slides it under Summer.

"I can't believe I have to walk down the aisle with this...this fucking giant blood-looking stain." Summer collapses into the seat and closes her eyes. Her skin is beginning to flush and I can see the nerves are getting the best of her now.

Summer starts to breathe quickly, obviously distressed. I spoke too soon about everything being calm with her and probably jinxed it.

Olive gives me a *hurry now* look, and I pick up the bottom of my dress so I don't trip as I jog to the door.

As soon as I open the suite door and run out, I slam face-first into brick.

No, not brick. *Him.*

"Hi, Ivy," Donovan says in a deep, rough voice.

I slowly raise my gaze to meet his eyes and instantly regret it. The intensity of his stare makes me feel weak in the knees.

"It's been a long time," Donovan continues to speak.

Yeah, about six months.

"How have you been? You look breathtaking."

I bite the inside of my cheek, trying to find the words to

respond to him. I want to tell him to leave me alone—to not call me beautiful or look at me with those eyes. I want to tell him that I'm in a loving relationship now. One that isn't toxic or fickle or based on meritless hookups.

But after all this time apart...after all this time it took me to stop thinking about him, all it takes is just his *hello* to light that ember inside me again.

I ground myself.

I lie to myself.

I smooth down my gown from our collision, straighten up like I'm facing off with a bear, and clear my throat. He raises an eyebrow at me, but I hold his eye contact.

"Sorry, I've got to go. I need to get something for Summer."

With that, I step around him and quickly walk off in the direction of the long banquet hallway, refusing to turn around even though I can feel his gaze searing into my back the whole time.

Chapter 53

"Devil Himself"

Donovan

"I saw her."

"Who?" Ezra bends down from the couch he's sitting on in the groom's suite to tie the lace of his left dress shoe.

"Ivy."

Ezra cocks an eyebrow at me. "Oh yeah? And how did that go?"

I look at him like he's an idiot. Eddie walks past and claps me on the back. I smile at him before turning back to my cousin and responding in a low voice, "How do you think it went? Do I seem happy?"

Ezra slowly looks over my features. "Is this a trick question? You rarely look happy."

"Stop fucking with me." I undo the button of my black suit jacket and sit next to him on the couch. "I'm serious, dude. She wants nothing to do with me."

"I mean, she's in a relationship." Ezra shrugs. "You know that."

231

"I know." I've heard through the grapevine that Ivy and Lee have been together for months now.

That's also the main reason why I made an excuse to Eddie about not being able to attend the rehearsal dinner last night, telling him I had to run a late charter and couldn't cancel. I did all this because I didn't want to sit through the pain of seeing them together across a table from me.

"Which is also your fault...because you told her to choose him." He lifts up his right shoe and ties it next.

"*I know.*"

Ezra looks at me again and sighs. "So you need to be a man and move on."

"I can't move on. I can't do it, I need her."

Ezra takes in my pained expression and sits in thought for a moment before finally responding. "Then, I guess you have to talk to her. But she doesn't deserve your wishy-washy shit again."

"You know why I was like that before."

"Yeah, I do. You need to tell her about all of that, too." Ezra stands up and glances at the small grandfather clock sitting on the fireplace mantle across from us. "Do you think that thing is accurate? I'm pretty sure the wedding was supposed to start thirty minutes ago."

I blink and slide up my jacket sleeve to view my watch—3:42 p.m.

"Hmm, when I ran into Ivy, she did seem to be in a rush to do something for Summer."

Ezra scratches the back of his neck. "Shit."

Abruptly, Wes walks into the room with Hunter following him.

"Eddie!" Hunter shouts.

"In the bathroom," Eddie responds. "I keep sweating through my undershirt; it's so damn hot in here."

232

Wes grabs a bottle of tequila off the coffee table in front of the couch and pops off the cork before taking a generous swig. He walks up to the bathroom door and opens it without knocking. "Here."

I hear the sound of water shutting off, and Eddie steps out of the room, bypassing the bottle that Wes is trying to hand him. "What's wrong?" he asks Hunter.

"Olive said Summer is really upset. That she spilled something on her dress and it's not getting better." Hunter winces. "Olive said she's in tears."

"Not letting that happen," Eddie responds quickly and walks right out of the door of our room.

Chapter 54

"Yellow"

Ivy

E ddie bursts in through the bridal suite door like someone has lit a fire underneath him. His eyes are wide with concern, and as soon as he sees Summer, he walks towards her. We are all standing around her trying to help her with the stain—which has grown larger in size but has now faded to a soft pink instead of blood red—and blink in surprise from his sudden appearance.

I rush to cover Summer with my hands.

"Whoa! You can't be in here," I tell him. "She's in her dress."

Summer awkwardly steps up from her chair to a standing position and begins to move around me. Her chest is flushed a bright pink from stress, and her makeup is streaked with tears. "It's okay, Ivy. I've shown him the gown already."

Eddie makes it to his bride quickly and gives her a hug. Her slender frame melts into his chest, and she cries softly.

"There, there," he soothes her, rubbing circles on her back with his hand. "It will all be okay, my love."

"I don't even know why I'm crying." Summer laughs with

234

frustration at herself. "I don't even care about stuff like this! It's just a dress!" Summer turns to me and adds, "No offense, Ivy."

I hold up a hand in understanding. "None taken, you're going through it right now."

Eddie steps back from Summer and takes both of her hands in his. "The only thing that matters today is that I get to show everyone we love how much I love you. You're so fucking beautiful, and kind, and *way* smarter than me, baby."

Summer lets out a snort through tears and grins at Eddie as he continues to talk.

"If you want me to, I will stand at the altar in my underwear to distract people from the stain. I will do whatever you want, darling."

"Please *don't*," Leena groans loudly next to me.

Olive laughs, and I step forward. "Wait, I have an idea."

Twenty minutes later, I'm watching Leena walk down the aisle, followed by Olive. A beautiful piano cover of "Yellow" by Coldplay fills the small banquet hall. I turn back to face Summer and squeeze her hand.

"I'm so proud of you; you found your soulmate. And I'm thankful to Eddie for giving us all a new sister."

Summer's eyes swell with tears—happy ones this time. "Thank you, Ivy. I love you, and I never would have made it to this point without you."

I lean forward and kiss her on her forehead before taking the short, sheer blusher from her veil off her head and gently covering her face with it.

"I'll see you out there," I tell her and pick up my wildflower bouquet from a bench near the double doors.

Taking a single step forward and pausing for a beat until Olive finishes walking, I take a breath and look around. I instantly meet eyes with Lee, and he smiles at me, looking handsome as ever in the crowd of familiar faces. He winks at me, and I bite the inside of my cheek as I grin. He looks incredible—his navy-blue suit complements his blond hair, and he radiates positivity like always.

I look back in front of me and realize it's my turn to go. *Shit.* Planting a large smile on my face, I begin the delicate, slow steps forward down the petal-lined walkway.

Feeling comfortable after the first few awkward steps down the aisle, I look around at the seated guests with a smile on my face. I make eye contact with someone standing at the altar and instantly regret it.

Donovan is staring at me like I'm his favorite dessert.

You stupid, beautiful, chiseled god of a man.

I look away and make eye contact with Olive before turning right to stand next to her. The music changes to "I Get To Love You" by Ruelle, and everyone stands to face the doorway as Summer begins to walk down the aisle.

As soon as I see her, emotion takes over me. No matter how many weddings I'm a part of, no matter how many times I've seen someone in a wedding dress, the magic will never be lost for me. It's breathtaking to witness two people choose to be together for life.

Nothing in the world feels like love.

Some of the guests gasp, and whispers begin to sound out in awe when they take in Summer's gown. She walks forward proudly, head held high.

The front of her gown is covered in the assortment of wild-flowers from her bouquet that mirrors the ones we carry as bridesmaids. With her permission I took apart her bouquet and cut off the stems before laying the flowers across the bust in a cascading pattern down the bodice and pinning them on. She looks incredible and unique. Summer resembles a woodland fairy now more than she ever has before.

She glows as she walks up to stand across from Eddie. He

steps forward and takes her hands in his before mouthing "beautiful" to her with a tip of his head.

The ceremony begins, and I swear there isn't a dry eye in the banquet hall by the time their vow reading is over.

And just like that, two people I love are married.

Chapter 55

"All I Think About Now"

Donovan

I vy's on the dance floor with Leena, laughing and twirling wildly, and although I know I'm being a creep, I can't take my eyes off her tonight. When I saw her walking down the aisle and we made eye contact, all I pictured was her walking down the aisle *to me*.

God, how I wish that was the case.

I've been a fucking idiot, and Ezra's right—it's time I tell her why I've been pushing her away since we first met.

I loosen the tie around my neck and stand up from my chair in the dining area of the reception room. If I don't do this now, I know I never will.

Making my way onto the dance floor, I'm reminded of our night together in Florida. Her grinding up against me and the intimacy we shared. I should have told her how I felt right then, and none of this would be happening. She wouldn't be here with Lee as her date.

As I get closer, I hear her laughing loudly as she sings the lyrics to a popular '80s ballad. Her back is to me, so she has no idea I've walked up behind her, but Leena does, and she stops moving abruptly.

"Hi, Donovan!" Leena shouts, out of breath. "Never thought I'd see you on the dance floor."

"Yeah, only once," I respond.

Ivy turns to face me, and I know she knows what I'm talking about from the look in her eyes. *Those damn eyes.*

I clear my throat as she starts to turn away from me to face Leena once more. "I need to talk to you, Ivy."

She stiffens. "Why?"

"Please," I tell her. "It's important."

I've never pleaded with her for anything, and I think she realizes that, too, because she responds.

"Fine. But I'm going to let Lee know where I'm going first."

I nod my head in understanding. "Meet me in the court-yard in five minutes? Please?"

"Okay."

She crosses her arms and walks off to head to the bar, where Lee is currently standing with Leena's boyfriend, Parker, waiting for a drink.

"What's going on?" Leena asks me.

"You know, you're nosy." I chuckle.

"Like I give a shit. Now tell me." Leena pokes me with her finger. I've known her as long as I've known Eddie since they are twins—he constantly had to drag her along to the skate park, or she would throw a fit.

"I just want to talk to Ivy." I shrug. "I haven't seen her in months."

"Yeah, you don't think we know how things were left off between you two? We all know now." Leena looks in Ivy's direction. "And we really like Lee. She's never had a boyfriend treat her this well."

I try to hide my wince at the word *boyfriend*.

Leena squints her eyes, peering at me more intently now. "You really like her. You're not fucking around?"

"I wouldn't need to talk to her right now if I wasn't serious."

"Damn." She raises her hands in surrender. "Okay, Donovan, do what you have to do, I guess. Good luck to you."

I thank her and step away to walk outside to the venue's courtyard. When I get outdoors, it's hot and muggy. Now that it's dark, lightning bugs float around in the expansive wooded area surrounding the wedding venue. There are lights strung up across the trees and a small brook nearby; the sound of water gently trickling combats the booming music from the reception inside.

Rolling my neck to try and ease some of the tension bubbling up inside me, I walk over to a small fountain in the middle of the sidewalk and watch as the water trickles out. If I wasn't so goddamn nervous to talk to Ivy right now, I might think about how beautiful this place is.

The sound of heels clicking on the sidewalk behind me makes me turn, and I instantly feel out of breath.

Ivy walks down the path towards me rapidly. Her expression is bleak, serious—not like the Ivy I've grown to know this past year. All the light and happiness I saw in her face while she was on the dance floor is now gone.

I walk towards her, offering her my hand to help her walk across the stone pavers in her heels and long gown but she shakes her head in refusal.

She stops in front of the fountain and stands across from me, arms crossed, with her body language completely closed off towards me. "Okay, Donovan." *Those eyes.* "Say what you need to say."

This is my moment to tell her how madly I love her. To tell

her that I need her like I need air to breathe. To tell her that the pain of not being around her for six months has nearly killed me.

The problem is I'm not great with words, and I'm scared I'll fuck it all up.

Chapter 56

"Apocalypse"

Ivy

I look up at the man I've spent months trying to forget. He is visibly nervous, and that makes me even more angry. How dare he look so helpless right now. How dare he try to speak with me when he told me to move on, to be with Lee— and now that I'm happy and have tried to move on, he wants to speak.

Donovan clears his throat. Not once, but twice. The third time I've heard him do this tonight.

"Frog in your throat?" I raise an eyebrow, unable to hide the anger from my voice.

"I'm nervous," he responds, wiping his large hands against his suit jacket.

I can't help but feel a little sympathy for him.

I blow out a breath and point towards a metal bench to my left. "Come on, let's sit down. My heels are killing me."

He follows me over to the bench, and I sit, letting out a groan for my aching feet before yanking off my heels and tossing them aside. My dress fans out around me, and I slide to the side, pushing it under me to make room for him.

Once he's seated next to me, Donovan leans forward, so his elbows are now resting against his knees, and stares down at his hands. I swear I can feel the nerves radiating out of him. I've never seen him anything but composed, so this sets me on edge, too.

"You're making *me* nervous now." I huff out a laugh. "What's going on with you?"

Donovan releases a loud breath and turns to meet my eyes. His own shine with emotion, like two dark endless pits waiting to spill over.

"Ivy, I—" He sits up straight and turns to face me; I lift my chin to meet his gaze. His jaw clenches.

I slide a little closer to him, knowing something is wrong with him right now and that he is struggling. The nurturing side of me temporarily blocks out the anger I feel towards him.

"It's okay," I tell him in a low, gentle voice. "You can talk to me. If there's something you need to get off your chest, just talk. I'm here; I'll listen now—no matter what terms we left off on, I'm your friend."

Donovan pushes his hair away from his face. "Ivy, I need to talk to you about my past. I think you might understand me better if you knew my history."

I look up at him and nod my head, encouraging him to continue talking.

He lets out a heavy breath. "I'm an alcoholic, Ivy."

This isn't a surprise to me since I found the chip in his shed the last day I saw him in January.

He speaks again. "I have had a lot of issues with alcohol throughout my life. I started drinking when I was twelve years old. Regularly." He looks at me for my reaction to hearing this; I just wait for him to continue. "None of my friends really picked up on it growing up, because I was just always the wild kid at the skate park, so they just thought I was bold and crazy

—which I was, but I was also drinking every day. The alcohol fueled a lot of my dumb decisions."

I think about the black and white photo I saw of him as a teen with all the guys that day when I was snooping. They all seemed so carefree and young; it makes my heart ache to know he was drinking like that back then.

"I was an angry kid. I never really knew my dad; he went to jail when I was young, and my mom thought it was better if I went away when she found out I was drinking so heavily. I crashed her car from drinking one night when I was sixteen— I'd barely had my license for a month. She didn't know what to do with me, and feeling the stress of being a single mother trying to make ends meet, she was desperate for someone to get me in check. She told me that she was moving up to Maine with my younger sisters and that she just couldn't stay in Clairesville anymore. So at the age of sixteen, I ended up at Onilley Lake with Ezra and his parents, my Uncle Gene and Aunt Mae. They were supposed to help me get my shit together, and for a while it did work."

Donovan looks up at the starry night sky, and chuckles to himself.

"That's where my love for boats and fishing started actually. Uncle Gene is the one who started Anderson Charter; it was his business originally. He taught Ezra and me everything we know, and that was one of the ways Uncle Gene taught me discipline and structure. He showed me how to fix up the boats, clean them, and do all the maintenance properly. I learned that I like to tinker with stuff. I like building and keeping my hands busy—when my hands are busy, my mind isn't. I was sober from the age of sixteen to the age of twenty-four."

The wind blows my long hair into my eyes and I push back a strand. "And then what happened?"

"And then I met a girl."

I feel a strange and unwarranted tinge of jealousy surge through me at the mention of another woman.

I love Lee.

He looks down at his hands. "I met a girl named Rya one day when I was working on the charter, and she was wild; I was instantly drawn to her. We started dating, and I discovered that she was a huge party girl, but I wanted to be in a relationship with her. I thought I could maintain my sobriety, and I did— until I caught her sleeping with another man. I was a fucking *wreck*. It was my first real heartbreak, and I really thought she was the girl for me—which is dumb looking back now—but I didn't know how to cope with the pain. So, I started drinking again. And once I felt the numbness of alcohol soothe my heartache, I didn't stop. It was like welcoming an old love back into my life. Rya and I broke up, but the drinking stayed.

"Everyone knew I was drinking again, but no one other than Ezra knew it was a problem. I convinced everyone else that I grew out of my addiction. I was a functioning alcoholic this time around, keeping my stash hidden throughout the house, only drinking when others weren't looking, unless it was a party. Then, I would have a beer in public."

Donovan adjusts his body on the bench, and sadness consumes his already dark expression.

"A year and a half ago, I was out on the boat with Ezra and some friends. I had been drinking a lot—since everyone else was busy having fun, I could drink without the nagging from Ezra. It was actually on a day that Hunter and Olive were hanging out with the crew at our place too," he tells me.

I'm shocked to hear this, thinking back to all the times Olive told me they would go out to Onilley Lake, no one having any idea what was going on with Donovan behind the scenes.

Donovan continues, "That night after everyone left the lake, Ezra and I got in a huge fight. He told me I was reckless and an idiot for drinking so much and that I was going to end up either killing myself or putting someone else's life in serious danger. He was right, but I refused to hear anything from him. I remember trying to justify it in my head at the time thinking *'he drinks a lot, too; who is he to judge me?'* which is ridiculous. He has never had a problem like I do.

"Ezra told me that if I didn't get help and stop drinking, that he wouldn't allow me anywhere near the charter and that he would tell his dad. I was immediately filled with anger. I didn't want him to tell my Uncle Gene; he was retired now and living in Maine with my aunt to be near my mom. I didn't want any of them to be disappointed in me."

He breathes out heavily. "So I lashed out at him. Physically. I started beating the shit out of my own flesh and blood—the only brother I've ever known—over the potential of having to let go of fucking *alcohol*. I was in a blind rage that night."

Donovan sits quietly, and I stare up into the stars thinking over his confession. "How did the night end?"

He blinks and meets my eyes. "Ezra eventually ended up pushing me off him and locked himself in his room. I finally tired myself out and went to sleep. The next morning I woke up covered in dried blood—his, and some of my own from Ezra trying to fight his way back from me. When I went into the kitchen, there was a note left on the fridge from him, saying he couldn't sit around and watch me self-destruct, but he would support me when I was ready to actually get help.

"When I went to the bathroom to shower after that, I couldn't believe what I saw staring back at me. My face was black and blue—my lip split. There was blood in my hair, and my shirt was ripped. I'd had enough in that moment. I hurt my family, and I was destroying myself. So, I forced myself to be better.

"I took a shower, changed my clothes, and left to go find

help. I found a community center about thirty miles from my house and forced myself to drive there every single day for a meeting and kept going. The routine was tough at first—I struggled not to drink, and wanted to hide that from the group—but the routine actually ended up giving me something to look forward to.

"I felt happy to have people around me that understood me. No one judged me if I didn't feel like talking or was having a tough day. After a little while, a few missteps, I was in control of my addiction again, and I felt like a new man. Ezra and I were on good terms after that and we decided to keep what happened between us private from the friend group."

Donovan glances at me. "You're the first one who has heard this story; everyone else just thinks I decided to stop drinking again as a means to better myself. And I did better myself. I put myself on a schedule daily. I started eating healthier, I started doing handyman work on the side to keep busy during the off-season, and I spent all other time on our boats and charter. I was able to go out with my friends, to live a life I wanted again —without a sip of alcohol. I was happy. Satisfied at least."

Donovan reaches out to touch the top of my hand, which is resting on the bench. I am so swept up in the moment that I don't pull it away from him. He gazes into my eyes. "Until I met you, Ivy."

I take in a sharp breath.

Chapter 57

"Turning Page"

Donovan

"I vy, from the second I first laid eyes on you at Whiskey Jane's, I was a goner."

I think back to that night when Ezra and I were there to watch Wes's band play and she first tapped me on the back. I turned to see a short and angry woman staring up at me with fire in her blue eyes as she insulted my head size, asking me to move.

I was at a loss for words—almost uncomfortable from her beauty. I felt like I wasn't worthy enough to even look at a woman like her. She has always been breathtaking.

When she went up on Ezra's shoulders, my jealousy grew as the night went on. I didn't want her to like him. I wanted her to laugh with me like that, to be on my shoulders having the night of her life. But I knew I already blew it by being a dick.

By the time Rinse and Repeat was done playing their show, my jaw ached from clenching it in frustration for the duration of the night. I leaned in towards Ezra, telling him "cardinal," our code word for when I feel uncomfortable in a social setting, for when I feel like drinking.

I know it wasn't something I should have lied about, but in that moment, I needed to get away from her. I couldn't handle being around her.

"Once we left after the show, I couldn't stop thinking about you. I tried to stop, but I couldn't. Then, the next day, Olive called me and told me that her friend needed help at her store and asked if I was available. I wasn't; I had some clients lined up back in Onilley to do repairs for, but when she said your name, I made myself available. I lied to you, Ivy, when I told you that I didn't know it was your shop. I only went that day because it was *your* shop."

I try to find an expression on her face as she stares back at me, but her look is unreadable.

I breathe out, continuing. "I looked forward to seeing you every single week at the bridal store. It was the high of every day, walking through the door and seeing you sitting behind the desk, and the low of every night, leaving you. Every time you were kind to me, smiled at me, or asked me questions about my life, I wanted to take you in my arms and kiss you.

"On Christmas Eve when you gave me the gift, I was so touched by the gesture. Touched by the fact that even when I was a grumpy asshole towards you most days, you still wanted to do something thoughtful for me. I let my weakness win that night—you looked so fucking good in that dress, I had to have you. After we slept together, I was freaked out by the wave of emotions I felt for you. I felt drunk on you. Addicted to you. So I told you it was just casual for me, trying to make it seem like it was something I did all the time. Which isn't true at all."

I let out a small laugh thinking about the fact that I haven't slept with anyone other than her since I've been sober these past few years.

"I tried to fight my feelings for you, telling myself that I only felt lust for you, and for a little while I was good at lying to myself. I believed that I could just sleep with you that one time and finish up the work at the shop and then be done with you. Until Florida happened."

I look up at the sky and shake my head. "That trip changed everything for me. I fell in love with you on that trip."

I hear her exhale loudly beside me.

"I fell so hard for you. I was actually planning on telling you that I wanted to be with you when we got back. I even waited for you after my flight at the airport. I was going to ask you if you wanted to ride back to Clairesville with me, and I was planning on confessing how I felt during the drive."

Ivy tenses next to me, probably knowing where this is going.

"You were there?" she asks in a whisper.

"Yeah, and I saw Lee had the same idea as me. When I saw him walking up to you with flowers, and then you jumped into his arms full of excitement to see him, I realized I must have gotten the wrong impression about things changing between us on the trip."

"Is that why you pretended to be sick that week? Why you didn't answer me?"

I lower my head, looking down at my dress shoes in the grass. "Yes. I couldn't face you after that—I was hurt. I was trying to get over you, and I thought maybe a little distance would help before I came back to finish the work. But then you showed up at my house with *him,* and I practically lost my mind with blind rage and jealousy. I couldn't stand seeing you with him. Watching him kiss you felt worse than any type of withdrawal I've ever been through. I was out of my mind that day; I had to have you close, needed to have a taste of you.

"When I got back with him after our boat ride and Ezra said you were exploring, I exploited Lee's trust in me and told him I was going to find you, asking him if he would help Ezra start the grill, knowing I was going to find you and kiss you." I shake my head. "I was a real piece of shit to Lee that day, and honestly I'm being a piece of shit to him right now, too. I have to get this all off my chest, though, or I couldn't live with myself."

Ivy reaches out and squeezes my hand. "Tell me the rest."

"When I saw you that day with him, I wanted to drink so badly. So desperately. I didn't know how to cope with everything I was feeling inside. I'm not a man who's comfortable sitting with my thoughts; they wreck me. That day put a lot of fear in me. Fear that I loved you and would never be loved back, fear that I was going to fall into my addiction again, and fear that I would never be able to get over you if you chose him.

"So, I made the decision for you. On our ride to the hospital the moment after Lee found out that we kissed, I saw the look on your face in the rearview mirror filled with sadness and worry—the bubbly Ivy that I was so used to, the one full of fire and passion, was gone. I knew I was going to tell you to be with him in that moment. I knew I was the wrong guy. I was an addict, and I'm always going to be an addict. Lee has it all together, and I might never. I had to tell you to pick him."

Ivy nods her head slowly. "I understand, Donovan."

"But I was wrong," I tell her. "I was so fucking wrong. I can be the best man for you, and I am more than just my addiction. I know you are the love of my life; I need you. I'm so desperately in love with you that sitting next to you right now and not having your lips on mine is killing me."

Her eyes spill over with tears as I speak.

"Ivy, I want you to be with me. I don't care what it takes; I will do anything to be with you. I will never go on a boat again if it means having you. I love you with everything in me. You're the most intriguing woman that I've ever met in my life—the

251

most beautiful thing to ever grace my existence. I love you, Ivy Penny."

Ivy is sobbing next to me.

"Say something," I whisper. "Please."

She sharply turns to face me. "How dare you tell me everything I've ever wanted to hear *now!*" She buries her face in her hands. "How can you confuse me like this?" she gasps through sobs. "I'm with *Lee*. I'm supposed to move in with Lee in a few weeks."

I breathe in a quick, sharp breath hearing this.

"I was fine, Donovan! And then you had to fucking show up here today—all handsome and vulnerable and now apparently *nicer* and ready to love me?" Her lip quivers as she continues to cry—I hate seeing her like this; I can't handle it.

I lean forward and take her into my arms, holding her tightly as she shakes with tears. She surprisingly accepts my touch, relaxing into my hold. The smell of flowers fills my nose as her small frame leans against me, and I instantly find what I've been missing all these months.

"I love you, Ivy," I repeat, smoothing down her hair. "I want you to choose me. I want you to choose me forever. I'm ready now. I'm not afraid to feel."

She pushes back from me suddenly, mascara streaming down her cheeks. "I've got to go. I'm sorry, Donovan, but it's too late." She begins to stand. "I love Lee."

"Please don't go," I plead with her, standing up as well. She bends down and scoops up her heels in her hands.

"I'm sorry," Ivy tells me with one last look, wiping her eyes quickly with the back of her knuckles. "I'm happy that you're doing well, and I am so glad that you're sober. Thank you for sharing your story with me." She backs a step away from me, but I follow, taking a step towards her.

"Ivy, I promise I'm ready."

"No." She shakes her head. "I've got to go. I can't do this with you again; don't contact me, Donovan. I love Lee."

I stand struck—an arrow in my heart. I watch as she turns away from me, running back towards the building, trying to leave me as quickly as possible. She opens the door and walks inside without even a glance back.

I know this will be the last time I'll see her, and my world shatters.

Chapter 58

"Never Once"

Lee

Two weeks later

Something's not right. Ivy's different—not in an obvious spoken way, but in subtle moments that I have been picking up on as her partner.

She's anxious, she's spaced out, and she's smiling at me, but there's no light behind her eyes. We have been packing up both of our apartments this week, preparing to rent our first house together, and the excitement just isn't there on her end.

I feel sick.

I think her seeing Donovan at the wedding changed everything. She couldn't keep her eyes off of him. I don't even think she realized that she was doing it. She's just that drawn to him.

He wasn't at the rehearsal dinner the night before the wedding, so I thought maybe he backed out as a groomsman, but that wasn't the case. On the day of the ceremony, he was there and she was there; that's all it took.

When I was in line at the bar with Parker waiting for a drink, I saw him walking up towards her on the dance floor, and

I prayed that he wasn't going to stop and talk to her. I watched, unable to swallow, as she spoke back and forth with him, nodding her head in agreement before heading my direction.

I quickly averted my eyes, not wanting her to know that I saw their interaction. I didn't want to come off as a weak or insecure boyfriend.

She walked up and bit her lip self-consciously before asking me if she could talk to Donovan outside for a minute. I told her she could do whatever she felt was right. I'm not her keeper; she can make her own decisions.

What do I have to worry about? I told myself as she walked away, trying to reassure myself. *She chose me.*

After twenty minutes of watching the door, waiting for her to return back inside, she finally did, beelining past some guests to the women's bathroom. She had visibly been crying. Her face was flushed, and makeup was smeared across her cheeks.

A hole grew in my stomach when I saw that, and it's only grown larger every single day since.

I know Ivy would never cheat on me. She has spoken to me many times about how guilty she feels for hooking up with Donovan and I at the same time—even though we were just dating back then. I don't take it to heart since it was before we were exclusive. So I know she didn't do anything with him that night, but I also haven't asked her what went down between them; I don't want to know what they talked about because I know I will dread the answer.

The past few times we have had sex, she hasn't even looked at me during. Her eyes have stayed closed, like she's shutting out all chances of connection with me. Some people might not notice that, but I do. I notice everything she does; I love everything about her.

I set my phone down on the couch next to me and glance at her. Her long hair is in a messy bun on top of her head, and she's wearing a pair of my old sweats with a sports bra. She just got back from a workout, and instead of kissing me hello at the door like she usually would when I meet her at her apartment, she just opened the door with a smile and let me in. She's been typing away on her laptop, working ever since I showed up an hour ago.

Her legs rest between mine and I wish I could just sit in this moment, comfortable and complacent, pretending I don't feel the change in our relationship.

"Ivy." I breathe out deeply. "I think we need to talk about something."

She peeks her head over her laptop. "Oh...okay, sure." She shuts it gently and slides it onto the coffee table in front of her. "What's up?"

I scratch the back of my neck and turn towards her. "Do you actually want to live with me?"

She lets out a half laugh. "What are you talking about? Of course I do."

I look into her eyes. "I'm serious, Ivy. *Something's different.* Ever since the wedding, something has been different between us—we both know it." I sigh, exhausted. "What happened with you and Donovan that night?"

Her body goes rigid, but she says, "Nothing happened that matters." She leans forward and places her hand against my thigh—her eyes stare into my own intently. "I love you, Lee."

"I don't doubt that you love me, but I think you're *in love* with him."

Ivy draws her hand back quickly as if I've slapped her with my words. "What are you talking about?"

"I think when you saw him, you remembered exactly why you had feelings for him before. And I think the same might have happened for him, too, right? That's why he wanted to talk to you."

Ivy tilts her head down and shakes it.

"Cut the bullshit, Ivy, please," I plead with her, "and just give it to me straight. Tell me what happened that night. Because I know that the woman you were that morning was not the same person who left that night."

She continues to look down at her lap; her hands are shaking violently now.

I feel bile rise in my throat; my worst nightmares are about to be confirmed—I know it.

"He told me that he is in love with me." She gazes up at me, and her eyes are glossy with tears. "That he has been for a long time."

"Shit," I whisper under my breath.

"And he told me that he wants to be with me." Ivy looks away now, unable to look at the pain that is likely visible in my expression.

"So, why aren't you with him, then?" I respond, unable to keep the hurt from my tone. "If he loves you and you love him... seems like I'm the only thing standing in the way, huh?"

My mouth tastes sour from the hopelessness I feel inside, but I continue to tell her what needs to be said.

"Ivy, I don't think you understand what kind of man I am. I'm the type of man who loves you so much, I would put your happiness over my own. I would tell you to go do what makes you the happiest. I want you to live the most amazing life you possibly can, and I hate to say it—it kills me to say it—but I don't think it's with me."

I can't hold back the tears that start to drop from my eyes, knowing I love her so desperately, but she loves someone else more. My love is not enough, and it never will be.

"Lee, I do love you." She's almost in my lap now, sobbing.

"But it's not the same." I shake my head. "It's not the same way you love him. Right?"

She buries her head into my shoulder.

My stomach sinks, wanting her to instantly reassure me that it's not true. But she says nothing.

I repeat myself. "Right, Ivy?"

"Right," she whispers into the crook of my arm.

I feel like my body is no longer attached to me.

I thought she was going to be the person I would marry in the future. I had visions of her walking down the stairs of our home one day, with a wide smile across her face and our baby in her arms, a place filled with love.

That's all over now; all it took was a five-letter response to change the outcome of my life.

She begins to cry harder than I've ever seen her before. I hold her, unable to do anything else, and let the emotion take over me, too—knowing this is the end of us.

"I'm so sorry, Lee," she cries repeatedly. "I'm so sorry."

Falling in love with Ivy was like breathing in fresh air—easy and pure. Watching Ivy fall out of love with me has been like slowly ingesting poison for the past few weeks and being unable to stop it.

Chapter 59

"Golden Light"

Ivy

Two months later

"Are you sure you're okay?" I ask Summer, who's currently vomiting on the other end of our phone call.

She groans, and I hear her pick back up her phone. "Yeah, just food poisoning," she coughs.

"More like the baby type of food poisoning," I joke.

"*Fuck*," Summer says, and then silence.

"You okay?" I laugh.

"Uh, Ivy, when's our period due?"

We have been on the same cycle for almost a year now; Mother Nature is a funny thing.

"*Our* period started six days ago, Summer. Mine just ended."

"Shit, I have to go—" The line abruptly beeps, and my dash screen flashes with the words "call ended."

Holy shit, is Summer pregnant?

I would absolutely take a baby in the group at this point—

we need something cute and precious to snuggle with. I will be the first to nominate myself for free babysitting duty.

Pulling into the Vera Bridal parking lot to pick up some gowns that I need to have cleaned, I see a large white moving van in the center of the lot. I look at my clock: 8:27 a.m. Too early for a normal delivery, and we aren't even open on Mondays. I hop out of my car quickly and make my way over to a guy standing beside the cab door.

"You the owner?" he bites out as I approach.

"Yes, I am. How can I help you?" I glance at the truck. I wasn't expecting any gown deliveries today, and they have *never* come in a vehicle like this before.

"I've got a piece of furniture for you in the back," he responds gruffly. "Tell us where to put it."

"I think you're mistaken; I didn't order anything," I tell him.

He reaches into his back pocket and pulls out a crumpled sheet of paper. "You Ivy Penny?"

"Yes."

"It's yours."

I try to protest, but he cuts me off.

"This paper"—the man waves the sheet around wildly—"says you did, and I have more deliveries, so tell us where to put it so we can get on with our day."

I'm ready to give him a piece of my mind about his attitude when I see another man step out from behind the truck and set down a table.

A wooden table.

I step closer.

With a small knot on the surface of the table that resembles a smiley face—I want to sink to my knees.

"I—I can't take that," I say to the young guy. "It doesn't belong to me. It's for someone else; they should have it."

The delivery guy opens the driver's door to the truck and

begins to get in. "Well then, you better take that up with that person." He slams the door and motions to the other employee through the open window. "Tell Dylan where he can put the table."

"Uh, okay...just put it inside." I rush to grab my keys out of my bag as the Dylan guy struggles to carry the table towards the front door of the shop.

I unlock the door and move out of the way, showing him an empty spot by the front door where he can set the table down.

He does and then turns to me, holding out his hand.

I reach forward and high-five it.

"No, lady," the teenager stares at me. "A tip."

"A tip? I don't even have cash on me. I didn't even know you guys were coming here."

He scoffs and begins to walk towards the exit.

"Sorry!"

The sound of the truck tires makes a loud squeal in the parking lot a minute later as the men peel out. *Lovely customer service*, I think, as I walk over to the pink front door and shut it.

Turning to face the table—the elephant in the room—I groan and slide down slowly against the door, letting my body slump in defeat when I make it to the wooden floor.

I haven't seen Lee in two months. The day he confronted me about my feelings for Donovan was the last time we saw each other. We both knew it was easier that way. We didn't live together yet, thankfully, so it was a clean breakup for the most part.

We just both went back to our lives.

I miss him constantly. I still love him, but he was right that it was different than how I feel about Donovan. It wasn't fair to Lee to stay with him, to lie in that moment just to keep the sense of security I had with him.

So, now I'm on my own again. Funny how things start and end the same way.

I don't feel like it's right to talk to Donovan until I've healed from my breakup with Lee. I didn't want to disrespect what I had with Lee by running into another man's arms the day after our breakup.

Forcing myself to get off the ground, I stand and walk over to the table, running my fingers over the smiley face. The table is breathtaking, with intricate patterns cut into the wood around the trim. This must have taken the man that made it forever and also must have cost Lee a fortune. It feels wrong to have this here. Wrong that he had this made for me when he loved me, and it's a gift I have received now when we have broken up.

I know what I need to do.

Chapter 60

"Blue Jeans"

Ivy

Looking through my front windshield at Main Street Café, I'm trying to convince myself to get out of the car—grow some balls and go inside. During the drive over here, I didn't feel anxious, knowing that it's not my item to keep, but now that I'm here...I want to back out.

Who wants to go inside a place and see their ex there—*on purpose?*

Even though we left the relationship on cordial terms given the circumstances, I know it was gut-wrenching for Lee, and he probably doesn't want to see me anytime soon. He only brought up us separating because he could tell my heart was pulling away. I feel guilty every single day that I stopped loving him the way I once did.

The deep regret that I couldn't make myself feel the way I do about Donovan when it came to my relationship with Lee follows in the back of my mind, always.

Lee forced me to finally be honest with myself—to face the truth that I didn't want to speak into existence. He was never going to be the love of my life, just one of the loves.

Leaning up out of my seat, I check my appearance in my rearview mirror. I look okay—a little flushed and sweaty from stress, but at least I'm having a good hair day.

Stop stalling.

I groan and force myself to open my car door. There's a small penny lying face down on the ground outside of my door, and I lean over to turn it right-side up. That has to be a good sign, right? *Ivy Penny sees a penny and creates some good luck for someone else?* I'm reaching.

Someone walks out the front entrance of the brick shop I've grown to know so well in the past year, and when I see the man is holding it open for me, I jog over.

"Thanks," I tell him, quickly stepping across the threshold into the shop.

Band-Aid ripped off.

The familiar scent of cinnamon, banana bread, and coffee fills my nostrils, causing a feeling of homesickness to wash over me violently. I used to come here every single day before work, and then things ended up so messy. I handled everything so wrong.

The shop interior is covered in fall décor. Cora's touch, I'm sure. Shades of brown and orange leaves hang down like streamers from the high ceilings. I can imagine her standing with her baby, Henry, in the body carrier, bossing Lee around as he stands on the ladder exasperated and trying to figure out where she wants them hung. She started doing stuff around the shop back in May, slowly getting used to a few hours away from Henry and has brought him with her on days where he's extra clingy.

I was surprised when Lee told me months ago that he was going to stay working in-house shifts at Main Street even after her return. He told me that he really ended up loving the atmosphere and getting close with the staff. Also, he didn't want to sit in his apartment office alone anymore just staring at invoices.

The day that Lee came to my apartment and told me that the baristas had added him to their group chat, I jumped up and down in celebration for him. I'm glad he found passion for his business—that it's not just his sister's dream now, but also his.

The counter has a long line, and I see Blaise making multiple drinks at once. We meet eyes, and he turns to say something to a petite barista that I don't recognize next to him before they both face forward and stare at me. The barista gives me a final once-over before turning away and shoving a muffin in a paper bag with tongs.

Great, they all hate me.

Blaise tilts his head to the left, motioning for me to meet him on the other side of the counter. I walk over and wait for him to set two lattes down on the edge of the drink pickup, calling out the name "Megan," and wiping off his hands on his apron before heading to me.

"Hi, Ivy," he greets me in a low voice, then looks around. "What are you doing here?"

"I need to talk to Lee. He's here, right? I saw his car in the parking lot."

Blaise bites his lower lip, looking at me skeptically. "Yeah. He's here. But I don't want to be the one to ruin his day by telling him you're here."

Damn.

"I'm not trying to ruin his day or make him upset," I respond quickly. "I just have something of his I need to give back to him."

The small barista calls out Blaise's name, telling him that she needs help with a drink.

"Go sit in your booth. I'll get him for you when I have a second."

"Thank you," I tell him, relieved.

Blaise lowers his head and rubs his brow—his neon green and pink cheetah-print buzzed hair is on full display. "It's fine. Just please don't make him upset. He just started laughing at our jokes again." With that, he raps his knuckles against the counter and walks off to help the new barista.

Well, now I feel worse than ever.

I walk towards the booth that I've spent many days and nights in—some with Lee, most before I even met him.

Usually I sit facing towards the giant glass window so I can people watch, but today I sit on the opposite side so I'm not blindsided when Lee walks over to me.

Not even five minutes later, I see his golden blond hair appear from the doorway that leads to the back office. Blaise looks at me and then says something to Lee, but I can't see him well enough to be able to read his expression since he's standing directly behind the bakery display. All I see is his familiar hair until he cuts around the counter and we lock eyes.

He gives me a small smile that doesn't reach his eyes, his dimple not even showing, and makes his way towards me. This isn't the Lee I've known for nine months, though. This Lee is rugged. More relaxed. He's wearing his glasses instead of contacts, his hair has no gel in it, the top few buttons of his blue shirt are unbuttoned, and for crying out loud, he is wearing *blue jeans*. I have never seen him in anything but khakis in public.

Great, I broke the man.

"Ivy, good to see you." He smiles politely as he slides into the seat across from me in the booth. "What are you doing here?"

The words make me want to wince. He said them in a

friendly manner, but it really sets in stone the fact that this is no longer a place I can come and feel welcome.

I look down at my hands resting against the table and begin to trace lazy circles around a spot where a child decided to add their own artistic expression with a crayon.

"I received something today that belongs to you." I glance up from my hands to read his expression.

Lee pushes his hair out of his eyes. "Oh yeah?"

"The table." I look for any type of reaction at the confession, but he gives none.

"Oh, right. My dad's friend mentioned last month that he was almost done with it."

"Well, they delivered it to Vera Bridal by accident," I tell him.

"No." He scratches the five o'clock shadow growing lightly across his chin. "Not by mistake. I told them where to deliver it."

"But why?"

"Why not? It's yours. I want you to have it." Lee cocks an eyebrow at me. "You don't like it?"

"No, no," I respond quickly. "It's incredible, one of the most amazing pieces of furniture I've ever seen."

"So." Lee shrugs. "What's the issue then?"

I breathe out. "You had it made for me when you loved me, and receiving it now just doesn't feel right. I don't deserve it, and I feel guilty."

Lee shifts in the booth and looks over my shoulder at the sound of the door jingling as more customers enter. "Look, Ivy, accept the gift. I still love you now, and I'm giving it to you. Is your basis for not accepting it because I first gave it to you when I was in love with you?" His expression does little to mask the hurt in his words. "I would never give you something just to take it away from you out of spite."

I nod and chew the inside of my cheek. "Lee—"

"I want you to take it. Seriously. It will actually piss me off if you don't," he jokes and gives me a smile. That dimple that I loved—that I playfully poked so many times—finally appears. "Okay?"

"Okay." I stare at his face; the man that was once so clean-cut and structured is nowhere to be found.

"What?"

"Nothing." I shake my head. "You just look different."

Lee laughs. "Is that a bad thing?"

"No, you look good. I like you wearing your glasses in public. You look relaxed."

He clasps his hands together. "Well, I guess I got a case of the *I don't give a damns* after we broke up and just kind of stuck with it."

"I see you're wearing jeans." I grin at him.

"I'm trying out something new."

We stare at each other for a moment in silence. Not an awkward one, but a comfortable one, like we are studying every feature on a face we once knew so well for the final time.

"You look good." I lean a little closer. "Are you doing okay?"

He tilts his head. "Yeah, I'm okay. It was rough at first, but I'm doing fine now. The café keeps me busy."

"Good."

"You know"—Lee looks up at the ceiling for a moment, like he can't believe what he's about to say, and laughs—"I now understand what you were saying on our first date. About the romance book thing and the girl picking the guy you didn't want. I get it...because I was that guy."

He laughs again, but it's hollow and inauthentic. I don't fault him for it at all; he has every right to feel bitter towards me.

I've felt that way, too, with my ex-boyfriend years ago. You feel so much animosity towards the person, but you can't just move on as easily as you'd like. You still wish you were with them.

I cringe. "I'm so sorry, Lee. I didn't think it would happen this way."

"It's alright. At least the other guy got his happy ending."

I sit across from him in silence but nod my head.

"I don't even know if I want to know the answer, but I'm going to ask anyway. How is Donovan?"

I bite my lip and look down at my lap. "I—I don't know."

"What do you mean?" Lee turns serious.

"I haven't talked to him."

"At all?"

"No. Not since that night at the wedding."

"Why not?"

"Because I didn't feel like it was right." I meet his eyes. "I didn't want to go straight from you to him."

"Well, that pisses me off."

"What? Why?" I ask, stunned.

"Because now there are three unhappy people that came out of this situation instead of just one."

I stare at him in shock as he continues.

"Do you think I stepped back from the relationship because I just didn't want to be with you? I stepped back because I knew you were in love with someone else. I know you can't help that you're in love with him, and I also know you didn't plan to love him and for everything to get fucked up. Now, stop punishing yourself about our relationship not working out and go be with him."

I'm absolutely speechless.

"The best thing you can do for me, is go be as happy as possible. I will feel better if I know you're happy." Lee leans forward and takes my hand off the table, squeezing it tenderly inside his own. "Seriously, I forgive you for not loving me the same way I love you."

I can't help it; I burst into tears. Hearing that Lee doesn't hate me causes a weight to lift inside of me that I didn't even realize was suffocating me. He's right. I have been punishing myself for the way things ended between us, not allowing myself to talk to Donovan so that I would also suffer like Lee is.

"Go tell Donovan you love him."

I nod my head, trying to wipe the tears away; I'm a mess.

"Right now!" Lee laughs, and I jump from his sudden outburst.

"Okay!" I stand from the booth, sniffling. "I'm going."

Lee stands from his side as well, and I can't help but give him a hug. His familiar scent of cedar and ocean surrounds me, and I take a mental snapshot of this moment in time.

I squeeze one last time and then look up at his face. "Thank you, Lee."

He grins down at me. "You're welcome, Ivy; now go. I'm busy, and I'm sure you're about to be, too."

I thank him one last time and start to head towards the door.

"Ivy!" Lee calls out my name.

I turn back to face him. "Yes?"

"You'll never guess...I like some coffee now; I drink mochas and sometimes cold brew! And I also like to bake now."

I laugh through my still watery eyes and smile at him. "Wow, that's great, Lee. Maybe all you needed was just to try something different. You always need to be open to trying new things; you might like it."

"Trying something new," he repeats with a smile.

"Something different from what you would usually go for."

He chuckles, and we both know I'm not talking about coffee now. "Goodbye, Lee."

270

"Bye, Smiley."

I push through the door and make it out to my car before I start sobbing again. I spy Lee through the café window, and the brave face he was just putting on for me slips. His posture sullen again, and I see how much I have truly hurt him. How much strength it must have taken him to tell me to go be with Donovan.

Suddenly, I realize that the fortune teller was right once again. Someone did end up heartbroken—only this time it was Lee's heart that was shattered and not mine.

Chapter 61

"Make It Wit Chu"
Ivy

Two hours later, I follow the gravel path down the wooded clearing to Donovan and Ezra's house. My car awkwardly bounces over the stones, and I will probably end up with a flat tire after this, but I couldn't care less.

I'm on a mission.

When I stop in front of his house, I curse when I see his truck is nowhere to be found. I drive around the property to the garage shed, hoping that maybe I will see either him or Ezra there. But it's empty.

Now what? I wait?

I had all this adrenaline on the one-and-a-half-hour drive over here, and now I'm supposed to just sit here.

Tapping my fingers against my steering wheel, I glance at the clock: 11:35 a.m. Maybe they went out to lunch, I think. Or maybe they are working...it is charter season, I think.

Throwing my car in reverse, I back out from behind their house and return to the main dirt road.

I have no idea where they run their charter, but I have a

272

feeling it probably starts around the boat ramp that we went to in January. I follow the curve of the road along the side of the lake; there are a few boats in the water as I drive, but none that I recognize. I am almost to the dock when I see Donovan's truck up ahead under a canopy of trees.

My heart begins to race.

There's an empty spot next to a few cars parked in the grass, so I pull in and quickly unbuckle my seat, hopping out before even considering checking my appearance. I've already been on an emotional roller coaster this morning, and Donovan needs to know what he's in store for if he wants to be with me forever.

I see a tented canopy near the left side of the shore with the words "Anderson Charter" printed on it. There are two yellow canoes, a few paddles, and a large cooler on the grassy ground under the shade.

So, this is what he does every day.

I look for any sign of him around the lake but don't see anything except for a boat about fifty feet ahead in the water going away from the shore.

Stepping closer to the lake, I squint with my hand above my eyes to block out the sun and recognize the boat instantly. It's the one Donovan fixed up at the beginning of the year. The only thing I don't recognize is the name painted in script along the back of the boat.

Her Eyes.

I swear my heart stops beating.

My throat feels tight with emotion when I see a man with tattooed forearms and long, dark hair standing in the center of the boat, speaking to what looks like a few people seated.

"Donovan!" I yell out, cupping my hands around my mouth. "Donovan!"

Nothing; no one even turns their head from the boat.

273

"Donovan!" I try again as I see the boat getting farther away. *Fuck.*

I begin to weigh my options. Then I remember the charter tent and run over. I look at the canoes...am I really about to try to canoe after him?

I look down at my leggings and tank top, thankful that I'm dressed casually today since the bridal store was closed. *Yeah, I can do this.* I'm already dressed for success, and I work out all the time. But what about the *water? Stop thinking, Ivy,* I tell myself. Just go.

What's a little rowing?

I try to pick up one of the canoes to bring it to the dock—it lifts only an inch off the ground. Okay, the thin-looking plastic is heavier than I thought. I use both arms to drag the canoe across the grassy area and get behind it to push it the rest of the way on the shore until it reaches the water.

Realizing I need a paddle, I run back up to the canopy tent and grab the closest one. By the time I make it back to the canoe and gradually push it into the water, my shirt is soaked with sweat.

Again, he will have to take me as I am.

Making sure I don't touch the water, I hop into the canoe and hold my breath as it teeters from my weight. I slowly scootch to the middle and place the paddle on my left side, pushing it against the bottom of the lake to give me a little momentum.

I begin to paddle.

Left, right.

Left, right.

Left, right.

I tell myself this mantra over and over again in my head as I make slow progress into the lake. I can feel myself start to grow anxious when I think about the fact that I'm in deep, dark water and try to distract myself while continuing to move forward.

I chant:

Hairy, balls.

Hairy, balls.

Hairy, balls.

I'm surprised how well it's working to calm my nerves—I'm almost enjoying myself now.

At first I think I'm moving so quickly that I'm catching up to the boat, but then I realize that the boat is stopped, which is why I'm making progress.

I try yelling out Donovan's name again, but I'm out of breath and my throat is dry, so it comes out more like "Dnnvnn" as a squawk. Sweat is pouring from my forehead now, and I stop for a second, setting the paddle down across my lap, so I can wipe my face with my hands.

That's where I fuck up.

The paddle falls off my lap into the water, and as I rush to grab it, the boat tips. I quickly sit up, feeling nausea churn in my stomach from the fear of falling into the water. *Shit.*

Breathing deeply, I try to reach out to get it again, but the paddle is now too far to my left, following the current of the water away from me. The only way I would get it back at this point would be if I were to get out of the canoe and swim to it.

I stand up and shout his name again. "Donovan!"

He turns his head, so I think he hears me, but he just looks away a moment later, turning to grab some fishing poles that are lined up on the side of the boat. I hear faint music playing and realize that between my dry throat, the boat's motor, and the music, he can't hear me.

I try yelling his name again one last time and realize I'm getting nowhere. I can either sit here and wait for help or figure something out.

Then, I see Donovan start to lift his shirt off over his head and toss it aside. He reels a fishing pole back and tosses the line out into the water on the other side of the boat. I watch from a distance as his muscles flex in his back as the sun beats down on him.

All rational thought leaves my head, and I jump in.

Chapter 62

"Panic Switch"
Donovan

"Uh, Mr. Anderson?"

I turn at the sound of my name to face Mrs. Snyder at the same time Ezra turns from the wheel. Right, we're both Mr. Anderson.

"Yes?" Ezra asks as I continue to add bait onto the fishing poles for the elderly couple on the charter. This is their first time going fishing, so we wanted to start out simple for them; we didn't go too far out in case they got overheated.

"Do people usually swim this far out?" Mrs. Snyder asks, concern lacing her tone.

"No, not usually," Ezra responds. "Maybe if they are local like us, but the current can be a little rough if you're not used to Onilley Lake."

"Okay." She looks at her husband, who is staring up at birds flying above us, unbothered by her questions. "Because I think there's someone that needs help in the water." She points behind the boat.

"What?" Ezra and I both ask at the same time. Ezra stands

277

quickly from the captain's chair, and we both hurry towards the stern of the boat.

Sure enough, about forty feet behind and to the left of us, I see someone in the water trying to swim but starting to panic and flail.

"Holy shit," Ezra says, and speedily gets behind the wheel to put the boat into gear.

"Hold on, please," I tell the couple, and they nod, Mr. Snyder now paying complete attention with the potential for action ahead of him.

Ezra drives my boat in the direction of the struggling swimmer, and as we get closer, I see that it's a woman.

"I'm going to jump in and help her," I shout to Ezra. "Get as close as possible without creating too many waves."

He tilts his head, the only acknowledgment that he's heard me, and slows when we are about fifteen feet away from the woman.

Her long hair is wrapped around her face, but I can tell she's young. The fact that her hair is reddish blonde sends a feeling of panic through me, thinking about how terrified I would be if something like this happened to Ivy.

Ezra stops the boat, and I dive off the side into the chilly water.

I swim over to the woman as quickly as I can and hear her crying, panicking, and trying to tread water as I approach.

"Here, I'll help you," I yell to her, and she starts to slip under the water from the wake the boat is causing. I grab her arm and pull her out from under the water sharply.

When I yank her arm, her hair pushes back as she is pulled above the water, and my heart drops out of my body.

Because it's the love of my life.

Chapter 63

"Wait For Me"

Ivy

Someone pulls me out from under the water with a strong arm, and I release a much-needed breath after struggling in the water.

"Ivy?!" A deep male voice, smooth as velvet and music to my ears, calls my name.

Am I in heaven?

"Ivy! Baby, are you okay?"

I open my eyes and see Donovan treading water in front of me, his arms extended to hold me up.

"Ezra!" he yells. "Throw me the buoy."

I choke on another wave of water that splashes towards us as the boat rocks, and Ezra tosses a circular floatie off the boat towards us. Donovan lifts me up higher when he hears me coughing on the lake water.

He grabs the red ring and forces my body over it, placing himself around me protectively as he starts to swim closer to the boat.

"Holy shit. Is that Ivy?" Ezra stares down, his mouth gaping open, before running to the back of the boat to help.

I can't even respond; my adrenaline is so high right now that I'm violently shaking. My teeth feel like they are going to chatter out of my skull.

Ezra reaches down to lift me onto the boat, and Donovan pushes me upward out of the water at the same time. As soon as I am lying on the deck of the boat, I vomit.

"Oh my," I hear a female voice say. I open my eyes, squinting against the sun's powerful rays to see an old woman with long white curls come to kneel by my side. "Are you okay, sweetheart?"

"Mary, please give the poor girl some space," a gruff old voice exclaims. "She almost just died."

Donovan is up in the boat a second later, kneeling behind me and pushing my hair away from my face. "Come here," he tells me and helps me sit up slowly.

"Are you okay?" the old woman asks me again, and I slowly nod my head. I'm still unable to speak from the burn in my throat.

Ezra lets out a huff of a laugh. "Well, alright. That was something, wasn't it?" He claps his hands together and smiles sheepishly at the couple. "That's a first for Anderson Charter; congratulations, you two got to assist on our first ever rescue mission. We made history today, folks!"

The old man seems proud of himself and happy to hear this news. "I can't wait to tell Jimmy about this. He'll really get a kick out of it—you know he loves a good story." He lends a hand to help his wife back to the bench; at her age I'm sure it was painful to get on her knees.

Donovan helps me stand up slowly and move to sit on the white padded bench that runs along the deck. He takes a seat next to me, putting his arm around me protectively, not even giving me an inch of space. He's holding onto me for dear life— I feel an undeniable sense of safety wash over me.

He looks down at me, worry and question in his eyes. "Ezra, can you take us back to shore?"

"Yeah, no problem." Ezra begins to walk towards the wheel and turns back to the couple. "I'm sorry about all of this; today's charter will be comped, and I will throw in some free tickets for another trip on us."

"Oh, it's no problem at all. We don't even nee—" the woman starts to say, but her husband cuts her off.

"That will be great, Mary. Free tickets and a rescue. Who'd have thought this was where our day would go?" the man says, chuckling.

"I promise next time there will be less cussing on our end, too," Ezra adds with a laugh. "We usually keep it more professional than what you saw today."

The couple laughs at that comment, and even I let out a hoarse chuckle. But Donovan remains serious, staring down at me with intensity.

Not even a ten-minute ride on the boat later, we are back near the shore. Ezra hops off to attach the boat to a metal T-shaped post on the edge of the dock.

I begin to try and stand, but Donovan still doesn't move. He's completely frozen next to me.

"Donovan, let go of her. We are on the shore now...it's okay, man," Ezra yells with a grin in his tone. "She's okay."

"I'm okay," I respond in a raspy whisper, standing. "Come on."

He slowly stands next to me and places his arms on my shoulders as we step towards the side of the boat to get off.

I turn to the couple and try clearing my throat. "I'm sorry," I tell them. "That was a lot, and probably not the experience you wanted."

The old woman faces me, smiling, and I feel like she looks

familiar, but I can't put my finger on why. I glance at her husband and find his face to be one I recognize as well.

"Don't even worry about it for a second, sweetie," she says. "Reggie and I are just so glad you are okay."

And then it hits me.

This is the elderly couple that I saw outside of Main Street Café the day that I first met Lee. This is the couple that was walking slowly together, hand in hand, and made me long for what they had.

I have an insane sense of completeness wash over me with this memory—a full circle moment.

I'm standing here now, next to a man that I love with a burning intensity, not even a year after I first saw this couple that stuck in my head.

"You guys are from Clairesville, aren't you?" I ask.

The woman looks surprised. "Why, yes, how did you know?"

I put my hand up to my chest in explanation. "I am, too; I've just seen you guys around town. I recognize you."

"Well isn't that something," the man says, smiling. "Small town, isn't it?"

"You've got that right." I laugh, my voice squeaking. "I won't hold you guys up anymore. I hope you catch a lot of fish, and sorry again."

"No need for any more apologies," the woman tells me. "I'm Mary, and this is my husband, Reggie." He holds up a hand in greeting. "I'm sure we will see you around town. Ivy, is it?"

I nod. "That's right."

Ezra hops back onto the boat, and I wave one final goodbye to them before turning to step off onto the wooden dock. Donovan holds out his hand, already on the deck, helping me across as I make the awkward leap over the foot-length gap of water below.

Once I'm across, he mutters to me, "My truck. Now."

He takes off in the direction of his black truck, and I quickly follow behind him. I can tell he's angry with me.

What I just did might be the stupidest thing I've ever done in my life, and that's coming from a girl who has smashed her ex-boyfriend's windshield with a bat at three a.m.

Chapter 64

"Take It Off"

Donovan

I can barely look at Ivy when she gets up into the passenger seat of the truck next to me. I'm trying so hard to hold my composure together right now, but I feel sick, and I feel terrified. The woman I love just almost drowned in the same water I was in, and I didn't even know.

Thank god for Mrs. Snyder.

Ivy shakes in the seat next to me, still dripping wet, and I shut off the AC quickly. Turning around and digging through my back seat, I toss her one of my clean work shirts.

"Thanks," she whispers and wipes the water off her arms with it.

I run my hands across my face. "What were you thinking?" I ask her in a low voice. I try to keep the anger out of my tone, but I know she can sense my frustration. "You could have died."

"I wasn't thinking."

"You can say that again," I respond and pull my hands back from my face to look at her.

She's smiling.

She looks thrilled.

"Why are you smiling right now?" I ask, completely exasperated with the situation; she has to be insane. "You almost fucking *died*, Ivy."

She just keeps grinning and shrugs. "But I didn't."

I run my hands through my wet hair, pushing it away from my face, and turn to her. "I could never live with myself if something happened to you. Especially at the lake next to where I live, where I grew up, and *where I work*."

Her face grows somber, like she is finally taking in what I'm saying. "I'm sorry I scared you. I just wasn't thinking. I just wanted to get to you, and I thought I could swim the distance."

I shake my head.

She reaches out and takes my hand. Hers is warm and soft, a stark contrast to my rough hands, calloused from manual labor.

"I really am sorry, Donovan. But I'm so happy to see you." She squeezes my hand.

I look into her eyes, swirling with depth. "Why are you here?"

"Because I want to be with you." She smiles.

My heart stops.

"Say it again."

"I. WANT. TO. BE. WITH. YOU," Ivy dramatically repeats, emphasizing every word, and damn, it's a beautiful thing to hear.

"Lee?" I ask.

She shakes her head *no*.

"Then what the fuck are you doing over there? Come here, baby."

Ivy jumps up from her seat, and I meet her instantly, pulling her towards me and onto my lap. Our lips connect instantly, a tornado of touch—kisses full of fervor and desperate need for each other.

I've missed this so much. I've needed her so much.

Ivy yanks her tank top off over her head, exposing her bare skin underneath.

"No bra?" I ask, my tone turning dark.

"I wanted to dress for the occasion," she responds, breathing against my lips.

"You certainly did."

I can't hold back any longer. I bury my face in her chest, taking her left breast in my mouth and slowly teasing her nipple with my tongue.

She lets out a moan of pleasure, and I smile at the sound as I nip against her skin.

"I want you, right now," Ivy begs, reaching her hand to feel my hardened length that pushes against my board shorts. "Please."

She strokes me up and down with her hand, and I spread her legs apart, pushing her up against my dick. She begins to ride me, and I can't take the teasing anymore.

"One second, baby," I tell her and push up so I can slide my shorts down.

As soon as my penis springs free, Ivy bends down and instantly has her mouth on me. She moans as she takes me in, licking me with her tongue and stroking me with her hand simultaneously.

The sensations are all too much, and I'm ready to come.

"Baby, stop. I want to be inside of you before I finish," I pant out.

She looks up at me, her cheeks flushed and lips plump from sucking on me. "Okay, Donovan."

Ivy straddles me, and we begin kissing again as I start trying to pull her leggings off. The material is stuck to her skin because they are still soaking wet, and I growl, frustrated.

"How much do you like these leggings?" I ask against her lips.

"Not much."

That's all the answer I need as I draw back from her and grab my Swiss Army knife that I always keep in my door pocket. I open it without even looking and lean her back against my steering wheel before gently pulling the fabric away from her crotch and cutting a hole. I close the knife and toss it onto the passenger seat. Then I take the fabric and rip the hole open wider with my fingers.

Ivy watches me, panting the whole time.

I smile and look at her as I insert a finger into her. "Better?"

"Mhmm," she moans, and I let her ride my hand for a minute as I watch her find her pleasure.

She grabs my wrist suddenly and stops me. "I want to finish with you."

"Good." I gently pull my fingers out of her and grab her hips, pushing her down onto my dick.

She cries out and opens her eyes to look at me as she begins to ride me slowly. I lock eyes with her and watch the look on her face as every sensation crosses it.

"I love you," she tells me.

I freeze.

She rides me faster. "I love you, Donovan."

I lean my head back from the sheer amount of pleasure I feel in this moment. "Say it again."

"I fucking love you, Donovan—I want to be with you forever," she yells out, and I can no longer hold myself back from release. I let the wave of euphoria wash over me as I come inside her, and I feel her muscles clenching around me as she finishes at the same time.

Nicole Mikell

We both breathe heavily with our heads pressed together, neither of us daring to pull away from each other. She strokes my hair gently with her hand, and I tilt my chin forward to kiss her soft lips.

In this moment, for the first time in my life, I feel complete.

288

Chapter 65

"Sea of Love"

Ivy

"So, I've got a serious question for you." I look up at Donovan, who's currently sitting behind me with his arms wrapped around me tightly, staring into the crackling firepit in front of us.

He shifts his weight backwards, resting his hands against the blanket on the ground so he can meet my eyes better. "Okay, sure."

I open my eyes wide. "How many fish do you think I swallowed in the water earlier?"

Donovan groans and shakes his head. "Too soon."

I start laughing. "What? It's just a joke." I swivel my body around on the blanket so we are facing each other now. "My fear of having a fish in my stomach days are over; don't worry."

"Good," Donovan replies and leans forward to kiss me on the lips.

I melt against his mouth and let out a sigh of pleasure as he draws away slowly. Donovan breathes against my lips. "You probably did swallow a couple, though."

I scoff and push him back playfully. "Rude."

289

"Don't worry, you definitely threw up at least half of them," he continues to tease me. "You did puke all over the deck and stern today."

"My apologies, Captain; next time I drown, I will try to keep that in mind."

His expression turns serious. "There will be no next time, Ivy. I will never let something like that happen to you ever again. If I have to put a bell on you so I can hear what your impulsive ass is doing—I will."

I turn and lean back against him, looking up at the night sky.

"You know, I saw that you named your boat."

Donovan responds "mhmm" from behind me, running his hand up and down my arm in slow circles.

"So is that about me?"

"Of course. You are the only person on this planet that has eyes that affect me the way they do."

I smile to myself. "When did you do it?"

"Two days after I last saw you at the hospital."

"Way before the wedding," I respond.

"Yes," he says, his voice clipped.

"I'm sorry I ran from you that night."

"I'm sorry I confused you."

"We don't have to worry about that anymore, though," I tell him. "It's just us."

Donovan wraps his arms around me and hugs me tightly. "So, what now?"

"Now our lives can begin. We will figure everything else out: location, work, telling our friends—it doesn't matter to me. I just need to be with you."

Donovan kisses the top of my head. "Me too, baby, me too."

We sit in the dark listening to the fire pop and whistle as a soft breeze passes us. I look up at the Anderson house and grin, seeing all the skateboards and fishing poles—all the hobbies that make Donovan who he is.

Until I remember something.

"I, uhhh...have one more thing to tell you," I say.

Donovan stiffens behind me. "Okay?"

"One of your canoes is floating somewhere abandoned out on the lake."

Chapter 66

"Who Knows"

Ivy

Spring

"Y ou know, I think I'm really starting to enjoy this boat thing," I say, smiling as I look out over the windshield from the captain's chair, where I'm currently steering the wheel.

"I wonder why," Donovan responds, looking up from between my spread legs and wiping off his mouth with a grin.

I laugh, and he grips my thighs with both hands before kissing up them till he reaches my mouth. I kiss him passionately—this touch of our lips is just as amazing as the first time.

Donovan pats my side playfully, and I break our kiss to slide out of the chair so he can take over.

"I'm going to lay out on the *bow* and tan," I tell Donovan, reaching into my tote to pull out my book.

"Oh, I love when you talk dirty to me. Tell me more boat terminology," Donovan teases.

I lean in towards his ear and whisper, "Hull. Cleat. Big fat *mast*."

"You better stop"—he spanks me as I back up—"or I might rip that pretty little dress off of you."

I laugh and walk across the deck towards the front of my favorite boat that the Anderson cousins own—*Her Eyes*. I think that's a personal bias, though.

Lying across the bench, I open my fantasy novel, holding it above my face to block out the sun, and begin to read. I get lost in the story about dragons and a heroine who shows bravery instead of fear, making stupid choices that end up paying off in the end. It reminds me of the day I came here in September to confess my love to Donovan.

Was I an idiot for jumping in the water? Yes.

But I also conquered my fear. It was like some form of exposure therapy, I guess. I wanted to get to the person I loved so badly, I threw all logic aside to make it happen.

Falling in love is a lot like fear, I realized; it makes your heart race, and you feel completely out of control in the moment. You no longer care about anything but the emotions swirling inside of you, and you know that you won't be the same from that day forward.

Donovan has become the greatest blessing in my life. My true love. I would give up everything else in the world if it was asked of me, as long as I got to have him still.

We have been living together for almost seven months now, and it's been bliss. We made the distance work easily, deciding to live in Clairesville through the whole winter season—when the charter is closed—in a small house we bought together. During charter season, we travel to Onilley Lake on the weekends so the guys can work together.

I'm lucky to have such amazing women work at Vera Bridal; they have been nothing but incredible with me taking the weekends off now. The only thing they've been pestering me about is when Donovan and I are going to get married—they want to see me in a wedding dress.

I don't want to pop their bubble by telling them we already secretly eloped.

On Christmas Eve, one year exactly after our first kiss—amongst our first of other things—Donovan proposed to me in our apartment. It was right before we were leaving to go to Eddie and Summer's Christmas party; I was so excited to tell everyone.

On the ride over to their house, we passed a shopping center, and Donovan pulled off and parked in the almost empty lot.

He turned to me, and I will never forget the look on his face when he asked me if I wanted to get married right then. I instantly told him yes.

I wanted to be his wife as soon as possible.

It's funny because when I worked in bridal stores before I owned my own, I would get so emotional, wishing and wanting it to be my turn to stand on the podium and try on dresses for my big day.

But now that I had found the right person, I realized that none of that mattered. I didn't actually need all the glitz and glam that I'm surrounded with in my job when it was my turn to say "I do."

Donovan handed me a single pink rose that he had in the back seat of his truck—the color matching my favorite pink dress. Then he took my hand and walked me into a little wedding chapel in a strip mall five miles from Eddie and Summer's house, and we got married. Just us, the minister, and his wife as a witness.

It was perfect.

We planned on telling people when we got to the party, but Summer ended up announcing to everyone that she was pregnant. Donovan and I instantly met eyes with each other, sharing a knowing glance that we didn't want to take away from her and Eddie's moment—so we kept it to ourselves, and it just stuck.

I kind of like how we have kept things private from the start; it's easy that way. Real. We don't have anything to prove to anyone.

Sure, I will tell my best friends soon, and we will end up having a big wedding ceremony to celebrate one day, I'm sure. But for now, I just appreciate being in this perfect little bubble together.

I stand up from the bench and walk back towards the stern of the boat, where Donovan is still steering.

I run my fingers across his face, and he cups my hand with his own before pulling it away to kiss my ring finger, adorned with my wedding band.

"How did I get so lucky?" Donovan asks.

I'll spend the rest of my life asking myself the same thing.

Epilouge
"Unwritten"

Lee

May

"Lee, are you okay with finishing up inventory for me today?" Cora calls out from the stockroom.

"Sure." I step away from the register and walk towards my sister. There's a lull in customers right now, and Arlet should be here any minute to take over up front.

As I head in the doorway, Cora steps down from the metal ladder and glances at her watch. "Shit, my friend will be here in less than thirty minutes. I'm going to the bathroom to freshen up. I did all the filters, espresso beans, and that wall." She points behind her. "I just need to finish up this top shelf."

"Noted," I tell her, stepping out of the doorway so she can walk past.

I glance around, looking for the notebook that I always use for taking inventory. Cora and Blaise always make fun of me for using a giant old notebook instead of tracking things directly on

297

the iPad like they do. They tease me for taking twice as many steps to get the same result, but it doesn't get to me.

I just like the simplicity of things, I suppose.

Searching under a stack of folders on a shelf full of training manuals and binders filled with our recipes, I find my notebook covered in stickers wedged near the back.

I grab a pencil and then climb the bottom few steps of the ladder so that I can pick up where Cora left off.

After opening the notebook to where I last left off, I start writing down the items that are low in stock. My numbers and words are tiny and close together as I scribble the info down—another thing the staff complains about, the fact that they can't read my "minuscule" handwriting.

Setting down my notebook on a step, I climb the ladder higher to reach the very top shelf. My knee accidentally knocks my notebook off. "Crap," I whisper to myself and groan as I climb back down to grab it.

When I reach down to pick it up, I freeze. My notebook has fallen open to a blank page towards the back that I haven't reached yet. Except the page isn't completely empty; there's a small note written in pencil in the upper right corner. I pick it up slowly and read the small script.

> *You're amazing and I'm so lucky to know you.*
> *I hope something good happens to you today.*
> *Your Smiley*

My breath hitches—Ivy must have written me this almost a year ago. I read over the message again to decide if I want to rip it out or not.

I don't feel any anger towards her anymore. The hurt has taken a long time to recover from, but I know I'm healing. I go a lot longer without thinking about her nowadays.

I even saw her walking down the street with Donovan, hand in hand, around Christmas time and didn't feel upset. That's when I knew I would be okay—that I will find love again one day.

The door jingles. *Arlet must be here to start her shift,* I think to myself.

"Uh? Hi? Is anyone in here?" I hear a female voice call out a moment later.

Shit, it's a customer.

Setting the notebook aside, I walk out from the stockroom. "Sorry about that!" I rush to the register. "What can I get for you?"

A woman with jet-black hair and tattoos stares back at me from the other side of the counter. She's gorgeous but intimidating.

"Can I get a matcha?"

"Sure." I punch the item into the POS and look back at her. "Anything else?"

She scans the bakery display to my left. "Hmmm." She taps her index finger against her chin. "How old are these things?" She points to our signature banana bread slices.

I cock an eyebrow. "Fresh. I just made them today."

She raises a brow now. "You made them?"

"Yes."

"Well, I guess I have to try one now." She smirks.

Is she flirting with me?

"Alright." I add banana bread to her order and glance back at her. "Anything else?"

"That's it." The woman grins, her eyes a piercing shade of green.

She begins to dig around in her bag, and I notice a Black Sabbath pin on the outside of it.

"Hey." I point to the pin. "I love Black Sabbath."

She looks up at me, hand still in her bag, surprised. "Really? You?"

"Yeah." I straighten. "Do I not look like I listen to metal?"

The woman gives me a once-over. "You look like you listen to frat boy pop country."

I place my hand over my chest, feigning insult. "You wound me with your words. Who wouldn't like the prince of darkness?"

She breaks into a full-on grin and holds out her hand for me to shake. "I'm Dove."

I look down at her hand, turquoise and silver rings on every finger, tattoos trailing up her wrist.

"Lee."

Her expression shows just a hint of shock for a moment before she instantly masks it again. "Well, Lee, it's nice to meet you."

She reaches back in her bag and pulls out her wallet to hand me her card, but I hold up my hand. "No, please, it's on me."

Dove smiles and puts her wallet back in her bag. "Okay, thank you."

We stare at each other for a moment longer, and although she's the opposite of girls I've dated in the past, something makes it impossible to draw my eyes away from her.

Something different.

"What?" She laughs.

I decide to be bold. "Would you, uh...would you like to go out with me sometime?"

Dove looks down at the floor, contemplating for a moment before nodding her head and grinning at me. "Okay. Sure."

"Great. Let me make that matcha for you now."

She bites the side of her lip with her teeth, and I turn away, trying to mask my own smile as I begin to make her drink.

A second later I hear a squeal and see my sister running out of the women's restroom like a maniac. I turn to see the commotion and watch as she runs up to Dove and gives her a huge hug.

What the hell?

Dove laughs, and Cora pulls apart from her, taking her hand and guiding her to the counter where I'm currently holding Dove's drink, mouth agape.

"Hey, Lee! Shut your mouth or a fly is going to make a home in it," Cora jokes.

I snap out of it and relax my expression as Cora continues to talk.

"Do you remember my best friend from elementary school, Ann?"

"Ann?" I ask, unable to hold back my confusion. "I thought you said your name was Dove."

"It is." Dove shrugs at me. "But I went by my middle name growing up because boys would always make bird sounds at me in class, and I got pissed."

Cora starts laughing. "Oh my god, I remember that. I still call her Ann out of habit."

Dove smiles at her. "I don't mind."

I stare between my sister and the gorgeous woman that I just asked out, my throat dry.

"Why are you being so weird?" Cora asks me and then turns to Dove. "Sorry about my brother; I swear he usually talks more than this."

Dove chuckles. "It's okay...he's cute, so he can get away with it."

Cora shoves her playfully. "You better not be flirting with my brother in front of me." She rolls her eyes. "Are you ready to go? I only have two hours until we need to go pick up Henry from the sitter."

"Yup, I can't wait to meet the little guy in person," Dove says, clapping her hands together—her rings making a clinking sound.

She takes the matcha off the counter and begins to follow my sister out of our café. Cora steps outside and holds the door open for Dove. I look at her and then at the counter, realizing I didn't give her the bag with banana bread.

"Wait!" I call out, and Dove turns back. "I forgot to give you the bread."

"I'll meet you at your car," she tells my sister, and Cora nods before going outside.

Dove walks back over to me and takes the small bag with the bread from my hand. She opens it up and pulls the slice out, taking a bite.

Her face shows surprise. "Wow, you're a good baker. I wonder what else you're good at..." She winks at me and begins to walk away.

"I'll be seeing you around, Lee. We'll plan that date soon."

Dove gives me one final breathtaking grin as she pushes open the shop door and exits. I watch as it closes behind her, and I can't help but feel that I'm already a goner.

Acknowledgments

Well shit, another book completed. I wrote and published TWO books? Twelve-year-old me would be shaking right now but probably not too impressed since it's not Twilight fan fiction or The Clique.

In all seriousness though, I am so appreciative to everyone that has been on this writing journey with me, and this is the sappy part where I give my thanks.

Thank you first to my readers, yes, you, sitting there, looking gorgeous and well hydrated while reading these words. THANK YOU. Every single person that has picked up one of my stories is helping me create the life that I've always dreamed of having. The words "thank you" don't even cover how grateful I feel.

MY ARC READERS—Thank you, you brave souls, for cracking the seal on my stories before they are officially published. You are all an indie author's dream team, and I'm eternally grateful for you.

To my BETA readers: Jesse, Caroline, Katie, Breanna, and Edith... Um, I love you? I thank each and every single one of you for all the incredible feedback and suggestions to help me write the best possible story I can. Having all of your feedback makes me feel so lucky as a writer.

Nikki—Thank you for helping me with my blurb. You helped me with amazing suggestions for literally the worst part of being a writer—the blurb is my kryptonite—and made it so I could breathe easier!

Thank you to Rattle The Stars PR—Jess and Heather, you guys have been a dream to work with and have been the clear heads that I've needed as I figure this whole process out. You are both so sweet and fun; I've loved getting to know both of you and can't wait for many more releases with you in the future!

Thank you to my street team! I love all of you and I'm so appreciative to have such amazing people on my team! Did you know you are the coolest people ever? I'm giving every single one of you a hug right now. Can you feel my arms wrapped around you?

Thank you to Jesse for proofreading...you're ICONIC. Can we please burn all the commas in the world now? Blink if you agree.

Katie—a little birdie told me that Dylan Efron said he loves you because you are so sweet and supportive and are always there for me whenever I need. (For legal purposes, Dylan Efron didn't say that... but we can manifest it, right?) Thank you for being there for me night and day.

Jesse—thank you for letting me bounce a million and one questions off of you daily and for listening to my twenty-minute voice notes without strangling me... lol. YOU'RE THE BEST. Also, we should take a cruise.

A big thank you to Jerrika, Brooke, Ashlyn, Breanna, Sarah, Joy, Jenia, and Jessica! Love my Jane Doe's! You guys are my day one.

To my editor, Danielle Barthel, working with you is a joy. I appreciate everything you do to help me polish my novels, and I'm so excited to have found such an amazing editor!

Now for the really sappy part, my family.

Thank you to Jordan, Gwen, Ollie, and Rowan for accepting the sudden change I made in all of our lives. I know I have been a lot busier recently, but I appreciate all of you for accepting the changes with open arms and understanding me, even when I'm stressed and overloaded. I love you guys so much.

Thank you to my parents for encouraging me to do something I love.

   My mom was the first person I ever told when I thought about writing my first book a year and a half ago, and she immediately told me, "You should do it!" without a second thought. Thank you for also reminding me to keep my strength when I get harsh reviews or feedback; you have taught me how to be a strong woman by leading by example.

   Thank you to my dad for always going above and beyond to help me out when I need it. You are always willing to run around with my kids to give me a break and also provide some comic relief when things feel too serious. Everyone calls you "Captain America" for a reason. I love both of you.

Finally, thank you to G.B. I hope you are proud of me.

About the Author

Nicole Mikell lives in sunny Florida with her husband, three kids, and two dogs. When she's not busy reading, you can find her thrift shopping or watching K-pop music videos with her daughter. Nicole loves reality TV, anything artsy, and a good Youtube dance workout.

She also really loves music, so send her some song suggestions.

You can follow her for future book updates on Instagram and TikTok:

Instagram: @nicolemikellauthor
Tiktok: @nicolemikell

Also by Nicole Mikell

Baby, It's You

You Can't Hurry Love